THE ART OF LIES

N.K. Napier

ISBN Paperback: 979-8-9889443-2-4
ISBN Electronic: 979-8-9889443-3-1

Library of Congress Control Number: 2025910978

Publishing Consultant: PRESStinely, PRESStinely.com

This work of fiction takes place mostly in Hanoi, Vietnam. While some of the locations, artwork, and artists mentioned do exist, most names, places, and events are products of the author's imagination.

Printed in the United States of America.

TMM Press
N.K. Napier
NancyKNapier.com

For Tony, always

List of Characters

Family:

THUY (twee): Pham Thao Thuy – museum business director who wants to become a curator

LAN (lahn): Pham Cho Lan – Thuy's father, called "Bo"; former war photojournalist

CHI (chee): Nguyen Van Chi – Thuy's mother; former employee for Ministry of Culture during wartime

QUANG (Quahng): Nguyen Son Quang – Thuy's son; talented artist

BAC (Bahck): Nguyen Lom Bac – Thuy's ex-husband; former marine, now bar owner

VU (Voo): Pham Ly Vu – Thuy's paternal great-uncle; famous artist

Friends:

Nguyen Thi HANG (Hahng): – Thuy's best friend; head of IT development at big tech firm

ANNA Stilton – Thuy's American friend for twenty-plus years; works in Hong Kong

Work colleagues

Vuong Hien TUAN (too-uhn) – museum director

Nguyen Anh HAI (Hi) – newly promoted curator

Lang Van CHIEN (Chee-in) – recently hired security operations manager, former gallery employee

Nguyen Son MINH (Ming, aka Thomas) – Vietnamese art collector based in Paris, France; Great-grandfather was a contemporary of Thuy's great-uncle VU
Nguyen Lam HIEN (He-in) – cleaner at museum
Vuong Le NGOC (Nop) – museum custodian

Others

"The Vietnamese Andy Warhol" – mysterious artist who paints copies in the museum
Morris TELLER – Bangkok based art dealer
Geoffrey Tan LEE – Singapore-based art authenticator
Le Quynh CHI – principal at Quang's school
Nguyen THUC ANH (Took Ang), expert in stolen art, Ministry of Culture, Sport and Tourism

Want to dive deeper into Vietnamese culture and history?

For additional context about Vietnam's art world, cultural traditions, and historical background that enriches this story, visit the *Art of Lies* section at **NancyKNapier.com**

Introduction

(Probably the shortest introduction to Vietnam's history you'll ever read)

For this work of fiction, a short description of key points in history is important for those unfamiliar with Vietnam's long story, much of which comprised war and conflict. The Chinese occupied Vietnam for 1,000 years; the French did so for one hundred years; the Americans were in Vietnam for twenty-five-plus years and fought "The Vietnam War," which the Vietnamese call "The American War" (to distinguish it from Vietnam's many other conflicts). American troops left Vietnam on April 30, 1975, which the Vietnamese call "Liberation Day from the American Imperialists," a startling phrase for Americans. Following that, the country faced more conflict—with Cambodia and China in the late 1970s.

During the Subsidy Period (1975 – 1986), called *Bao Cap,* the Vietnamese people experienced rations on rice, cloth to make clothing, and other staples. They lived with constant hunger and remained isolated from much of the world, except for Vietnam's main trading partner and supporter, the Soviet Union. Starting in the late 1980s, the Vietnamese government began a move toward a market economy under a set of policies known as *Doi Moi*, officially known by the mouthful English title of "Moving toward a market-oriented economy under socialist guidance." After the Soviet Union fell in 1991, Vietnam lost its main supporter and had to learn how to do business with the rest of the world. And it did, quite remarkably. The economy picked up real steam in the 2000s. Today, Vietnam is one of the fastest growing and most dynamics economies in Asia.

The intense economic changes ushered in cultural shifts as well. Vietnam has long been a collective, community-focused culture, where the group is more important than the individual. Confucianism, with its ordered hierarchy and behaviors regarding who was more senior, more important, and more revered, offered rules of behavior: wives followed their husbands' and fathers' requests and orders; children obeyed parents' expectations in what to study, what job to pursue, and often, who to marry. A misstep or wrongful action could lead to loss of face—how others may view a person or family or organization—and was scrupulously avoided.

But as the economy changed, Vietnam opened to the world through Internet, travel, and global exposure. Vietnamese professors and businesspeople scooped up mobile phones before they were widespread in Europe or North America. Children studied in the United Kingdom, Canada and the U.S. and tapped their feet to the sound of K-pop and Techno music. All of this exposure brought material goods but also a subtle shift in culture. A country heavily grounded in family and community, in hierarchy and following the advice of elders began to change. Young people more often chose their educational majors instead of studying what their parents demanded. Those same young people often worked abroad for long periods before (possibly) returning to Vietnam. Some Vietnamese married non-Vietnamese and divorce, once a taboo, became more common.

Finally, the art scene in Vietnam has also undergone dramatic changes, from a time during the 1920s and 1930s when some Vietnamese moved to France, including Nguyen Ai Quoc, a young kitchen worker who became known as Ho Chi Minh. Vietnamese artists also moved there to study; some stayed, some returned. In Vietnam, during the many conflicts, the government often drafted artists to help document and spread news about the fighting through drawings, posters, and photographs in newspapers, which had captions like "the brave Vietnamese fight off the cowardly French" (or Americans).

More recently, in peacetime, Vietnamese artwork has become widely sought after in and outside of Vietnam. This is the story of the family of one painter who lived through many of those periods.

Chapter 1

On her way to her boss's office, the kitten heel on Pham Ly Thuy's Ferragamo shoe broke. *"Chet Tiet!"* She'd bought them at a store in Hanoi that sold imitations of high-end shoes and paid the price: faulty quality.

She rushed to her office on the third floor of the Hanoi Museum of Modern Art and yanked her sturdy Vietnamese-made shoes from her desk drawer: one-and-a-half-inch chunky heels, one inch by one inch. Square toes. Comfortable, not fashionable, but practical. Thuy straightened her black linen tunic and black slacks, her personal uniform since joining the museum six years before, first as an assistant in the gift shop and later as business manager. The black tunic never distracted from the art, which had to shine in any museum, and it was easy to wear, even though some friends urged her to wear more fashionable, tighter clothes that would flatter her shape. One friend had said she reminded her of a long Coca-Cola glass bottle: long neck, curvy but not too much, and bubbly, at least some of the time. Thuy's one fashion vice was fancy shoes, or at least the look-alike versions she could afford: knockoffs Ferragamos, Jimmy Choo, and Manolos sat tucked in her closet, and sometimes they fell apart, like today.

Backtracking to Tuan's office, she replayed her argument to herself, one more time. The previous curator had retired a month before, and Thuy wanted the job, or at least a chance to apply. And she should qualify: she'd been the museum's business manager for four years, had a Sotheby's certificate, and had started a successful blog to boost the museum's visibility. The curator job was a respectable position for her conservative parents to appreciate and would cement her artistic family's legacy. *But I can't say that.* And Bo would finally show some parental pride in her. *Can't say that either.* And she craved the status. *Definitely couldn't say that.* But most important was the benefit she knew she could bring to Vietnamese art and artists in connecting them to the broader art world. As buyers and visitors clamored for more art from Vietnam, she relished the chance to help promote the artists and the museum that could show them. *Or maybe that all sounded too sappy. Surely, though, Tuan would appreciate it.*

Cutting through the gallery would shave three minutes, so she slipped into the third-floor gallery space. The room nearly echoed: artwork rimmed the walls, two wooden benches floated in the center, and the guard sat hunched over her phone, chewing on a strand of hair.

She halted and stared. A girl stood frozen in front of a painting, one of Thuy's great-uncle Vu's pieces. It was one of his alleyway pieces, the neighborhood where he lived in the 1970s. Flat, solid buildings with bags of sand out front to protect against bombs.

The little girl stood like the famous Degas ballet dancer sculpture, leg jutting forward in third position, hands clasped behind her back. Her head tilted up toward the painting. Thuy recalled the gut punch of falling in love with a painting for the first time. She missed that feeling.

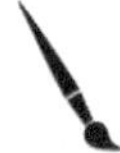

Down two flights and one hundred four steps until Thuy knocked on a tall wooden door.

"Enter!" Tuan shouted. He raised his hand without lifting his head and continued to scribble. "Prosperous Tuan," she called him. He'd grown up surviving on two bowls of rice a day, like she had, during the period after the American War, but he'd made up for it in middle age and become prosperous enough to afford more food. And it showed. She could probably outrun him, even in heels. *But maybe not in the fake Ferragamos.*

She gritted her teeth. *Patience.*

Tuan's office mirrored Thuy's in size, bland walls, and not-very-elegant plywood desk and table. A portrait of Ho Chi Minh, surrounded by children, looked over Tuan from behind his desk. Four piles of paper, each nearly a foot high, covered the desk. *How could he find anything?* Ashes from a cigarette dangling from his lips threatened to drop.

Twenty seconds passed. He glanced at his watch, removed his glasses, and placed his chewed-upon Bic pen on the desk. "Ah, you. So sorry I missed our meeting this morning. Busy day. Now what did you want? Would you like to sit? Make it snappy."

"I'll be fast," she said. *I'll stand, so you have to look up at me, like that little girl.* She cleared her throat and spread her feet under her to be sure she didn't fall over. *Stay firm.* "I would like to offer myself as the new curator. Or at least, I want a chance to apply."

His head jerked back, he blinked at her, and his breathing stopped. Three seconds later, he blew out a breath with a whistle and stared at his desk. "Anything else?"

Her mouth opened and closed. "I… I know the collection better than anyone. And the business side."

"I am surprised. Your outburst is… Where does this come from?"

"I've been interested in it for some time, and I've waited long enough. You must open it up so people can apply… So, *I* can apply." Her stomach crunched, but she couldn't bend over in pain. *This isn't going how I hoped.*

Tuan stood and shook his head. "With this outburst, you've made the decision easier." His shaky voice was so low, she took a step forward to hear him. "It's Mr. Hai." He plunked back down.

She felt like a cold towel covered her body, draining any warmth. *Hai? Mr. "phone glued to his ear" Hai? Constantly distracted, that Hai?* Voices passed in the hallway, and a thud came from the upper floor. "But, but why? I'm more qualified."

"Simple. He's senior."

That makes no sense. He has no seniority in matters of art. He is simply older. She felt she was pulling away from a stable shore, losing her bearings. "But he doesn't know art like I do—"

"He has a bigger family." Tuan tapped his desk. "And he needs more money."

Heat flushed back up her chest. "So, if I was older and had more children, I'd be qualified?"

Tuan gripped his pen. "You showed today that you are impetuous and unprofessional. You need more experience, more time, and you have modest training in art."

Her heart pounded and her mind jumped to the diploma on her office wall. "But he has none! I have a certificate from Sotheby's and—" She halted and closed her eyes, forcing herself to slow down.

"He is in training, learning," he said. "He'll do fine if you help him."

She looked at the ceiling. She had to make him see.

"I refuse to argue. You have my answer." His jaw clenched, and he looked at her above his glasses, gauging her reaction. "Was there something else? My papers call." He reached for the chewed-up pen and bent down.

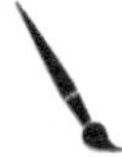

Thuy raced to her office, grabbed her poncho and red notebook, and fled to the museum's outdoor plaza. She tugged up the hood on her plastic rain poncho and blinked her eyes from the sting of the rain but looked away from the building. No one could think she was crying; her eyes might well up but tears never spilled. With all of the suffering her family had faced during those years of famine, she'd learned to hold emotions tight to her chest. *Crying wouldn't help. But a good dumping of her feelings never hurt.*

She pulled out her small red "Francis Underwood" notebook. Francis Underwood was the name of a main character in an American television show called *House of Cards*. He wore cuff links with "FU" on them. She was shocked to learn what the meaning in English was, but it fit the purpose of the notebook, and the nickname lived on, at least until more colleagues learned what the initials stood for.

She plopped on a concrete bench under the museum's overhang, out of the sputtering rain. She'd start with little Mr. Hai, who was nearly a head shorter than Thuy. *I could do so many things to make Mr. Hai's new life as the curator miserable. Offer to support a new project and then let other priorities get in the way. Delay requests for contacting other museums about special exhibits.* Her pen flew over the paper. *What else? Hire the wrong people to design an exhibit. Offer to attend community events and then skip them.* She paused. *Wrong track.* These acts would hurt the museum, which she didn't want since she'd put so much into making it better. She simply needed to make Hai's job harder. Tuan expected her to teach him about art. *She could make excuses and delay doing it. Or be busy every time he asked for help. Overwhelm him with information whenever we talk so that he's confused. Arrange for him to be on some panel of experts and expose his ignorance of the art.*

A man with an umbrella sat on another bench further away. After a minute, smoke drifted up.

Maybe it was time to start smoking. Umbrella man enjoyed a cigarette and she sat plotting to finish off her bosses.

She took one large breath, turned away so the man wouldn't see her scribbling, and imagined her damp black tunic had bled onto her skin. She would be grey and splotchy by the time she undressed tonight. She turned to a new page in the notebook. *How to embarrass Tuan: mess up the books, mischarge vendors, not pay the electricity bill for a couple of months.* He wanted partnerships with other museums, with collectors. She could arrange for museums to contact him and then not tell him about meetings. She could put the wrong paintings up for deaccession, and when they disappeared, he'd be furious. Perhaps another museum could recruit him for a job that was fake. He'd be mortified when he found out it wasn't real, and word would get around. She closed the notebook with a snap.

These men, these old geezers, they should retire and let a new generation in. Especially brilliant women, like the ones she knew who were still fighting the bamboo ceiling. Women. There's a thought. She could look into working at the Women's Museum. She loved the wide-ranging museum with its focus on women's lives—at home, at war, all aspects of life. She jotted that in her notebook.

She looked at the grey clouds and then sketched two men, one bald, with five children circling around him, holding a piece of chalk (the educator), and the other with big glasses sitting crooked on his face and a cigarette hanging from his lips. She tilted her head back and guffawed. If anyone doubted, this made clear that she was not the family artist. She stopped scribbling. She'd lost track of time and her conscience. *But damn, that felt good.* She sighed. Back to reality. She needed a plan.

Chapter 2

In her office, Thuy pinched the front of her tunic between thumb and index finger and puffed it out over and over, trying to dry the material. She slipped out of her wet practical shoes, and reached for the fake Ferragamos, the heel, and glue. *At least I'll have dry shoes.* Tuan's voice sing-songed in her head: "It's Mr. Hai. He's senior… has a bigger family."

Dismissed. Without a chance to try for the job. She scanned the office, taking in remnants of her predecessor, a retired accountant and former Viet Minh army major. On her first day in the office and his last, four years before, Mr. Long had waved his arms at the propaganda posters and pointed to a scar that ran from the back of his right ear to the top of his skull. "Heavy fighting. Bad times."

She had kept the posters to honor men like him, soldiers who'd fought for Vietnam in so many conflicts. One of her favorites was a poster made to commemorate the 5th Communist Party Congress in 1982. Three young Vietnamese, looking straight ahead: a boy-almost-man wearing a blue worker's uniform and cap, a young woman farmer in a red and blue bandana, and a soldier wearing a pith helmet with red and gold stars, and epaulets, a gun slung on his shoulder. A hammer and sickle peeked from over his shoulder. Their black eyes filled the sockets: no irises, just black, radiating fierceness and grit.

Grit and fierceness. She faced the wall behind her desk. Her diploma from the National Economics University and the museum management certificate from Sotheby's online program gleamed. She straightened the diploma, and Tuan's comment from several years back roared into her head: "Fancy degrees don't count as much as good hard work."

She'd heard Tuan's background was limited—a degree from a lower-ranked university than hers and construction work in Bulgaria during the subsidy era. He'd learned English late in life and never appreciated that hers was the new generation, the future of Vietnam. He deserved a little slack, since he'd done time in war and suffered like everyone else during the subsidy period. But he'd closed her down awfully fast. *That stung.*

She needed a break. She pulled open the center desk drawer and pulled out an envelope stuffed with postcards of her favorite paintings. She gazed at Chanh's *Going to the Rice Fields* painting, which she knew by heart. Done in 1937, he'd used watercolor on silk and made magic. A water buffalo anchored the scene—its whole body, except the feet, filled a third of the frame. Four people, only partially visible, trudged next to, in front of, or behind the beast under a muted blue and orange sunrise. Two men wore conical hats: one carried a scythe and the other a bucket. A woman in the background had draped a wooden yoke across her shoulders. A child led the buffalo on a lightweight rope. No doubt they both knew that if the buffalo decided to go in a different direction, that rope was useless.

Thuy leaned over and crossed her arms, eyeing the expressionless faces and drooping shoulders. *Worn down. Such a message in a few strokes. The power of art.* She wondered if Uncle Vu had worked in a rice field—so much about that man she didn't know. Even so, he'd probably known how those people felt—drained, forced to toil, hour by hour without hope of anything better.

She pressed her hand to her heart, released the tension she'd had and thought about the galleries, where she felt at home—mostly a benefit but sometimes an unwelcome weight of growing up with the spirit of her famous great-uncle.

But it was that spirit that had lulled her into assuming she was a candidate for the curator job. Humiliation prickled up her neck. She was blindsided in thinking she had a shot at the job. Instead, Hai got it. Hai, a former agricultural analyst who'd been a security guard before taking on the job of education tours at the museum. Despite her training and degrees, the blog, her passion for art—and yes, her family legacy—she'd been shunted aside without so much as a pat on the head.

I earned it. At least the chance to apply. All that extra work I did for him.

When the former operations manager retired two years earlier, she'd taken over many of his tasks, at Tuan's request. An honor—at the start—until it overwhelmed her. Six months after she'd stepped up, he'd complained about her performance.

She'd been doing two jobs for him, one that was completely new. When she'd threatened to leave the museum, that scared him enough to seek a new operations and security manager, with her help. Chien joined a year ago, with experience in galleries and an auction house.

"A good decision, Mrs. Thuy. Your input was very useful," Tuan had said after Chien was on board.

She had stood straighter. *A compliment. From Tuan.*

"Yes, your progress is steady, but slow. You need more experience. We can't rush into any big changes here. Not just yet."

Thud. Her shoulders had folded into her chest, but she heard the "mother noises" of Chi's voice in her head: "*Be strong. Get on with it. Your time will come.*"

She went back to one of the galleries to calm down. Murmurs from the other end of the gallery roused her. The child she'd seen upstairs on her trek to Tuan's office stood with her mother, who urged her to move on, but the little girl slipped from her mother's hand and walked to another painting. *Mom, get used to it. She's a born art lover.*

Thuy rubbed her thumb over the silver bracelet Chi had given her after university. Its chunky pieces had "Courage" and "Strength" scored into them in Chu Nom, which she couldn't read—no one could anymore—but she trusted that Chi had known what they said.

After Chien's hiring, she'd decided to give the business management job another year. Then she'd push for a promotion or leave. Now, a year in, she'd done what she set out to: created new business processes, started the blog, and become a regular visitor at openings around town. Some people thought of her as the face of the museum.

And today she had pushed for that promotion and failed.

"Ah, here you are. I wanted to see how you're doing."

Chien's sonorous voice startled her. "Oh, Mr. Chien. I'm well. You?" *Don't need an audience right now.*

"We have a new curator, I heard?" He muffled the last part of his comment and pulled on the sleeves of his suit jacket.

He must be sweltering in that jacket, but he looked like a fashion plate. More than she did in her limp, droopy clothes. "Where'd you hear that?"

"Oh, I didn't, officially." Chien Stared at the painting before them. "But I saw Tuan and Hai at lunch having a grand time, like they'd been buddies in the war or something."

She blinked fast, willing herself not to yell some obscenity that would make Chien blush. Or probably wouldn't, but she didn't know. *Squelch those feelings.*

"You should be running the place, you know."

You're right. I should. "You're kind to say."

"I could help you if you decide to leave."

She whipped her head. "No thanks." *Not yet. But soon.*

Chapter 3

For the rest of the afternoon, Thuy reviewed financials and then treated herself with drafting ideas for a new blog—"The Painted Ceiling: How Women in the Art World Deal with Discrimination"—which, of course, she'd never post. *But it felt good writing it.*

On her way out, she made one more gallery tour, this time for inspiration. The second floor housed several pieces by "her famous great-uncle, the artist," as the family sometimes called him. She zeroed in on *Ba Dinh Neighbors*, one of her favorites. The oil painting displayed several white-washed single-story houses with people meandering in front. A boy pushed a bicycle on the dusty road. Men and women wore loose black trousers, white shirts; more women wore cone hats. It reminded her of one of Bui Xuan Phai's, also of his neighborhood. It showed a concrete light and utility pole with a man walking on a dusty road. *They painted their neighborhoods. Made sense—they had no money to travel, and barely enough for materials.*

The guard passed her on the way out. "Toilet break." He winked but held a cigarette in his fingers. "Five minutes."

At the far end of the gallery, in front of another Uncle Vu piece, a man who looked like a Vietnamese Andy Warhol gripped his white bushy hair and pulled on it. He'd visited the museum before but usually sat on a stool, painting. Today, his easel and paint box rested by the wall, under the painting he studied. From his smock's front pocket, he pulled what looked like a measuring tape, which he stretched across the width of a portrait called *A Woman in the Countryside*. A young woman sat alone in long grass, staring into the distance while she twirled a daisy in her hand. Warm tones on a spring day. *Daydreaming? Waiting for someone?* The painter squatted, jotted on a piece of paper, and rose to stretch the tape vertically.

She glanced around and saw no one else. *Looks like he's measuring the piece—to copy it?* Nothing against copying; artists did it all the time to practice, to learn from better painters. But she'd never seen anyone measuring a painting.

Thuy picked up her pace. "Excuse me. Sir? I've seen you here before and wanted to introduce myself."

The man spun around, and his cloak billowed around him. *Cool robe.*

"What? What did you say?" His right eye drooped.

Her fingers played on her thighs. "I said I've seen you before. You're a painter... or student?"

The guard shuffled back in, tipped his invisible cap, and slumped onto the stern wooden chair at his desk.

"Of course, I am. We're all students. Always." He gestured at the paintings. "I learn from these masters."

"Were you measuring this?" She approached the painting.

He scooped up the paper on the floor and jammed it in his pocket. "Yes, I want to paint like Vu, and I need to understand scale. Copying the masters is allowed."

"Yes, of course. It's Friday, when many artists come. But... why did you choose this one?"

"This one? I sketch older artists, ones from the academy." He pointed to the art. "Pham Ly Vu was one of the best of his generation."

She stiffened. *I should have talked to him before. If he knew Uncle Vu—or of him—I could learn something.* She put her hand on her chest. "He was my great-uncle. Did... did you know him, by chance?"

The Vietnamese Andy Warhol froze and again that robe swelled in front of him. "He influenced me. A lot. I copy his work to improve."

Her heart raced. "And do you know anything… about his life?"

"Why these questions?"

She stepped back. "I don't mean to pry but I'd like to learn about him. And you seem to know or at least you're interested."

He snorted. "He was famous. I wish I could paint like him."

She had grown up with Uncle Vu's spirit, the man her father worshipped as a famous artist. She'd seen family photos that included Uncle Vu, and yet her parents rarely said anything meaty about him. *If he was such a great artist, they should know more. Or maybe they knew but wouldn't give it up. Perhaps the Vietnamese Andy Warhol could fill in the gaps.* "Could you tell me—"

"Artists of his generation… they had complicated lives. They…" He stared at the portrait.

Please. Say more. She clenched her fists.

He picked up the easel, and it vanished in the swirling cloth of the robe. "You seem like a serious student of the arts. If that's true, you know that the work is most important. Study paintings. Most artists say this. No need to learn their lives." He jerked the easel higher under his arm. "I don't mean to be rude, but my time is short."

"I'm sorry, I didn't—"

"That is fine. But be mindful of older artists—like me—who come here." His right eye, the one that drooped, had a silver ring around the iris. *Striking.* "We come to learn, and our time, unlike the young ones, is not endless. Show patience for our impatience." He glided to the exit.

She watched him leave and gasped. A few days before, four of Vu's war sketches hung on the wall next to the exit; now there were four empty spots. The sketches were gone.

They must be in the vault. Thuy detoured to the vault in the basement of the museum. She unlocked the door and stepped inside, shivering as she went from the warm corridor to the climate-controlled space, which they kept at At about 70 degrees Fahrenheit. The consistent temperature protected the art not on display. Rows of sliding doors with art pieces hanging on them, cabinets with narrow drawers for artifacts, and a large center table filled the space.

The sketches, tied together with a string, leaned against the wall just inside the vault's entrance. *Odd. Like someone stashed them in a hurry.* She lifted the set and placed them on the large table in the room's center and closed the door.

The framed sketches, laid out side by side, were ones she'd seen all of her life and thought she knew. This time, though, she bent over each, giving her full attention for three to five minutes. None of the sketches included guns: the soldiers didn't carry them; none lay on the ground or propped against a tree or hut. They were all of men in uniform, sitting, lying on the ground, standing, but at least one or two writhed in pain. She called up images of war sketches on her phone and glanced at them. Soldiers, village residents, young people and old. Almost all had some evidence of weapons. But not these by Uncle Vu.

Chapter 4

Rain threatened as Thuy slid her motorbike in the ground floor of her family's narrow four- story house on Pho Hue. She shoved the kickstand down, opened her seat to pull out her purse, and slammed the seat shut. *What a day.* And now, she had to tell her family the bad news about her meeting with Tuan. She hoped for, but didn't expect sympathy. Not much had gone right today. The one good part was the young girl fascinated by the art. *Hold onto that that memory.*

Lang strolled out from the back of the garage, wiping his hands on a cloth. "Welcome, back, Ms. Thuy. You look tired."

With the family for years, Lang had come to know Bo when they both fought the Americans. Later, he'd been stationed in Cambodia and on the Chinese border. One night, after lots of moonshine drinking, he'd shown her a scar on the side of his head and said, "Metal plate." But she never knew if he was telling the truth or embellishing.

"Hard day, yes. How're things here?"

He shrugged. "Broken brakes. But I've fixed it. Your father's bike."

She nodded and traipsed upstairs, never telling him that she was glad or thankful. She chuckled remembering her American friend Anna, who had once asked Thuy why she never said "thank you"—why most Vietnamese never said "thank you" to others.

"If we are friends, then you know I am grateful. I don't need to say it."

Anna had raised her eyebrows. "That explains a lot."

Thuy climbed the concrete steps from the ground floor to the kitchen and sniffed. Hints of pork meatballs, Nuoc Cham sauce, and scallions filled her nose as she recognized Bun Cha. Her favorite.

Quang sat at the kitchen table, sketching. She peeked at the landscape of the neighborhood, mostly shops across the street: Café 51, Lan Anh's Dress Shop, and the Goladi travel office. Someday, she'd use their services and take Quang to Hue or Hoi An. But for now, she'd dream. "Nice work, son."

He never lifted his pencil.

"Welcome home, daughter." Chi dropped a batch of sliced onions into the pot on the stove. "What news from the outside world?" She offered Thuy a mug of blue butterfly tea.

Thuy wrapped her fingers around the Warm mug. *Chi used the same welcome phrase every day.*

"You need to get our more," Lien said.

"I'm perfectly happy with my world—the market, the house, the neighborhood. Someone has to keep Bo in line." Chi winked.

"Do you miss work, after all those years?"

"I had my day but can't say I miss it. The Ministry? I do miss some people. Wartime? I did learn to fight, but when would I need that? You and Quang bring all the excitement we need now." She poked at the sizzling pork patties and looked at the scars on the backs of her hands. Long ago, she had told Lien that she was caught in a fire once in the war.

"Bo told me you worked in the police." Quang looked up at Chi.

"Bo says a lot of crazy things." Chi waved her long cooking chopsticks. "I helped a long time ago in a small way with some police in the countryside. Not a real job. Now, what's the news of the day?" She lifted her eyebrows at Thuy.

"Lots of news, but it will wait. I'll change and help you. Where's Bo?"

"Beer. But he'll join soon."

She walked to the family altar and knelt. She said a short prayer and then scanned the photos of her grandparents, an uncle, and the offerings her mother refreshed so regularly: beer and Buddha fingers. Quang offered Choco pies to the mix. *The photos are all from Bo's side of the family. Chi was adopted; maybe that's why. Need to follow up on that sometime.*

Twenty minutes later, Thuy plunked vermicelli noodles from the large center bowl into her soup, added coriander and sliced chilis, and leaned forward.

"Smells great. I overdid the chilis at lunch the other day. Took all afternoon for my mouth to get any feeling. I never seem to learn."

Quang put two chili slices back into the serving bowl.

"I have some news, but it's not good." Thuy slid her eyes from Bo to Chi and back.

"Oh dear. It can't be that bad?" Chi spooned more broth into Quang's bowl and lifted her eyebrows.

"No. Thanks. I… I didn't get the job." *And I lost my cool. Bad move.*

"What job?" Bo gulped his beer and mumbled. "I don't remember you talking about a job." He placed his palms on the table and covered his right hand with his left. He'd been a sniper in the war, lost his right index finger, and became a photojournalist instead. But he'd never gotten over the shame of losing his finger.

She glanced at Chi and swung her head toward Bo. "The curator job. You know I've wanted it for ages—"

"What happened? Please tell us." Chi lifted her hand toward Bo.

"The curator retired a month ago, and I've waited for Tuan to let us know when we could apply. But he didn't."

Quang looked at her. "Why didn't you apply?"

She wrung her hands under the table. "I didn't have the chance. He made a decision without telling anyone, without letting anyone else be considered—"

"That's not fair," Quang said. "Can he do that? Just give a job away?"

"Sure, he can," said Bo. "Not much is fair in the world." He turned toward Thuy. "Did you do something wrong?"

Don't assume the worst. I give myself enough pummeling for both of us. Keep still.

"You are known to have a temper, my dear," Chi whispered. "Did you get angry with Tuan? He would not take well to that. I remember his outbursts from years ago. But then he could be so kind."

"How so?"

"When you were a child, he went to visit his family in the countryside, maybe twice in a year. Each time, he brought back two eggs: one for Bo and me and one for you. We almost never ate eggs, so we had some luxury because Tuan's compassion."

Thuy coughed, unlodging a piece of garlic. "I know you knew him at the Ministry. And maybe that's why I hoped he'd give me a chance. I've done more than he asked—"

A siren blared outside the kitchen window.

"But you have a good job now, don't you?" Quang looked worried.

"Yes, I do." Bits of coriander and noodles covered the Formica table. "But I want to be more in the art side of the museum. And it pays better. You'll need academy fees soon, and I want to be sure we can afford—"

"It's fate." Bo's beer glass hit the table. "You're trying to act like an artist with a job like that and you can't. You'll never be an artist. Leave that to Uncle Vu." He reached under Quang's chin. "And this one."

She didn't expect him to console, but she hadn't anticipated hostility either.

Quang reached for a toothpick.

"I deserved that job, or at least the chance to apply. I've been the business manager, got some training, and with our family background—"

"Stop right there. You shouldn't use your uncle's notoriety to gain benefits." Bo swished his right palm over the table.

"But it wouldn't harm the legacy."

He glared at her.

Thuy flexed her fists. *Especially gruff, even for him.*

Chi cleared her throat. "That's enough, you two." She turned to Thuy. "You haven't told what you did, what you said. Please tell us what happened. I'll get more noodles."

Thuy sucked in air. "Well, yes, I was a bit short with him."

Quang gasped, and the toothpick fell out of his mouth. "But we'll have money for my fees? Do I need to get a job?" His head swung from Bo to Chi.

Chi touched Quang's arm. "Please don't worry. We'll find a way. But now, it's time for homework. You still need to do well in school even if you become an artist." She waited for the kitchen door to close and turned to Thuy. "Tell us more. Do you want to stay at the museum? Do another job there? Archives? That would be interesting."

"And a demotion." Thuy's shoulders sagged. "I've begun thinking I might be better off somewhere else. Maybe the Women's Museum."

Bo's eyes looked bleary.

From the beer? From weariness? From something else?

"I hope you stay at your museum," Chi said. "You're good at your work and I love hearing what goes on there. And what else would you do?"

"None of us had the stomach to be doctors," Bo said. "And Chi and I hope that we're the last to go into the military. Stay where you are."

Just once I'd like to be enough for him. Good lesson for me with Quang. She raised her shoulders and breathed out. "I went to see some of Vu's work on the way out. Always good inspiration. And I met a painter there, copying one of Vu's pieces. Got me thinking of doing a blog about that generation, those artists who went to the art academy and then painted during wartime. But I'd need to know more about them. Figured I'd start with Vu."

Bo looked sideways at Chi. "Waste of time. I'm going to watch the match. We're playing Laos. Where'd Quang go?"

Chi patted Thuy's arm. "That's interesting, dear. But not sure how much help we can be. Barely knew him. Just saw a few photos over the years."

Photos. That's it. The photos.

Chapter 5

After the family had gone to bed, Thuy tiptoed two floors down to the kitchen. She reached to the back of a lower cabinet until her fingers scraped a small family photo album that she pulled out every few years. Her fingers danced over the hard black cardboard and grey thread binding of the album.

Photos and a few news clippings of sketches during war time—the thirteen photos, all taken during Tet, celebrated the entire family's annual get together. Even as a child, she'd known that her parents saved all year to buy extra meat or sweets for New Year's. Food heaven for two or three days and then back to two bowls of rice a day.

She carried the album to her bedroom and shut the door. The brittle pages contained cracked, faded black and white photos. She slipped four from their frames and placed them on her bed. In the later photos, the adults looked the same, but the children got taller. Or rather, two children.

The photographer had staged the family members the same way each year. Grandmother and Grandfather sat on chairs in the center foreground. Grandmother wore a thick quilted cotton coat over a polyester ao dai, grey in the photo but probably red in color. Bo and Chi stood behind them. Bo's sister, Auntie Le, stood frowning next to Chi.

Bo stood behind Grandfather and next to Uncle Vu.

She stroked the photo. The Vietnamese Andy Warhol painter had reminded her how little she knew about Uncle Vu. *Surely, Bo and Chi knew more than they claimed.* He'd been a great artist. They were proud of him but never said much about him—where he grew up, his friends, his work during the war.

She had been in the photos, starting February 1979, when she must have been days or weeks old. Then she was in one marked 1982 and each year after. In six of the photos, a boy about a head taller than she was, stood next to Uncle Vu, who draped his arm on the boy's shoulders. In one, Bo made a side glance and smiled at the boy.

She didn't remember if she'd asked who the boy was before—surely, she had, but it'd been years. He seemed familiar to the family, or at least to Bo and Uncle Vu. She had memories of everyone else in the photos but not of this mystery boy.

Chi drummed her fingers on the bedroom door and poked her head in. "Still awake? I wanted to see how you were… after our discussion. It got a bit heated. Sorry. Bo's not always himself these days."

"Thanks, I'm okay. Is there something wrong?"

She waved her hand in front of her face. "He forgets, but he'll be fine."

"Well, please, do come in." Thuy patted her bed.

Chi wore her polyester pajamas with peonies on them. "Photos. Where'd you find them?"

"The ones from the kitchen. I look at them every few years."

Chi placed her hand on the photos in the album and then on the four laying on Thuy's bed. "Such good times. We had some happy days and funny stories."

Thuy stayed still. "What stories?"

Rain drops pinged on the window.

Chi leaned back. "Oh, I remember one year that Grandfather had bought firecrackers. A whole batch so each of us could have a few to light. A real treat."

Thuy clicked on the bedside lamp.

Chi became a silhouette. "He put them into an empty rice cooker to store them. Somehow, though, the cooker came on and the whole thing exploded!" She laughed. "Grandfather was so angry at himself."

Wish I could remember more. "How about this one?" Thuy handed her another photo. "When was it, do you think?"

"Hmmm. Probably about 1982. You look to be around three. I was working at the Ministry at that time, with Tuan. He was kind to us. When he went to visit his family in the countryside, I told you, he brought back two eggs for us. A real luxury." Chi ran her thumb across the photo. "But Tet was the one time of year we made photos. And had extra food."

Thuy's stomach growled, and she chuckled. "My stomach remembers that hunger." She pointed to the lineup. "Who are all of these people?"

Chi leaned into the photo. "You know them. Your grandparents, us, Auntie Le. Her husband fought in the American war, you remember."

"Vaguely. Tell me."

"He fought at Quang Tri. That's where our largest cemetery is—more than 10,000 martyrs."

"But he didn't die there?"

"No, he died later. February 1979. Just after you were born. When the Chinese invaded." Chi teared up. "Auntie Le never smiled after that."

"Ah. That's why she frowned in all of those photos." Thuy sucked in a big breath. "Do we have any photos of your parents?"

"You know I was adopted. Grew up with a woman who adopted me, and she's long dead."

"Does that ever bother you?"

Chi patted Thuy's hand. "What's to bother? No way to change it. Just the way things were then. What else do you have here?"

Thuy picked up another photo. "OK. Look at this one. What about the boy next to Uncle Vu? Who is he?"

Chi shivered and wrapped her arms around her. "Hmmm. Why do you ask? Is it cold in here?" She looked toward the window.

"Raining. The boy…" She pointed again. "He's in a few of the photos when I was pretty small. I don't remember him, but he must be someone close enough to be in the photos."

Chi shook her head. "No… I don't think he was there that often."

Thuy jabbed at three other photos. "But look. He's getting taller, so it must have been over several years."

"Sorry. I can't remember." Chi's voice rose. "It was a long time ago, and you were a child. You kept me very busy."

If she didn't know better, she'd think Chi was trying to divert her. "But Bo looked at him like he knew—"

Four raps on the door jolted her, and Bo stepped in. His singlet hung crooked, exposing his collar bones and tops of his bony shoulders. "I heard your voices. What are you doing up so late? I worry about you getting your sleep."

The closest he'll ever come to an apology. Thuy glanced at Chi.

"Lan. Thuy found the photos again. She's trying to learn more about Uncle Vu and the rest of the family." Chi squinted at him. "Our daughter has a lot of curiosity."

If they talk, I'll take notes. Thuy reached in her purse for her black notebook, the one she used for ideas for the blog, for new artists to investigate, and articles to look up. She fished out the black notebook and glanced around for the red one.

"Uncle Vu?" Bo rubbed his chin. "I've told you all I know."

"Uhhhh. But I have so many more questions. Vietnamese art is getting more attention, and he'll be one of the artists people want to know about. So, I could use help with these photos."

Thuy handed him three. *The red notebook's got to be there.* "I just asked Chi about them. Trying to figure out who everyone is. She told me, except for one person. This young boy." She pointed.

Bo pursed his lips and shook his head. He placed the photo back on the bed. "History. Old times."

"But who is that?" She peeked again into her purse, and her heart rate went up.

"Can't recall."

"That's what Chi said."

"Then believe her. We don't know."

Maybe they truly did not remember. Or maybe they're evading the question. "But in this photo, you're smiling at him? And Uncle Vu seems to know him."

Chi squeezed her jaw. "Too many questions this late at night. I'm going to bed."

She had to go for it. "Wait. I also wanted to ask about Vu's sketches. The ones the museum—"

"Chi's right," Bo said. "You are too curious. Look at his work. Don't worry about his life. Enough for tonight."

Before the door closed, Thuy dove into her purse again. She shoved aside her makeup kit, an extra bottle of water, and her keys. Nothing red. She turned the purse upside down and shook it. A lipstick, mechanical pencil, and old receipt fell out. The notebook was gone. The one she'd spilled her vile thoughts in. The one that would get her fired if anyone found it.

Chapter 6

The next morning, Thuy left early to grab Pho at her favorite shop on Tu Mien. She reached the museum at 8:17 a.m., well before her normal 9:00 a.m. start time. She skirted around the plaza benches on the way in since that was where she last recollected having the notebook but couldn't remember if she'd brought it inside with her. Nothing on the bench where she had been sitting. Nothing on the ground around it. She raced to her office, scanning the desktop, bookshelves, even the waste bin. *No luck.* She stepped into the hall and saw Mrs. Hien.

"Ah, Mrs. Hien, I need your help."

"Whatever I can do, child." Hien leaned on her string mop and pushed the scarf on her head backward. A mole right below the edge of her left eye gave her a "come hither" look that must have enthralled young men. She had stopped going to school at age ten to work in her family's rice field, then joined the military during the American War. She knew Chi from the time they'd been in the military, when they both worked on the Ho Chi Minh Trail. Chi had been a sapper; Hien had carried supplies. When Chi started working at the Ministry, she helped Hien get the museum job, almost forty years before.

"I've lost a notebook," Thuy said. "A small red notebook. It looks like this black one but it's red."

"Must be important."

Thuy felt her face redden. "I must find it. Have you seen it, by chance? Last, I had it was in the plaza last evening."

Hien chewed, an old habit from the days when she had betel nut in her mouth. She looked at the ceiling and the floor. "No, I'm sorry, child. I can't remember seeing it. What was in it?"

"Just some bad thoughts of mine. Shouldn't have written them. I'll never do that again. But I do need to find this one. If you find it, please don't read it. Can I trust you on that?"

Hien winked. "Sounds like a racy novel. Can't promise I won't peek." She chuckled. "But I will bring it to you. Please do not fret." She shuffled down the hallway and laughed under her breath.

Thuy scurried to the lobby to look around once more. At the edge of the space, near the front doors, the ticket desk sat unmanned until 10:00 a.m. when the museum would open. She spotted a splotch of red on the corner and caught her breath. *Maybe another custodian had found it.* She rushed to the desk and found a red kerchief folded into a square shape.

At least she hadn't put her name in the book, but anyone who knew her could figure out. She made a fist, pounded her thigh, and shuffled toward the coffee shop.

Chien stood behind the counter. "Helping out before we open," he said. "And you? Here so early?" When he smiled, the pockmarks on his cheeks indented. Other than the marks and his operatic voice, he blended into the woodwork: grey slacks, white shirt, round body.

"I… uh… just looking for something."

"Any luck?" He leaned on the counter.

She couldn't read his expression. *Surely, he isn't sneering.*

"Ah. Just a moment." He reached under the counter and brought up a red notebook. "Yours?" He tapped it on the counter.

Her heart sped up. She snatched the notebook and flipped through it. *Yes, mine.* "Where did—"

"I saw you yesterday outside, writing. Quite furiously, I thought. You left it on the bench, so I picked it up." He winked. "Big plans for some people we know."

Thuy clutched her throat. "Could we keep this between us? I overreacted and should never have put such awful thoughts on paper."

He shook his palm in front of her. "Don't worry. I like fanciful thinking. And it's nice to know someone else is not the biggest fan of Mr. Tuan." He snickered. "Or Mr. Hai."

Thuy clutched the notebook. Even if Tuan was loathsome, she'd overstepped. "You're not a fan? But Tuan just hired you." *Actually, we both did, but he took the credit.* "What, a year ago? Are you leaving already?"

"No, no. And I don't recall if I thanked you for your support of my application. Tuan told me you had played a big role."

"Kind of you." *Tuan is full of surprises.*

"But sometimes he can be… a bit over his head. And given what you wrote…" Chien said, chin tucked.

She leaned over the counter to hear him.

"You might consider a murder—"

She reeled back.

He swept his eyes side to side. "No one's here. Yes, a murder mystery. You could write 'The Case of the Sabotaged Curator.' We would know the perpetrator, wouldn't we?"

She half-laughed and tucked the notebook away.

"And you? Any thoughts about a new job? I could help. I have friends in Ho Chi Minh City." He saluted. "Let me know. I'm here to help."

"No, I don't think so." *But stay tuned.*

"Like I said before, you should be running the place."

Or a place like this.

Chapter 7

In her office, Thuy pulled up her blog draft.

A new book sits on my desk. The first four words of the title—The Story of Art—are in minium red, somewhere between fire engine red and dark orange. The author's name—Katy Hessel—is in something close to cobalt blue. Both stand out on the mustard-colored hardcover background. From a distance the book cover looks like "The Story of Art," by Katy Hessel. But the words in the second part of the title, after "The Story of Art," are formed by tiny white lines and from ten inches away, I see the whole title: "The Story of Art Without Men." Some days the art world feels like this title in reverse—the art world without women. That's why breaking the painted ceiling in Vietnam must be our focus for the future.

Not a bad start. Her phone buzzed: Anna. She pushed the volume button lower, punched "Accept," and got ready for it.

"THUY!"

Anna. Big, bold Anna. Her voice filled Thuy's office, even with the volume turned down.

"Anna! So good to hear you!"

She'd met Anna years before when they both held internships at the Women's Museum. In her early twenties, Anna had come to Vietnam to learn the language and stayed for two years, teaching English before getting into the art world. She'd charmed anyone who gave her a chance, if they weren't intimidated by the tall, blond American. But almost everyone was, until they knew her.

Anna had been in Hanoi when Chi was undergoing cancer treatments and stepped in to be there. She sat with Chi and cheered up Bo when he was down. And through it all, she had said to Thuy, "Don't thank me. I want to be your friend."

Thuy stood to stretch, ready for a long intro from Anna.

"I was thinking about you and had to call." Anna huffed. "Sorry, I'm walking up to my apartment. Hong Kong hills never get easier." A bus whooshed past.

"So glad you called. Been a rough week."

"God, I'm sorry to hear that. What happened?"

"I didn't get a job I had hoped for. Or at least hoped I could apply for, and Bo was his normal judging self. He knows how to bait me. I shouldn't feel like I need his approval. But I do."

"That's awful. I'm sorry. Can I do anything?"

"Not right now. I'll let it sit for a while. But what about you?"

"Well…" Anna huffed. "Speaking of jobs, I just joined the *Financial World*. Culture desk."

Thuy's heart sped up. *Excitement or envy or both?* She gritted her teeth. "That's great news. Really. I'm so happy for you. Will you stay in Hong Kong?" She shoved envy away and kept the excitement.

"Yes. Still here. But the best news is I get to find my own projects—dream job. I called because I'd like your help. Ideas. I need ideas for possible projects. My boss has given me some time to find one—or he'll assign one. Figured you would have some ideas."

Thuy's office door opened, and skinny fingers wrapped around the frame. Hai's upside-down pyramid shaped head appeared. "Mrs. Thuy, come now. Conference room." He stood by the door.

"Thuy? You there?" An ambulance siren played in the background.

The city that never sleeps.

"Uh. Yes. Sorry. Can I call you back? Someone's here."

Hai tapped his foot.

Rude.

"OK, but don't forget. Ideas. Next week."

"Mr. Hai, what's so—"

"Come now. Mr. Tuan wants you." He slipped out as quietly as he'd slipped in.

Either Tuan would formally announce the new curator, or, for some reason, she'd get another dressing down. Either way, she dreaded what was coming.

Chapter 8

Thuy slipped into the conference room where Tuan and Hai shook hands with a tall Vietnamese man.

"Mr. Thomas, please meet Mrs. Thuy, who takes excellent care of our money so we can take excellent care of our art." Tuan chuckled and clasped his hands over his ever-expanding prosperous stomach.

Someday he'll make that joke once too often. And calling her Mrs. Thuy was so old fashioned. She bit her tongue.

The man held Thuy's hand for a split second longer than most people. "How nice to meet you at last." His upper front tooth had a small chip.

Charming. And I'll bet he knows it.

"I read your blog with great interest."

Not a way to start. Tuan won't be happy. I'm getting credit, not him.

"Mrs. Thuy, could you kindly make coffee for our distinguished guest?" Tuan gestured to the side table and tilted his head.

She stiffened. She wanted respect, and he gave her coffee duty. *That's why he wanted me here. Delights in putting me down.* Moving to the table underneath the wide rain-spattered windows, she plugged in the red-hot water thermos and took the Celadon ceramic demitasse cups—imitations, of course—tiny tin spoons, and packets of instant coffee to the conference table.

Thomas pulled out a chair for her, next to him, across the table from Tuan and Hai.

She hesitated. Normally, she and Hai would flank Tuan on one side and visitors would sit opposite. Thomas must have been away from Vietnam too long or had forgotten meeting protocol. *Or he was breaking with tradition on purpose.*

He removed his jacket. A big gold watch peeked out from his shirt cuff, and taut muscles showed through his silk shirt. She imagined him in a gym—bulky calves and thighs, flat stomach. *Cut that out. Focus.*

Tuan gestured to the coffee cups. "Welcome to our museum, Mr. Thomas. When did you arrive?"

"Saturday night, from Paris. Direct flight. My first time in Hanoi since I was a teenager. It's completely different. And please, call me Minh. 'Thomas' is for foreigners."

"What do you remember from those days?" Thuy stirred her coffee.

"Doi Moi had begun, of course, but the 1990s were still early days. No tall buildings, no stop lights, no sedans, almost no electricity." Minh spun his Mont Blanc ballpoint in his fingers. "My family lived in the old quarter and cooked on the street. Like all families."

Tuan opened his mouth to speak.

Thuy jumped in. "And why did you leave?" She gripped her coffee cup and glimpsed at Tuan, who was snarling at her. *Serves him right.*

"I received a scholarship to study in France. And never returned." He hadn't yet made a move toward his coffee. "I got interested in art because of my grandfather. He went to the Hanoi College of Fine Arts."

She made a fast calculation. *About the same age—or younger than Uncle Vu.*

Tuan leaned forward. "We have several artists from the academy here." Mr. Tuan sat taller.

"I'm aware. In fact, I think Mrs. Thuy's grandfather and mine were at the academy around the same time. The 1930s?" He turned toward her.

"That could be." Tuan leaned in. "What little we know—or Mrs. Thuy knows—"

Minh frowned at him. "Should we let Mrs. Thuy tell what she knows? And I'm sorry. I didn't know you were married. You look far too young."

She laughed. If she didn't know better, she'd bet he was toying with her—the handshake, the chair, now this? *No, that sounds crazy.* She was so out of practice. "You are too kind, but I'm old enough to have a son. Twelve. I'm divorced."

"Oh, I am sorry." His eyes widened.

"No need. It's been a while." *And no future prospects.*

"Ah." He winked at her.

Seriously? She had to stop thinking like a schoolgirl.

Tuan cleared his throat. "Enough on personal talk. We are curious to hear about why you have come to us, why our museum?" He tugged on his jacket, tight across his chest.

A man who doesn't go to the gym. Thuy sipped her coffee to stifle a chuckle.

"As I said, my grandfather studied in the academy—his name was Nguyen Tho Nam."

"Of course. We know his work." Tuan lifted his palms. "Even though we have none of his paintings here."

"I noticed that this morning." Minh raised his chin.

Ouch. Thuy peeked at Tuan's narrowed eyes. She knew that look. A vacuum cleaner whirred in the background. *That won't make him happy either.* She stared at the three silk pieces on the wall behind Tuan and Hai: a group of flowers, lotus blossoms. Traditional Vietnamese style. She knew he'd bought them from a market downtown—not authentic, but no one would put originals in a conference room.

"When he moved to France for more study," Minh said, "he stayed. Several of his friends also went." He looked at Thuy. "But I'm sure you know all about those artists?"

A cluster of school children scurried down the hallway. She went to close the door completely and tensed. "A little. But please, fill us in."

"Well, several left Vietnam. Like Le Pho, Trung Thu Mai. Then there was the metal sculptor, Vu Cao Dam. He shifted to painting during wartime because the metal went for weapons."

She leaned forward. *If he knew about them, he might know about Uncle Vu.*

Tuan tapped his pen on the table. "To be truthful, we do not know much about artists who went to Paris."

"I see," Minh said. "Some went and never returned, like my grandfather. Others came back." He put his palm on the table near Thuy. "I don't recall if your grandfa—"

"My great-uncle, actually."

"Oh no. Once again, I am wrong." He smiled, and his dimples went deeper. "But if I'm accurate, it was my great-grandfather Nam, but it's easier to say 'grandfather.' They were probably about the same age."

She scooted her chair to face him. *More, please, about artists, about Paris, about you.*

"He—my great-grandfather—collected work by Vietnamese artists, mostly friends of his. They've stayed in the family, and I've added more over the years."

On the side table, the water thermos's red light clicked off. Fresh hot water ready. Tuan stared at Thuy and glanced toward the thermos.

She didn't react. *He was a man who liked the titles but wanted others to do the work, even the basics of making tea.*

He brought the thermos to the table, poured water into his empty cup, and set it on the table with a thud. "You must have quite a number." Tuan said and crumbled an instant coffee packet.

"Mmm. Probably around two hundred paintings and sketches. Artists from the 1920s to the 1990s. A few from the 2000s, but they've become so expensive."

Thuy bit the inside of her cheeks. She couldn't imagine living with so much artwork. Even the museum didn't have that much from the era of those artists. She'd give up Ferragamo shoes for a year to see that many.

"I can't imagine so much art in one place," she said.

"Sorry, not in a single place. In three places. In France, England, and Monaco—and also free holds."

Thuy gasped. *Three houses. Unbelievable.*

Minh pulled a tin box out of his briefcase and waved it in front of them. "Would you allow me to make some tea for you?"

Tuan stiffened. "Of course, but you are our guest. Let Thuy—"

She squeezed her lips.

"I wouldn't hear of it." Minh shoved his chair back and walked to the side table, where he dropped the leaves into a separate tea pot and added hot water. Steam floated up from the pot. "I carry my own tea when I travel. From Bhutan. I must be the only Vietnamese not enamored with coffee." He filled four teacups.

And in the process, he took control of the room.

"Cordyceps," he said. "From a particular mushroom." He handed cups to her and to Hai.

"Quite strong." Hai wrinkled his nose, took a sip, and pulled his lips around his teeth.

Minh chuckled and handed a cup to Tuan. "You may not like my tea, but I'm sure you will like what I have to say." He looked at Tuan and Hai and back to Tuan. "I think your museum might benefit from showing some of my art. Not to be impertinent, but when I walked through your galleries I… forgive me, but I found them lacking. And old fashioned."

Old fashioned. Lacking. A smack on the museum. On the previous curator. On Tuan. She braced for Tuan's reaction. She imagined him vacillating between anger and salivating. Hai looked at the ceiling. *Surely, he isn't bored?*

"Mr. Minh, I'm… I'm surprised," said Tuan. His neck turned pink. "But please. Say more of what you mean."

Kudos to him. He held his temper, if not his pink neck.

"As I said, my great grandfather and his friends made lots of drawings, sketches really, on whatever paper they could find:

newspaper blank pages, backs of receipts. He and many others were part of quite a robust Vietnamese community in Paris in the '20s and '30s. I once visited the neighborhood where they lived. Some descendants live there still."

"And you ended up with many of their pieces of art," Thuy said. *Unbelievable.*

"True. But many of the pieces—here and in Europe—disappeared. Foreigners who worked for embassies, aid organizations, and a few businessmen bought art in Vietnam and took it when they left—to Russia, Europe, Sweden. Now, I want to bring some of my collection to show here."

"And how many do you have? In those three places of yours." Thuy swallowed the bitter tea and tried to keep from pinching her mouth.

Minh shrugged. "Not sure, so I hired some students in France to do an inventory."

Thuy nearly choked. *No idea. Mon dieu.* He had so many paintings that he didn't know the number. She stared at the lotus blossoms on the wall.

"But Mr. Tuan. My offer. Your collection is dated and without a clear theme. Modern, yes, but not really curated, don't you agree?"

Mr. Tuan's pink neck flushed red and began to seep up his jawline. He tucked his finger into his collar and pulled. In meetings with her, he would explode. But so far, he held it together.

An assistant knocked on the door, slipped to Tuan's side and whispered in his ear. He lifted his eyebrows and murmured to Hai, who nodded. "Let us take a break. I must answer a call."

Minh tilted toward Thuy. "And I must find some time alone with this lovely person. But first, a cigarette."

Thuy blanched and curled her toes in her fancy shoes.

Chapter 9

Thuy returned to the conference room before the men. She'd looked for Minh, but he had vanished during the break. *Misread that one.* Once they gathered, she closed the door, and the ceiling lights flickered. *Oh no. Not a power outage.*

Minh looked at the ceiling. "I remember those. Now, to business. You could use some of the Vietnamese artists I have. Especially ones that have not been to Vietnam, as far as I know. Will you allow me to loan you some?" He lifted his chin and ran his hand down his shirt front.

She held her breath and glanced at Tuan, who stared at his teacup and did not move.

Rain drops sounded like bullets on the windowpane.

"Mr. Minh, what a kind offer." Tuan shook his head. "In principle, we agree but we must consider. It takes time."

"I understand you have requirements, but I wish to do this soon. Several buyers are interested in these works, and I am interested in selling. Once they disappear into private collections, we may never have access again."

"How soon could you send some of your artwork? And how many pieces are you willing to offer?" Mr. Tuan twitched in his chair like he was sitting on hot coals. "Not that we have accepted what you offer. We must consider, of course."

Thuy's foot jiggled under the table, and her shoe fell off.

Minh flashed a smile. "By soon, I mean whenever you receive government permission. Certainly, before Tet. Late January. We could negotiate the number, but less than forty, more than twenty?"

"Are you talking with other museums?" Thuy stared at her hands.

"Not yet. But a large museum in Ho Chi Minh City has shown interest."

She froze. The Ho Chi Minh Museum of Modern Art. Hanoi's biggest competitor and one of the best in the country. *They'd leap at the chance show those paintings. But he came here.* "Excuse me, but why?"

Minh slid his glasses on, startled at her outburst. "Sorry?"

"Why do this now? And why this museum first?" She glanced at Tuan, who squinted with a vengeance. The lotus blossoms in the lacquer piece behind him stood for rebirth. *Not the case right now with Mr. Tuan.*

Minh winked at Mr. Tuan. "Blunt. More than most Vietnamese women."

Smack. *A put down or an invitation. Hard to read this man.*

"How could you ask? Because of you, your blog, of course. You advocate for Vietnamese art, which is gaining more notice on the world stage. You are the reason." He swiveled toward Tuan. "And… because of my great-grandfather and Ms. Thuy's great uncle. An exhibit like this will give my paintings more exposure, especially to Vietnamese people." Minh sipped his tea. "And because you have a museum in need of masterful art."

Pow. The normal Tuan would keel over. And yet, he didn't move. *A male standoff, with Tuan on the defensive.*

"An expert in Southeast Asian art who has worked for some of the big auction houses is my advisor. He'll probably have information on many of the artists you show here. And the ones I may send to you."

"This advisor. What is his name?" Tuan picked up his pen.

"Name? I'll pass that along" He touched the table in front of Thuy. "He also found many of the works I have. Some by your great uncle. What do you think, Ms. Thuy?" Minh held the teapot over her cup.

She nodded. *A chance of a lifetime.* "Art never before displayed in Vietnam? Remarkable." *I've got to be the one to oversee it.* "We're honored you would consider our museum."

Tuan spun his cup around and turned to Thuy. "Let us not get ahead of ourselves." Tuan's lowered voice had an edge of threat.

She felt her face redden. "I'm sorry… it's exciting."

Tuan folded his fingers into his palm and brought it to his lips. "Let us review what you have and what we might show."

Oh no. He might kill the opportunity because this man had criticized the museum.

Tuan droned on. "… catalogue or inventory of these pieces you wish us to consider? And we must see the pieces in person, of course."

"Of course, any of you would be welcome to see them." Minh looked at Hai, then Tuan, and flashed a smile at Thuy. "But I do have a thumb drive—here's a catalogue of the pieces I'm thinking of showing."

Hai's phone buzzed, and he scooped it up.

Minh pulled the drive from his briefcase. He reached for Thuy's hand, opened her palm, and placed the drive in the center. He closed her fingers but didn't look at her.

Brazen. She opened her fingers and stared at the drive. "Thank you. We'll take good care of it."

Tuan cleared his throat. "Yes, of course, please give that to Mrs. Thuy. She may review the first round."

The spell was broken. The last few minutes made her dizzy.

"And who will come to Paris?" Minh's forehead wrinkled. "To see the paintings before they travel to Hanoi?"

If she'd been ten years old, she would have raised her hand, bounced in her chair, and screamed, "Me! Pick me!" Instead, she stared at Tuan.

"We shall discuss," said Tuan. "In principle, we agree that it would be a great opportunity to show paintings from Vietnamese artists in that time period." Tuan jabbed his elbow toward Hai. "Our curator will make the final decision."

Hai looked up from his phone, stunned. "Yes, yes. We are very happy to meet you."

He looked at Tuan and Minh and blanched at his blunder of speaking in English. "Sorry, distracted. Personal matter," he whispered to Tuan and screeched his chair back on the cement floor. He bowed as he backed out of the room.

Thuy seethed. *Tuan chose a man who couldn't stay focused during a simple meeting. Hopeless.*

"His wife is ill." Tuan made a tut-tut sound and shook his head.

Minh raised his eyebrows. "If that's the case, Ms. Thuy could visit and look at the paintings."

She caught her breath.

"That is very kind of you," Tuan said, "but unnecessary. Our curator will go."

"But if his wife—"

Tuan raised his hand.

Minh stood. "I need to make a call. And give you a few minutes." He looked at Thuy, blinked twice, and grabbed his phone.

The door clicked closed.

That blink—could it be a signal? If it was, she couldn't read it but wanted desperately for it to mean, "I'd like you to come to Paris."

Tuan lowered his voice. "This is a second time you have questioned my decision. It is not becoming or professional. Hai is the official curator and should represent the museum. He will go."

"But you agree I'm more familiar with that period of art—"

"And because of that, you will give him a short course on the artists and pieces that will be best for us." One more fast click with the pen.

She opened her mouth but closed it as Minh shoved open the door.

"All decided in here? Or should I withdraw my offer?" He chuckled.

She braced herself.

Tuan shook his head. "We're discussing Thuy's obligations in Hanoi, raising her son without a father. And her mother—"

"No need to burden him with my personal life." Thuy squeezed her fingers and thought about her FU notebook. *Hold those thoughts.*

"Yes, and she has much work here, of course," Tuan added. "Mr. Hai will make the trip."

"Are you sure, Mr. Tuan? I would take good care of Ms. Thuy in Paris. And perhaps in London if some of your requested paintings are there."

Tuan scoffed. "No, I stay with my choice." He placed his hands on the table, fingers pointing toward each other and pushed to a standing position, which was not much taller than his sitting position. "Mr. Minh. Again, we thank you for your visit and this kind offer. We will come back to you with our decision." He gestured toward the door.

"My absolute pleasure." Minh packed away his tea and turned to Thuy. "I leave tomorrow. Will I see—"

"Mrs. Thuy, one more word. Now, please?" Tuan nodded at Minh and held the door for him.

Tuan pushed the door closed. "Mr. Hai will travel, but you will oversee the art once it arrives. If it comes. Are you able to take that duty?"

What is this? A reversal? Belief in me? "I-I… of course."

He held open the door. "I believe you are the best for that part. You know the artists, you can succeed. But do not fail." He bit his lower lip.

Chapter 10

That afternoon, the office clock—brass rimmed with a white face—clicked down the minutes. Just past 4:00 p.m. Plenty of time to do a quick review of Minh's thumb drive. After the meeting, Thuy had walked back to her office with the drive burning in her hand. What a turn the day had taken, in a good way. A chance to show what she could do on the art side of the museum. *Tuan would see, and so would other museums.*

She stared at the wood veneer that had peeled from the front right corner of her desk. She stroked it, trying to push down the part that had lifted. She leaned back on the armless teak wood chair, which must have been designed by a cynical architect. The seat was a square flat plank; the back rose 90 degrees straight up and also had a flat plank for shoulders to rest against, if rest could be possible. The seat rose high enough that most Vietnamese found their toes touched the floor but not their flat feet. She'd considered sawing the legs to be shorter, but others had tried and never got the legs even, so they ended up with an uncomfortable chair that tilted.

First, a quick search on this mystery collector—she punched Nguyen Son Minh into the computer, and it turned up "Thomas Son Nguyen." *Bingo.* In his LinkedIn photo, he wore an open collared shirt, like Silicon Valley tech leaders. He managed a firm that manufactured lithium batteries. *Nothing about art. Hobby?*

Minh had said that his thumb drive included descriptions and photos of the artwork he would consider loaning. This was her chance to make the first selections—even if Hai and Tuan would do the final ones. If she couldn't be the museum curator, maybe this could be her break—an opportunity to show the art world—and Bo—what she could do.

Her desire came partly from having Uncle Vu in her world for so long and from wanting Quang to follow his dream. And it was her time, her generation's time, to make a difference and help bring this country from eons of poverty and war into a modern future, where Vietnam was connected to the world. Enough on the big ideas. She had to get to work.

She'd talked with Tuan once more after the meeting, and they agreed they should choose painters who had studied at the academy during the 1920s and 1930s, had worked through wars, and still produced work through the subsidy period and even into the 1990s or 2000s. *Do this the logical way. Step by step.* She pulled out a reference book on the academy and a pad of paper for notes.

- 1925 – Indochina College of Fine Arts founded. V. Tardieu (Fr): blend traditional VN craftsmanship with modern (i.e., European) approaches – he died 1937.

Mostly French instructors had taught mostly Vietnamese men how to be artists, how to move beyond crafts to fine art. They taught perspective, anatomy, oil painting on canvas but used local content and substrates, like lacquer and silk. She scanned the page. Some critics early on accused the academy of colonialism, but in the end, people agreed the academy created Vietnam's fine arts industry. *Right, I remember this part.* She flipped the book's pages.

- 1940 –1945: Japan occupied Vietnam.
- 1943: America bombed Hanoi, and the academy evacuated.

She rubbed her eyes. *Quite a rough first twenty years.* The museum had several Vu sketches during the French and American wars, so she assumed he and the other artists had also gone to war. *Those young men likely fought with their pens, not with guns.* She leaned back over the book.

- 1945: Independence declared.
- 1950: December. The academy opened w/new name—Fine Arts Secondary School. Thai Nguyen (in the resistance zone); aka The Fine Arts School of the Resistance.

Of the resistance. What a name for an arts school.

- 1957: Another name change: The Fine Arts College of Vietnam.

And why not? By that time the country was on the road to unification and should have a single college. But, of course, a unified country would take another twenty years.

She flipped through pages listing the academy's famous students. Her uncle, of course, but also Nam Son, To Ngoc Van, and Le Pho. And there was her pal, Nguyen Pham Chanh of *Going to the Rice Fields* fame, the picture that calmed her the other day.

Enough on the academy; now to the thumb drive. She scanned the list of artists, and her fingers tingled when she saw Pham Ly Vu. *Uncle Vu.* She wanted to open that file and see what Minh might have on Vu. She hoped it would be more than she knew or could get her parents to reveal. She positioned her fingers above the computer, relishing this moment and believing deep down that what was in this file could change her life.

Someone hummed in the hallway, and she heard a knock at the door. *Not now.* She pulled her fingers away from the keyboard and made fists.

Hien rounded the door. Her wrinkled blue linen uniform was spotted with splotches of water. "Mrs. Thuy. I wondered if you found your notebook? I'm so sorry I did not see it in the museum when I cleaned."

Thuy relaxed. "Nice of you to check. I did find it and will be sure never to lose it again."

Hien snickered. "Very sad. I wanted to read your spicy entries." She waved. "Say hello to your good mother. She should come by more often."

"I will." *Come by more often? Hien must be mistaken. Chi doesn't go anywhere.* Thuy shook her head and looked back at the screen. *Slow down.* She had to do this right. No mistakes, no jumping too fast: *be a logical curator, not an emotional family member.* She stacked four sheets of recycled paper on her desk, grabbed a pen, and made a list of what Bo had told her about his uncle over the years. A baseline to compare with Minh's information.

1. Vu – born in 1926. In Thai Binh.
2. Student – Indochina College of Fine Arts – late 1930s? Would have been around 12? *But that's too early.*
3. Peers at the time? Unknown.
4. Brother of Pham Quang Hoang (Bo's father) who died during the battle of Dien Bien Phu. 1954. 31yo when he died. Bo was 3yo.
5. Taught at academy –1940s. (Bo thought.) Didn't know how long.

Vu might have been at the academy during the Japanese occupation, or before, but then he would have been too young. She rubbed her temples. The academy closed in 1943 and reopened in 1950, Thai Nguyen, a resistance zone. *Maybe Vu had been there. Could have been a teacher or assistant.*

6. Sketch artist during 1950s – maybe at Dien Bien Phu. If yes, he could have been there when his brother died.

How little Bo knew about his uncle. She glanced at the clock again—4:31 p.m. *Speed it up.*

7. Lived in countryside (where?) during 1950s.

Painting, after his stint in the war. She'd noticed portraits by academy artists in the museum's storage vault made during that same timeframe. Maybe after the trauma of war, they wanted to paint People in peaceful settings. Something rustled outside her door and then banged against it.

8.   Worked as a sketch artist again during the American war – 1960s.

So much time at war. The museum had many of Vu's sketches—at least four of them hung in the third-floor gallery, and she thought at least 15 – 18 total, including the ones that had been removed, and she found in the vault. Bo never mentioned where Uncle Vu was based, but maybe Vu had scribbled location on the sketches. The ones that appeared in newspapers had locations, but not all of the sketches seemed to.

9.   Lived in Hanoi in the subsidy period, when he did the Ba Dinh neighborhood paintings.

She needed to look at the ones in the museum to confirm. Thuy skimmed her list. She felt like she had a skeleton of a man and not a full one at that. A human skeleton had 206 bones, and an arm had thirty, if her memory from ninth-grade biology served her correctly. But this skimpy Vu skeleton didn't even have enough "bones" to make an arm. *Push on.* She listed what else she'd like to know to have a fuller account of this man.

10. Did he ever marry? Bo says no, but is that true?
11. Did he have a lover? Any children?
12. Who were his friends? Are any still alive?
13. How did his paintings get to France?
14. Why doesn't Bo know more? Or tell more?

She stretched her arms and tilted her head side to side. Four loud pops competed with the ticking clock. 4:40 p.m. She glanced at the office door, willing it to stay closed, and tapped open Vu's subfile.

PHAM LY VU. B. 1920. Nam Dinh Province, Vietnam.

Her foot stopped waggling. *What the…? Born in Nam Dinh. Not Thai Binh. They were close, sure. But how could Bo get this wrong? And the date of birth—1920?* Bo always said 1926. Maybe Minh was wrong. Bo wouldn't miss something like this. She slowed her breathing, and she shuffled the mouse arrow over Vu's name.

PHAM LY VU. B. 1920. Nam Dinh Province, Vietnam.
Student at the Hanoi College of Fine Arts, 1936 – 1938.
Paris, 1938 – 1940.

She slammed back in her chair. Paris had never come up in all the years she and Bo talked about Vu. *Makes no sense.*

Teacher, Fine Arts Academy, 1940 – 1945.
War journalist, 1951 – 1954.
Teacher 1955 – 1960.
War journalist, 1963 – 1970.
Death, unknown.

She did a double take and leaned her head in her hand. Nothing after 1970. Death unknown. Bo had always said he died in 1991. Twenty years couldn't just disappear. Her stomach lurched. The file shattered too much of what she'd thought she knew. Minh's research had to be faulty. It was far too different from what Bo had told her. Something was wrong.

The wretched clock ticked on its relentless path toward 5:00 p.m., when she had to leave to reach Quang's school in time. Just two more minutes to read.

Pham Ly Vu was a fierce nationalist, painted and sketched in service to the homeland, and drew scenes of life among his neighbors in Hanoi, using a mix of styles.

She knew his style and content was flexible—he drew neighborhoods and portraits, war sketches and landscapes—and probably depended on the range of materials he could find. During conflict times or the subsidy period, he drew with pencil, charcoal, or ink. During the 1950s and late 1980s, he used oil. She couldn't remember seeing any paint on silk, which some of the other artists used.

She forced her shoulders down from her ears and heaved a sigh. *No, don't hurry this.* She would take the thumb drive home and review tonight, away from time pressure. She pulled the drive out, put it next to her purse on the desk, and rushed to the toilet.

When she returned to her office, her purse was on the edge of the desk and the drive was gone. *What the…?* She'd left it on the desk, next to her purse. She dropped to her knees, looked under the desk, swished her hands in the rubbish bin, and scanned the floor. *Nothing.*

Defeated and tense, she glanced at the clock. 5:02. *Dammit. No time for this.* She had to leave in five minutes. She paused at an odd twittering from the radiator by her window. A shadow skittered along underneath. She leaned forward to see and sprung back. *Chết tiệt!*

A rat the size of a small cat raced from beneath the radiator to the far corner of the office, where a patched hole had come unpatched. The varmint sprinted inside, its tail whipping the wall as it slithered in the hole. In its wake, she noticed a white strip on the floor. The thumb drive.

She scrambled up and her eyes darted around. She grabbed the desk to steady herself and put her hand over her heart to slow it down, but in these moments nothing helped. She felt detached from her body, watching from a few feet away, scrutinizing herself like a doctor might diagnose a patient—disconnected, objective, and clinical. But her real body cringed in horror.

A grey blur stood at her door. Chien. "Everything all right?"

She still grasped for air. "No. No. A rat just invaded my office."

"In this city? That's got to be a first." He peered around the desk, snickering. "We have so many…"

Thuy backed up until she felt the chair against the back of her legs and sank to her seat.

Chien stared at her. "It wouldn't be—wait. You're not… Are you afraid of them? I'm sorry to make fun."

She nodded weakly, hands fluttering over the desk, straightening piles, keeping her eyes occupied. "Terrified. Always have been. Just let me get my breath."

His voice softened. "Do you need something? Water? Whiskey?"

She huffed. "Thank you, but no. I'll be okay." She waved her hand to dismiss him. "Thank you. I'm fine." She crouched on the floor, grabbed the drive, and pulled herself upright, still panting. *Breathe. Breathe.*

Her phone buzzed. A call from a number in Ho Chi Minh City. No voicemail, and no text, and she made it a rule never to answer unknown numbers, so she dropped her phone in her purse and hurried down the hallway.

Chapter 11

Thuy wanted Chi and Bo to be happy about the new exhibit but feared they'd not understand how important it was. Or at least Bo might not.

"Wonderful news! I am so proud of you!" Chi clapped. "You deserve this." Chi sat on a Naugahyde couch, nursing a lemon drink. She tapped the remote button to turn the TV sound off.

Bo scowled at Chi and then focused on the big television screen: Vietnam vs. Indonesia.

"What's the good news, Mum?" Quang walked into the living room and flicked on the fluorescent ceiling lighting. "Bo, what's the score?" His eyes shifted back and forth to the screen.

Thuy sighed and focused on Chi, since it wasn't clear if Quang or Bo would even hear her. "I'm going to curate a special exhibit. I'll be in charge of paintings by Vietnamese artists whose works have been in France for a long time. Maybe even some by Uncle Vu." Thuy looked at Quang and patted the couch.

Quang stayed in the doorway, eyes glued to the TV.

Relax, this is part of teenagehood. She'd talked about it with Chi, who promised her it was good news: a child who grew apart and more independent was more able to deal with life's problems, like she had, like Bo had. But it meant Quang wouldn't cling to her like he'd done even a year ago.

It's good news. But don't let him pull away completely.

Bo shifted in his chair. "I suppose it is a good thing to curate. What you've wanted." He looked back at the television. "I wonder if Vietnam will ever qualify again."

She cocked her head. *He seemed unable to focus, to concentrate. Probably just aging. But it seemed more frequent.*

Bo turned to her. "But why were Vu's paintings in France? He was never in France."

"The collector—he's called Nguyen Son Minh—is French Vietnamese. His great-grandfather may have been at the academy with Uncle Vu. In Hanoi. He went to France and stayed and, apparently, collected art from his friends. Minh has those paintings and bought more over the years. I don't know if the grandfather somehow had Vu's paintings or if a dealer did."

"If you want paintings that no one has seen before, I can find some for you," he said. "Some we never sold."

Never sold? She looked at Chi, who shook her head.

Bo looked dazed. If the game was the distraction, she could understand. *But it seemed different.* "Not sure you understand what I mean—these are paintings that have never been in Vietnam, not just that they've never been seen here. They come from Europe, from France—"

Chi leaned forward and raised both hands. "When does this happen?"

She shrugged. "As soon as we get permission."

Chi rolled her eyes. "Paperwork. I always hated that part of the Ministry."

"Another reason for me to help you," Bo said. "To be sure you have enough."

"Why not put a hold on that, dear? She has to follow the process." She nodded at Thuy. "Isn't that right?"

Chi, the peacemaker. Happens more often these days. "Right. But we can choose the pieces now. Then the curator goes to Paris to look at them—"

"Not you?" Bo punched the remote to bring the sound of the game back on.

"Well, I'm not the museum curator. But I'll oversee it once the pieces arrive. It's an opportunity. For the museum, for me, for the artists we bring. We'll create a catalogue sketch about each of them. Including Uncle Vu, if his work is included." She swung her eyes toward Bo.

He stared at the ceiling. "You know enough about him. You see his paintings all the time. If you want to know an artist, know his work."

I just heard that comment from the Vietnamese Andy Warhol. Still sounds lame. "But I don't know about his life, who he really was. You knew him—"

"Let's eat." Bo shut down the TV.

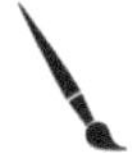

"Taking a walk. Anyone want to join me?" Thuy called to Chi, Bo, and Quang after she had cleared the dinner debris. No one responded. "I'll be back in an hour, then." She grabbed her umbrella.

She plugged in her ear buds: K-pop music, all the rage among young Vietnamese, and she tried to stay up with what Quang was listening to. At this time of night, runners jammed the sidewalk around the lake. Mostly Vietnamese, but plenty of foreigners who took two steps to the Vietnamese men's four. A young mother squatted on the sidewalk, resting her elbows on her knees, arms stretched toward the tottering baby who had left her husband's grasp and wobbled toward her. A grey-haired Vietnamese man in an undershirt and droopy basketball shorts faced the lake and swirled his arms around like windmills, loosening his shoulders. He then swung his arms horizontally and slapped himself on the back of his shoulders with his palms. Seven thick-bodied older ladies followed a Tai Chi instructor, lifting their feet from the ground and stepping carefully side to side. *My future.*

Her phone rang. She assumed it was Chi, probably to apologize again for Bo, but Anna's name appeared.

"Thuy! My friend! How are you? I was worried about you after our last talk. Any better?"

"Much better," Thuy said. "I'll tell you about it, but first, how're you?" She sidestepped a heavily made-up woman lowering her tiny poodle with green dyed hair to the ground.

"So much to tell you. Remember my new job—cultural projects? My boss and I just came up with an assignment. Might interest you as well. Maybe we can work together. It's in Paris! *Paris!*"

Thuy's head lurched, and she squeezed the phone. "Paris! Lucky you. What's the job?" *I should be going. If it weren't for Tuan.*

"I'll write about immigrants to Paris in the 1920s, starting with musicians, artists, and writers. I read an article about how many Cubans and Japanese and Chinese and African American artists decamped to Paris in the '20s and '30s. Lots of writers, like Hemingway and Fitzgerald. It sounded like a fabulous environment. Anyway, I wondered about Vietnamese? Do you know if any went then?"

Thuy's pulse picked up. "Well, yeah. Of course. Our Uncle Ho—Ho Chi Minh—is the most famous. He was a cook, but there definitely were others. I'm just learning about some. Your new job fits."

"Fits what?"

Thuy scanned the sidewalk and scooted around a child jumping up and down in front of a balloon artist, arms upstretched.

"A Vietnamese French collector from Paris just visited the museum. He wants to loan us some of his paintings. Pieces by Vietnamese artists who were in France, or whose paintings found their way to France."

"God. That's brilliant. And yes, these topics mesh. Tell me more. Maybe I can find a way to come to the show. Haven't been to Hanoi in way too long."

"Definitely come. Bo and Chi talk about you still. And Chi asked if you're still trying to hide from him."

Anna skipped a beat. "From John? Tell her I'm fine. Yes, I still avoid Seattle and the West Coast. So far, success. But don't we both deal with dodging our ex-husbands? Let's not go there. Tell me more about the exhibit."

"Right. The exhibit. We'd show pieces never seen in Vietnam. But I need to find out more about the artists we might show. Your new project could help."

"Absolutely. What do you need?" Sirens raced in Anna's background. "Oops. Sorry."

"Where are you? I hear all kinds of noise."

"The normal Hong Kong cacophony. Nearly tripped over a person. I'm going to meet friends."

Thuy had visited Anna in Hong Kong once years before and discovered she lived in a lavish mid-levels apartment. On an auction house salary.

"My real name's Anna Stilton Ballat. 'The Seattle Ballats,'" Anna had said. "Lumber barons from the late 1800s, early 1900s. Lots of money. My family managed it well. But that meant expectations. Lots of them. Vietnam was my escape from all that. No one knew me." After two years in Hanoi, Anna returned to Seattle and married an investment banker (mother's choice). When that soured, she had run away again to Hong Kong.

"Sorry for the noise. You know Hong Kong. If not a typhoon, then there's an accident."

"In Hanoi, the honking competes with smells."

"Ah, yes, the wafting scents from men who used—was it Bao Khanh Street?—as a public toilet. Ugh."

Thuy laughed. "That's all cleaned up. But now it's dogs and their business. Hanoi is overrun. But some are cute, even if their owners dye their hair. But back to you. What do you plan to research?" Thuy wove through the crowd to a cement bench next to fourteen stocky women rocking to Zumba music. One wore a flouncy white gauze number, half dress and half tunic with puffy sleeves. Another's leopard leggings clashed with her orange stripe top. They smiled with half closed eyes and swayed. All seemed right in their worlds, at least during thirty minutes of Zumba time.

"And now your noise is filling my ears. What is that? Zumba?"

"Yup, the ladies over fifty crowd. Go on about your project."

"Planning to look up several different groups. Right now, I'm thinking Cuban, African American, and Chinese writers, artists, musicians. And if I find something going on with Vietnamese, that too. I suspect some of these groups were the seeds for their countries' anti-colonial underground work for the start of their communist parties."

"Could be. Uncle Ho did some of his work there, for sure."

"Have you picked the artists you'll show?"

Thuy reached for a sprig from a Hoa Sua tree, next to her. "I've got a list of the possibilities. One would be Uncle Vu—"

"How about that! More recognition for the famous Vu family, eh?"

"That assumes I can find enough about the artists to put into the catalogue. I can find bios on some, but Vu is still a mystery."

"Where are you getting your information?"

Thuy sat up straight and tensed. Bac, or a man who looked like him, strolled on the sidewalk opposite the lake. He wore a shirt she'd given him five years ago when they were still married: a red jersey with the number 44, worn by Nguyễn Công Phượng, his favorite football player. *Couldn't be too many of those.* The man stopped, leaned against the wrought iron fence at the edge of a restaurant across the street, and stared in her direction. He lifted his chin, revealing his gang tattoo. She shivered and moved behind a tree.

A policeman strolled by, smiled at her, and then jerked his head in the direction she looked. He turned back and mouthed "You okay?"

She nodded and waved her hand.

He handed her his card with his name and number on it. "If you need help." He saluted and left.

She'd adored Bac in the early years, in university when they'd studied economics together, before he dropped out. They married against mild qualms from Bo and Chi. They'd thought he was too restless, too unknown.

"We've never met his family, his people. What do you know about them?"

"They're farmers. Good people. Poor, but good, from all he told me. And it's the modern age, when I should be able to make my own decisions on who to marry. No more arranged marriages."

Bo had gone to the wedding but never gave his full blessing; Chi had played peacemaker, as always, and tried to bring Bo around. Still, they had never warmed to Bac until Quang's birth, when they tried to welcome him more openly.

By then, Bac had taken a job in a retail clothing chain but complained that they never had enough money, especially with a child to care for. He had left his job and had begun activities that were shady, ones she never fully understood. She thought there had been drugs, black market schemes, and involvement with bad people, but Bac had denied it. They had divorced in a time when women were beginning to take charge of their lives and marriages, but the stigma followed her, especially when she moved in with Bo and Chi. She had expected Bo to gloat, but he never did.

"Hello? Thuy? Are you there?"

She let out a big breath. "Yes, sorry. I thought I saw Bac—"

"On no. I can't believe how small Hanoi is."

"So true. He's gone now. What were we talking about?"

"Your picks for the show. How many, and who do you want?"

Thuy glanced at the fence again. No sign of him. It probably wasn't Bac, just her imagination. "Uh. Right. I'm going to turn over my picks to the new curator—"

"That should have been your job. Still irks me."

She unclenched her jaw. "I'm over it. I've picked forty-one. The collector said we could have more than twenty and less than forty, so that's pushing it a bit."

"And who's the collector? Is it common for someone to approach you like that?" A door whooshed open, and suddenly the Hong Kong street noises became a cacophony of voices. "Hi all! On the phone with a friend. Be there in a flash... Thuy, I just got to the restaurant, but I'll go back outside till we're finished. Now, the collector?" Screeching car noises filled the phone again.

"Collectors do approach museums. But it's been a while for us. He found us through the blog." A fluffy dog, with orange dyed hair, pooped in front of her, while the owner faced the other direction. *Come on, pick it up.* "I think he made money in the tech world and inherited his great-grandfather's art collection from painters he knew in Paris. He also bought some from a dealer in Asia."

"Interesting. And you're sure they are authentic?"

"Huh? Of course they are… why would you say—"

"It's the former auction house in me. We had problems with forgeries sometimes. And now, researching these groups in Paris, I'm seeing similar problems. At least one source that says copying was rampant in those early days—mainly writers. I don't know about artists or musicians. You know that quote from Picasso that 'good artists copy, great ones steal.' There's talk about Fitzgerald using his wife's work."

Sprinkles hit Thuy's head; she stood, brushed her slacks, and pulled her umbrella from her bag. The Vietnamese Andy Warhol sprang to mind. "Is that so bad? People borrow, get inspired, copy to learn."

"I'm sensitive because there's a museum in France that's been showing fake paintings and didn't know it."

Another call beeped. The number looked familiar but not one she knew, so she declined it. "Sorry, another call. To your question, we'd never do that in my museum. But I'll admit, we do allow artists to come in once a week to practice. I ran into one the other day copying one of Uncle Vu's pieces. Sorry, you said something about France? "

"A piece by Le Pho—"

"One of the early ones to go to France."

"Right. Sotheby's sold one of his late 1930s family series. One called *Family Life.*"

"I remember that one. A mother, gorgeous green ao dai, and a little girl. Women in the background. Peaceful."

"Yes. Ink and gouache on silk. Well, Sotheby's sold it in 2017 for over a million dollars. Broke the record for his pieces. I think they'd sold one a few years earlier for eight hundred thousand dollars, so this was over the top."

She glanced at twinkling lights around the lake. "I remember. It made headlines everywhere."

"But some people thought it was fake. Big scandal."

"Geez. How awful. But we'd never let that happen."

"That's what you'd hope, but I'd caution you to be careful. Be sure your pieces are real."

"Is that your righteous American attitude?" Thuy laughed and clicked open her umbrella.

"Touche. But still, my one law course in college taught me that copying is one thing, but trying to benefit from it is a crime. Forgery. I hope your loaned ones are all good."

"I'm sure they are. I mean, I just read about how museums are the most trusted institutions—we wouldn't jeopardize that." A thunderclap struck before globs of rain drenched her shoes. "I need to run. Keep me posted."

She tucked under an awning to wait out the downpour and checked her phone. The number was the same as the other night—Ho Chi Minh City again. This time a voice mail popped up: "I am Nguyen Thi Linh, director of the Ho Chi Minh National Museum of Modern Art. I would like to speak with you. We have a position that might be of interest." Her heart pounding competed with the roar of the rainfall. *The best museum in the country! God, what a chance to make her own mark.* And, if she needed to, a way to put Bac behind her for good.

Chapter 12

A few days later, at a back table in Pho Thin on Lo Duc Street, Thuy took a slug of watermelon juice to celebrate her weekly lunch date with Hang, where they ate chicken pho and griped about work, life, and family. Clattering dishes, laughter, and beer glasses that slammed onto tables made it the perfect spot for deep discussions. No one could hear anything. The lunch rejuvenated her enough to get through the week. But today wasn't to vent. She wanted Hang's reaction and advice on whether to pursue a new job, the most exciting thing she'd had happen in a year and her chance for real independence. Hang was one of the best analytic minds she knew. And on top of that, she'd been Thuy's best friend from primary school.

Hang bustled into the restaurant, in her bright purple ADP polo, khaki slacks and ever present red high top basketball shoes. "Chuck Taylors," she had told Thuy. "The real thing, not fakes." On Hang's IT manager salary, she could afford them, compared to Thuy's museum pay, where counterfeits were her only budget option.

Where Thuy was a long Coke bottle in shape, Hang was a deck of cards: square torse, flat front and back, and cinched wait. "I'll never be a model," she had said in high school. "So, I'll have to dazzle with my brain." She threaded her way through the tables, turning sideways to pass through, and stepped back twice to avoid servers carrying aluminum trays of steaming soup. "Sorry. Traffic… whoa, what's up? Did you eat some bad fish?"

Thuy laughed. "Not at all. I have some news. Maybe good news. But something to talk through for sure."

A server stood over them. "Chicken or beef?"

"Ga," said Hang, holding up two fingers. "OK, I'm ready to listen." She tilted her head toward the server. "Raging rocks! Shouldn't she know we always get chicken since we've done that for three years."

"She's new. Only here two years. Are you quoting Shakespeare now?"

Hang chortled and knocked on the table. "What's going on?"

"Short answer: Ho Chi Minh Modern called—they want to talk about a new position."

Hang clapped. "The museum? That's big. What you've wanted, right?"

Thuy's heart drummed and she couldn't hold back a smile. "Well, yes, but slow down. It's just a cloud, nothing firm. I've only traded voice mails with them so far. I know nothing more than that. I'm probably not even qualified. The odds are not—" She leaned back as the server put the bowls down, sloshing broth over the top of hers onto the table. She sopped it up with a paper napkin.

Hang reached for two wooden chopsticks from the plastic container holding at least twenty. She wiped them several times with a napkin and placed two across Thuy's bowl. "Don't be so modest. You're qualified; you want a change. It's a big growth opportunity, don't you think? Go for it."

"I don't know—"

"Don't be a milksop." Hang stacked noodles on her tin spoon. "Means coward."

Thuy rolled her eyes. "Now what? You're learning Old English? Every week you get on a kick to teach those developers of yours something obscure."

"Yup, those baby developers need to know something besides code, so I'm teaching them Shakespeare's insults. They love it." She lifted her chopsticks.

"You always know just what to say." Thuy squeezed the small quarter of lime into her soup and added a scoopful of chili sauce and five chopped fresh chilis.

"You sure? That stuff's potent. You tried this last week and—"

"I need a burning mouth today to get ready for battle."

"You know best." Hang lifted her eyebrows. "Now, tell me what you're thinking."

"Told you I know nothing more. We've got a date to talk today later but…haaaaaa. Whew." She coughed and sucked in air. "More punch than I expected." She waved her hand in front of her open mouth and reached for water.

"Serves you right. Now let's talk it through. Why this job?" Hang stroked her left wrist: a tattoo of an infinity sign on its side. She'd told Thuy years before that the tattoo reminded her that she was a speck, a tiny piece of nothing in infinity. "Keeps me grounded," she'd said.

"Well, the challenge, of course. I want to be on the art side, not just business. I could be a curator, which Tuan won't let me do here. Whew." She fans her mouth. "And Ho Chi Minh Museum is the biggest and best in the country."

"And you'd escape your jerk of a boss."

Thuy laughed. "Tempting. Then again, Tuan did give me the opportunity of the special exhibit so we shouldn't be too hard on him."

Hang wiped a slick napkin the size of her palm across her lips. "And you want the status."

She cuts to the quick. "Jump right to that?"

"You're my best friend. I say what others won't. And what you won't admit out loud."

"I want to uphold the family legacy, true. Uncle Vu put this family on the map, and Bo wants to keep that. I do too, for Quang's sake."

"Nhaaaaa. Go ahead and be self-righteous but know that I know…" Hang snickered.

"OK, you got me. But to make such a change would mean upheaval."

Splat! An aluminum tray landed on the floor, spewing utensils and empty glasses. Silence for three seconds before two servers scrambled to pick them up and another brought a string mop.

Thuy turned back to the table. "Where was I? Oh yeah, cons to this job. I'd have to move, and that would be hard for Quang, if he couldn't do the academy."

"I thought he'd already applied?"

"No. So much to it. He's getting a portfolio together. Then there's the actual application. And, even in the Vietnam of today, you need connections to get in. Bo is starting to meet up with people from the academy and others who know the leaders there. Helpful here but worthless out of Hanoi. Bo and Chi and I are talking about how to make the tuition work. If I left, and he stayed, I could send money back, but I don't want to be that far away."

"Right. Or if Quang went, you leave your parents alone, and they'll need more help. Maybe not today but sometime."

"Another fallout of one-child families."

"What's the timeframe?"

"No idea. I'll know more after we talk. But if it's too soon, then I'd have to give up on the special exhibit, which I definitely don't want to do." She checked her watch. "Got to run."

She gathered her purse, pulled out money, and stood to leave. The restaurant had quieted and was two-thirds empty. Someone called her name. Thuy spun around, and her eyes landed on Chien, standing by the door.

He waved and mouthed "wait for me." He worked his way through employees, customers, and tables to reach her. He bowed to Hang. "I'm Chien. One of Thuy's colleagues… and a fan of hers. I don't mean to intrude." He smiled.

Hang reached out her hand. "Nice to meet you. I've got to dash. Later!"

"I need to go as well," Thuy said.

"Just a quick moment. I heard that you'll talk with the Ho Chi Minh Museum about a job."

Thuy stiffened. *How did he know? Or maybe he was the reason they'd called.*

"No worries. I'll tell no one. Just let me know if I can help in any way." He bowed and turned toward another table.

Chapter 13

Thuy met Hai in the hallway as she headed to his office and chuckled, thinking about the idea for a murder mystery—The Sabotaged Curator. She handed him the thumb drive with her choices for the special exhibit.

"Forty-one," she said. "I know Mr. Minh said no more than forty, but surely you can convince him. We need some women, some pieces that are unusual. My choices meet the criteria we talked about. Artists from the early academy, ones whose artwork spans decades Please consider—"

"I and Mr. Tuan will review. What else should I know? You must teach me before I go to Paris." His teeth, stained brown, would have dazzled her if they'd been white, but years of no dental care had taken its toll.

Thuy gritted her teeth. She had to avoid any emotion, any outburst. "Of course. Whenever you wish."

He motioned her to his office, and they stood at the threshold. His desk and side table were covered with flower bouquets, congratulations for his new job. The bouquets were large bunches, with stems taped and wrapped with pink and green and white paper.

He lifted his hand toward the flowers. "Beautiful, yes? People are so kind about the new job."

Nothing from me, though. She shook her head. *Maybe not over it after all. But maybe I won't need to worry about it soon.*

"I will inform you after we review. But Mr. Tuan said you are responsible for the final pieces in the museum." He tossed the thumb drive in his palm. "You understand my meaning?"

She gripped her icy hands. *Right. I'm your cover.*

One of the guards passed by. "Oh, Ms. Thuy! Congratulations on your first exhibit!"

She smiled with her mouth, barely.

Hai's cheeks puffed out. "And I will need some of your training on the artists before I go. Of course, I do not wish to be trouble for you."

She wished she could call up some of Shakespeare's insults. Something like "away, you three-inch fool." She shook her head to wipe out the insult. "By the way, how is your wife?"

He clapped his hands. "My wife rallied! I have my visa and air ticket. I will enjoy the weekend in Paris before the working days."

Her last hope thwarted: no Paris for her this time. As she drifted down the hall toward her office, her phone buzzed. The museum in Ho Chi Minh City.

"Ms. Thuy. I am Hoang Anh, of the Ho Chi Minh Modern Art Museum. We want to confirm the upcoming video interview. You will meet the director and curator, who will retire before the Tet holiday. If that goes well, we will invite you to visit us."

She stepped into a side room. "Yes, I am very interested to chat." Maybe she'd not need to worry about this special exhibit after all.

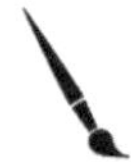

That afternoon, Thuy drafted a blog requesting information from readers about the artists she'd chosen for the exhibit. *Maybe others have access to places I don't—photos, articles, letters. Never hurts to ask.*

Tuan poked his head in her office. "Mr. Hai and I have a final list. We removed several of your suggestions."

"Did you replace them?"

"A few. The ones you chose were dark. Not vibrant. But I added new ones. Here is the final list. Twenty-four."

Her chest felt like he'd thwacked her. *Twenty-four? They had dropped almost half.*

He handed her a sheet of paper with his scribbles. "Much more beautiful. Showing the positive spirit of Vietnam."

"But that's so few—"

"You recall he said between twenty and forty. Mr. Minh will approve, I am certain."

She had no clue what Minh would think, and doubted Tuan had more insight. She scanned the list. "You removed the women artists?"

"No. I kept one. But your choices were mostly boring. As the museum director, my eye for this is stronger than yours. I know what people want—what they need—and that is to feel proud of our Vietnamese painters. We need to show upbeat paintings. You need to find information on their lives to include."

Outside the building, a loudspeaker strapped to the utility poles blasted the afternoon news and weather. The voice sounded robotic.

She braced. *Fight? Give him this one.* "I just read an article that says museums are places of trust. Visitors must believe that what we show is seeking to be honest and truthful. Vibrant, cheerful paintings may not represent our true history of conflict, losses. What the artists—and the people—experienced."

She had selected four by Vu, including two sketches from his war period. *Exactly because they were not "positive and vibrant."* They were sepia colored. Soldiers around a fire, or in a village. The faces on the villagers and the soldiers were drained, weary, not upbeat. *But they felt real, more than some of the pieces Tuan probably chose.*

"I kept two Vu pieces. Because of you, your blog, and his interest. Otherwise, I'd have pulled them. Too dark. Please look at the new list."

Final decision. She'd lose this battle, so best to give in this time.

"You must give Mr. Hai some training before he leaves for Paris. His success depends on you."

Of course. Not only the exhibit's success, but now Hai's success is my job. She craved the red notebook about now.

Chapter 14

Wednesday, the next week, Thuy finished her latest blog and answered a call from Chi.

"Shoving a child? He would never do that. What happened? He must have a reason for what he did." Thuy stared at her phone after Chi hung up. *Got to be more than a math test.*

Over the weekend, Quang had said he was nervous about upcoming exams, but this threw her. *Shoving another child?* He would never hurt another person, or animal. As a child, Quang had been the go-to kid in the neighborhood when another child wanted to play ball in the street or learn to draw. Five-year old Duc, from across the street, had come over just last weekend to ask if Quang could read to him, and he did. He read to the boy for thirty minutes, until Duc let him stop.

But teenage Quang sometimes retreated to his room for hours to draw; he didn't run to the kitchen to hug her when she got home from work like he had done even a year before. She had to pay more attention.

She lifted the two-pound replica of a Cham statue head from her desk and tossed it hand to hand. She'd bought it in the 1990s from Anh Antiquities, on Hang Buom Street. The owner said it was authentic, but she'd learned later that so many of the pieces were rip-offs. For years, robbers had chopped off the heads of many such statues near Da Nang. Later, forgers created the statue heads and sold them, claiming they had been part of a statue. The one she held reminded her to question everything, including what she saw in her son, his life, and changes. The exhibit and job possibility distracted her, but she still had to spend more time with him.

Thuy shut down her computer and grabbed her sweater. Her phone buzzed. *Hai, calling from Paris.* Where she should have been. She frowned and clicked her phone.

"Mrs. Thuy. It's Hai. I must return to Hanoi early—my wife has taken a bad turn—but I wanted you to know that Mr. Minh reduced the number of paintings even more."

"That's awful… I mean about your wife. I'm sorry. But what did you say about the paintings? How many?"

"Twenty-one."

She tried to swallow, but her throat seized. "Wha—"

"Yes. Very disappointing… you should have—"

"Only twenty-one? He agreed to only twenty-one?" Thuy squeezed the phone until her hand hurt. That would not have happened if she had gone.

Hai let silence hang.

She counted to seven.

He cleared his throat. "Yes. Twenty-one. I suspect he would have done the same if you had come. He insisted."

Thuy tilted away from the phone. *Geez. He could read my mind.* "Which ones? Did you see them all?"

"Sorry, please slow down. He chose ones from Paris. None from London—"

"I don't understand. What are you saying?" *Where are Hang's Shakespeare insults when I need them?* Her pulse slowed as she spewed venom to herself. "Seven of the best paintings were in London."

"I know that some of the pieces were in London. But Mr. Minh refused. He was very busy and could not take me. No one was available to welcome me. So, he removed those paintings."

"Then what did you see? And where were the paintings? His house? His office?"

"He said the paintings you picked were not good ones, so we made changes. Or rather, Mr. Minh changed some."

"But did you see them? The ones he picked?" She paced around her desk.

"Yes, some of them. At a store house—"

She heard raised voices outside her door. "I'm sorry. Are you saying you did not see all of the paintings he will send? How could you agree—"

"We had little time. He is the expert of his own paintings. He knows which ones will be best for us."

Ringing in her ears. *He couldn't possibly know what Minh thought was best.*

"I am needed in Hanoi. My wife."

And there's the rub. I should have gone.

"You should have come to Paris instead of me," he said.

Stop this mind reading! "I'm sorry for your wife."

"Thank you. The artwork arrives in a few days. Your job now. Make it succeed." He hung up.

This. And Quang. *Two crises. Never dull.* She grabbed her purse and shot out the door.

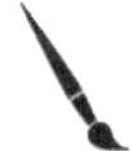

The hard wooden bench outside the school director's office offered no comfort to spirited young boys or their mothers. Thuy reached over for Quang's hand. "They'll call us soon. But I want to understand what happened and what made you push her. Can you tell me?"

"I didn't mean to," Quang said. He pulled his hand from Thuy's, faced the ground, and crossed his arms. "I'm sorry." He covered his face with his hands and sniffed. "I don't know. She said something… about Dad." He put his hands on his bouncing knees. "About a gang. I don't know what she meant. I only… I didn't push her. She walked away and tripped." His chin trembled and he pulled at the red "young pioneer" kerchief around his neck.

She'd heard stories about this girl. Her family had made lots of money from real estate, and there were rumors about corruption. She didn't think that Quang had much to do with her, but now she had to question everything.

His teacher claimed he'd pushed the girl from the back, and she had fallen forward. The girl's skirt had torn, her knees were scuffed, and she'd lost her bravado, but not her ire. She'd reported Quang, and the administrators had no choice but to pursue the incident.

She glanced at the name on the director's office and gasped. *Mrs. Quynh Chi. Chemistry, twenty years ago.* In Thuy's final high school year, Mrs. Quynh Chi had asked students to write a four-page paper about how they solved problems. Thuy thought about it for a week and then wrote a half page, describing her simple three step process: analyze the problem, brainstorm ideas, pick a solution.

Mrs. Quynh Chi rejected the effort and insisted Thuy write a "longer, more beautiful paper." Thuy had refused, and Bo was called in for a discussion. He backed the teacher, claiming that Thuy had to respect her teachers, that they knew best.

"But she's wrong," she'd told him later.

"She's the teacher. You must obey teachers and your parents. They are the most important."

"Why?"

Bo had shaken his head. "Whoever has position has power. Confucius says that teachers are high in our order. You must obey."

Thuy loved Bo and kept quiet, but the experience had rankled her.

Mrs. Qyunh Chi stood by the door frame. Despite a bent back, her face was wrinkle-free, and her hair was jet black. "I am sorry to meet you in this circumstance. Quang has been a model student. Up to now. I am sorry that he brings shame to your family, which I understand has a long artistic legacy."

Thuy's insides went cold. Mrs. Quynh Chi had no recollection of who she was, how she had humiliated her so long ago. *But she's had hundreds of students. Of course she couldn't remember all of them.* She shook her head. *Focus.*

"Quang must face a punishment."

She turned to Quang, who looked pasty in the room's fluorescent lights. He swiped his hand across his eyes.

"He will apologize to the girl and her parents and stay away from school for three days. And he will write a four-page paper about what he learned from this."

Thuy shivered. *Four-page paper. The woman hasn't changed.* She glanced at Quang, who hung his head, unmoving. *Should I fight for him? Or let it go, like Bo had.* She knew that Mrs. Quynh Chi had been at the school for twenty years and would likely remain long after any skirmish with her today.

Because Mrs. Quynh Chi had power.

In Confucius's day, power came from position or a ranking. These days, power could come from who had money or friends in the government, or other places where they could help. By now, in her position, Mrs. Quynh Chi would have a lot of power. Thuy had none. A sinking feeling joined with a growing realization that Mrs. Quynh Chi would always win.

"I will see that Quang satisfies the punishment."

Mrs. Quynh Chi dismissed them with a wave.

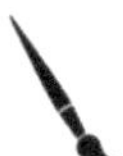

"Can we talk about it?" Thuy sat next to Quang on a bench outside his school.

"What's to talk about? You didn't believe me. She didn't believe me. I didn't do anything, but no one believes me." Quang swung his leg and stared at the ground.

"Unfortunately, Mrs. Quynh Chi has the power, right now at least. She can make your life easier or harder and I was afraid of it being harder. Sometimes, life isn't fair. You've heard Bo say that." *I even sound like Bo right now.*

"But it's not right. It should be fair. Why isn't it?" He looked up at her with eyebrows that peaked in the middle. This kid, who rarely cried, blinked fast to keep his wet eyes from overflowing.

"I'm so sorry, Quang. It's hard. You'll come to understand later. But for now, you must accept that when you push on something that is immovable, you will lose."

"But isn't that what you did at work? I thought you pushed for that job."

She caught her breath. "And I lost."

"But at least you pushed." The doors to the school banged open and a dozen kids streamed out, Two girls with linked arms, lifted their chins and glanced at Quang with smug smiles. A small boy with a bowl haircut walked by and wiggled his fingers at Quang, as though he didn't want anyone to see.

"Let's go home," Thuy said.

"No. Today is the day that Bo comes for me. You go."

She felt he'd punched her. And she deserved it.

Chapter 15

At last, something I know how to do. Four days after the school visit, Thuy stood in front of art crates from France in the museum's storage vault.

Chien had asked to watch her process the crates. "Since I'm head of security, I should understand this part too."

Today, he sucked a splinter out of his finger from one of the wooden art crates that stood amidst hundreds of art pieces—crated, packaged, or standing free like the metal sculptures. "How does this work?" He wandered through the vault, hands clasped behind his back. "Transport and unpacking?" The harsh fluorescent light exaggerated the pock marks on his face.

She held a clipboard to her chest. "People on the sending end do a 'condition report' on the state of each art piece before it leaves their museum or gallery or wherever it's coming from. We do the same kind of check when the art arrives. They packed each piece in its own crate. Sometimes, with smaller pieces, they're doubled up. If it travels by truck, a courier goes along to monitor heat and humidity to be sure the works arrive in the same condition that they left in." She waved her arms around the new crates. "These came by air, so the environment should have been pretty well controlled."

"When did they arrive?"

Thuy tapped her watch. "This morning. They have to sit for a while to acclimatize."

"Like people with jet lag."

She laughed. "Right. We'll unpack and hang them in a few days."

The basement's thick inner concrete walls kept weather out. Ceiling fans and air-conditioning controlled temperature in the space, which was jammed with art—oil, pastel, and charcoal paintings; lacquer paintings and vases; small pencil sketches; and large metal sculptures and ceramics.

Chien tapped on a bronze sculpture of a young female soldier kneeling on the ground, holding a rifle as if she was ready for battle.

Thuy cringed. That young woman was clearly a patriot. With a weapon. She still couldn't figure out the Vu war sketches and what they meant. For now, she had to focus on what was here. "Please don't touch them, even the metal ones." She scrounged in a drawer and handed him a set of bright blue latex gloves. "Here. Wear these. Your hands will sweat, but it protects the art."

He snapped on the gloves. "How much of all this is shown in the museum at any given time?"

"We're like most museums. About 10 to 20 percent of the items are on exhibit at a time."

"So few?"

"So much art, not enough room. And it has to rest now and then." She patted a crate. "In the vault, they're safe. It's dark, we monitor humidity and temperature levels, and no one's breathing on it. In one sense, we destroy art by showing it. Visitors are hard on art, and we have to protect it."

Chien pointed to a white sign, about half the size of an index card, plastered to the side of a crate. "And what do these numbers mean?"

"Ah, that's the accession information. When we got the piece, and from where. A description of the art piece that links the paperwork and computer records."

"So, what's this one mean?" Chien touched a sticker that read:

So Van Ly (1913 – 1991)
Young Boy by Pond, ca. 1943
1979. 33. 8

"First, it's So Van Ly, the artist, and his birth and death dates. The painting's title. And because we're not certain when he painted it, we add 'circa'—so it was around 1943."

He leaned in. "And acquired in 1979?"

"Right. It was the eighth piece of thirty-three art pieces that came into the museum that year. But we don't know how we got it—from a donor, or a purchase."

"Do all museums use the same format? And all of this is in the computer too database?"

"I think most use similar systems. And yes, it's on the computer as well." Her phone buzzed in her skirt pocket, and she peeked. *Ho Chi Minh. Perhaps confirming the video interview for later today.* She clicked decline.

Chien glanced at her. "Everything all right?"

"Of course… where was I? Inventory. We do one at least every year and match physical results to data in the computer." She moved toward the new crates. "Now, let's see what our collector sent us."

Chien squatted down to read the address on the crate that had arrived in the morning. "Huh. Look at this."

Written on the crate's side was: "Collection of Nguyen Son Minh, 456 Avenue des Fleurs, Paris, FRANCE. To: Museum of Modern Art, c/o Ms. PHAM Thao Thuy. Hanoi, VIETNAM."

No street address. Wrong museum name. Her heart rate sped. *Shocking.* "The paintings might have been lost."

Chien pointed to the wood crates. "Nine crates. How many did you expect?"

She snatched her clip board from a side table. Her fingers raced down the list, and her eyes flipped back and forth from crate to list. "Looks okay. At first glance, at least. But we'll know for sure when we unpack. If they were so slipshod on the address, who knows… I should contact the collector about what—"

"Oh, I'm sure they're fine," Chien said. "He sounded like an expert, from what Tuan said. When will you hang them?" He stepped closer to the crates.

"Uh… in three days."

"Good to hear. The upstairs gallery looks great—fresh paint, tape on the walls for each of your paintings," Chien said.

"We'll hang each piece right after opening the crate. Less stress to the art that way. Now, sleep time for the artwork." She clicked off the lights.

Chapter 16

After closing hours, Thuy went to her office for the Ho Chi Minh Museum video call. She checked her office wall background—her diploma and certificate—and signed onto the call. The director, Ms. Linh, gestured to two women next to her.

"Let me introduce our curator and archivist," she said. "You would be working with them."

Thuy winced. She'd thought the position they had in mind was the curator's. *Unpromising.*

Ms. Linh shuffled papers in front of her. "Ms. Thuy, we are considering creating a new job. We wish to become Vietnam's first museum that has an interactive exhibit space and is a creative hub for the country."

She felt tingling in her arms. Interactive museums were big recently: Huge iPad-like screens where visitors could change images, curate their own small shows, and generally access photos of paintings and artwork from around the world. She'd read about them but never seen one in in person. *Probably beyond me.* "Interesting. Tell me more."

Over ten minutes, Linh and the others explained the technology and offered to send articles.

"I'm not sure I'm the right—"

"I ask you to be open. We're interested in more than adding an interactive experience. We want other ideas for how to be creative. Two other candidates—from Singapore and America—are interested, but we hoped to find a local person. We hear that you're the face of your museum, what with your blog. And, apparently, you've improved some business systems."

"Not all my doing, of course."

"Don't sell yourself short, as they say in America. Most important for us, you know art and how it can help Vietnam in the future. But we need to move quickly if we are to retain the funding. Could you visit us in the next week or, at the latest, in ten days."

Thuy froze. *Slow down.* She stared at the wall behind the people on the screen in front of her. "That soon?"

"A problem?" Linh raised her eyebrows. "We'd like to move rapidly if possible."

Hang's logic darted into Thuy's head. *Take charge.* "I'll make it work. Let's plan on it." *Take charge.* That's what she should have done in Quang's meeting and regretted later. She cringed. *I need to talk to him again.*

She signed off and checked the blog. The site had a few responses to the questions she'd posted, asking about Uncle Vu and the other exhibit artists. She'd started with Vu as a test case. She'd hoped her readers might have information, especially if they had connections to France. Two responses:

1. *Don't ask so many questions about old artists. Including Pham Ly Vu. It can be dangerous to bring up old history.*
2. *Vietnam exiles in France have many stories, not all good. Some spied for France. Some spied on France. Be careful what you wish for. The information may not be what you want to hear.*

Lightning-rod responses. The topic of patriotism gone wrong ran underneath. *Surely, Vu couldn't have been on the wrong side.* But she'd read about artists putting codes or messages within their work. *Maybe he was sending a message within the sketches with no guns.* Her mind raced through options: discount the responses, put them up to quacks or trolls; ask for clarification. The notes sounded shrill, and she could sound the same if she responded. Or she could wait and see what else turned up. *A lame move, but it bought time.* And she had to hang those paintings first. She made small fist pumps.

In the meantime, she'd do more research on the Ho Chi Minh job.

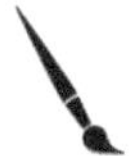

On her way out, Thuy planned to walk through the second-floor gallery, which had the most war-related work. She wanted to remember what some of the artists had done, in comparison to what she knew about Vu. But first, she looked at her postcards, several of which illustrated war. Mai Van Hien's *Vietnam War Meeting* showed an ethnic tribal woman greeting a Vietnamese soldier. Several pieces, in her museum and others, aimed to show how Vietnam sought to integrate ethnic groups into the country to meet the goal of the communists bringing people together in a unified, harmonious society.

Another in her set of cards was *The Mother in the Resistance War*, a lacquer piece. A young Vietnamese soldier filled the front of the painting. He sat underground, in a cramped space, with an outstretched bandaged leg. A pink plastic basket, holding a bottle and possibly a blanket, sat nearby. A bony-faced woman, gaunt and slumped, squatted behind a young girl, who stared at the soldier. The woman touched the soldier's leg, comforting him, as his eyes glazed over.

Propaganda again, but the vibe was solidarity in adversity. No guns, but clearly war is raging. Now she had to figure out where Vu fit into that world.

Chapter 17

To spend more time with Quang, Thuy had made plans for them to go to the Moon Festival with Hang and her daughter, who seemed likely to follow her mother's footsteps: a budding tech genius, coder and Shakespeare lover. As Quang's best friend, the girl balanced his art side with her clear-eyed logic, like her mom.

Thuy wanted to spend time with Quang and if it meant bringing his best friend along, she welcomed it. Soon, when he got older, he'd brush off the idea of going to the festival, but for the present, he was excited. She'd take whatever she could get.

At dinner before they left for the lake, Quang asked Bo to tell the story of the moon festival man, as he did every year.

One more year and he'll be too old for it.

"I'll tell the short version since you must get to Hoan Kiem." Bo cleared his throat. "Long ago, a man did a terrible deed and was sent away from his family as punishment. The police sent him to the moon, very far. He missed his family but couldn't return to this world. So, in autumn, he made a big smile that lit up the moon to be very bright. So bright that his children could look up and see the man in the moon. Their father."

Quang chuckled and pushed his rice bowl to the center of the table. "What a story. I used to believe it but now I just like the idea of a man smiling that big. Thanks for telling me." He moved to the door. "Mum?"

They walked barefoot down the concrete stairs in the center of the house, separating the kitchen from her parents' bedroom. At the base of the stairs, Thuy found her sneakers in the jumbled pile of a dozen sets of shoes and sandals. She pulled on her LV logo helmet and handed a smaller version to Quang. In another year, he'd need a bigger helmet and might be as tall as she was. She put her arm around his shoulders. "I'm glad we'll spend some time together. I've been so busy lately." She yanked a yellow jacket from her bike's storage under the seat. "Please wear this."

He slipped out of her grip but put on the jacket. "Can't wait to see Hannah."

She flinched. *Roller coaster reactions. Wanted me at school when he was in trouble but today, he's too big for a hug. I've got to do better while I have the chance.* "You call her by her English name?"

"Of course. We all do. I need one too. If I'm going to be an artist, I want people in America to say my name right."

An artist name. Another sign of him growing up and away. *Part of the seasons of life but I have to hold onto as much as I can, with him and for him. And for me.* She maneuvered the bike through Friday night's traffic, made worse by the throngs going to the lake for the festival. When another bike slipped in front of her too fast, she squeezed her hand brake to keep from slamming into it. Her helmet shifted forward, and Quang slid into her back. "You okay?" she said over her shoulder.

"Fine. Almost there anyway." His hands rested on his thighs. Last year, he would have held on to her.

The streets around Hoan Kiem Lake were closed to car and motorbike traffic, allowing masses of people to crowd the space. Children carried lanterns, magicians tossed fire sticks, and performers created balloon animals. "A snake! A dog! Or a giraffe?" Food trucks and peddlers sold moon cakes and wispy cotton candy.

Thuy parked, wiped her face with a handkerchief and plucked her shirt away from her chest.

"Here we are!" Hannah waved from the other side of a parade of costumed dragons that swished their heads and tails in the street, bumping into anyone in their wake. In bright red and yellow, two dragons walked on four feet (two people inside) and three others walked on two feet. Their mouths gaped and closed as they swayed.

Hannah, still in her white school shirt and red Pioneer scarf, scooted between the dragons, pulling Hang in her wake.

Quang hugged Hannah and jabbered right away. His face lit up when he talked to her like it did for no one else.

"Look at them. They've missed each other. Why was it he changed schools?" Hang slipped her arm through Thuy's.

"Bo thought it would give him an edge when he applies for the art academy. But it's been hard for him, making friends. Some of the teachers were there when I was in school. Battle axes." A teenager shoved her aside to get to a food truck.

Hang said something in the air.

Thuy leaned into Hang's ear. "Too much noise. Can't hear you." Another person jammed into her, and she lost her balance. She turned, and a woman, carrying balloons on long sticks, moved away. The music competed with cheering, and the dragon dancers wove their way through the crowds. Drummers pounded out of sync.

She glanced around for the children—scanned the crowd in front of her and to the side. She grabbed Hang's arm, yelling, "Do you see the kids?"

Hang lifted her eyebrows and screamed back, "They were just here. I'm sure they're around. But I can't see anything. Can you?"

Thuy stood on her toes and swept her eyes over heads around her. Nothing. No yellow jacket. No white shirt with a red scarf. "Can't see them. Let's split up. I'll go toward the lake, you to the food trucks."

Hang nodded her pinched face.

Jostling through the crowd toward the lake's edge, Thuy found multiple rows of children and parents holding and tossing lanterns into the lake. Colorful, lit-up paper lanterns bobbed on the water, making gentle ripples. Small children jumped up and down, pointing to the lights. She scoured the waterfront. Nothing but revelers who were not the children.

A tap on her shoulder, and she placed her hand on her chest. *Thank God.* She spun around, smiling.

"Excuse me, madam. I must go through." A thick-bodied woman in a white linen tunic and quilted jacket pushed forward a toddler, who thrust her sticky cotton candy into Thuy's shirt. "Sorry, sorry. But you must move."

Thuy saw a familiar profile and froze. A gang scar running down his left cheek—Bac—and a flash of yellow next to him. Quang. Her stomach flipflopped, from fear and relief.

"Quang!" She elbowed through the crowd to him. In a flash her wretched past rose up: threats, disappearances, people who'd come after Bac—and her—for money. She'd been afraid of him during the latter years of their marriage. Once he had threatened to hit her, and as part of the divorce, he was supposed to leave them alone. *Not following the rule, as usual.*

"Look who's here." Bac tapped Quang's arm and pointed to her. He moved in to peck her cheek.

She recoiled and clutched Quang.

"Mum! Dad bought a lantern." He thrust an orange paper lantern at her, swinging on a pole. "I'm going to put it in the lake. Want to come?" Almost a teenager, maybe, but a lantern turned him into a kid again.

Bac smirked at her. "Coming, Mum?"

Thuy gritted her teeth. "You shouldn't be here."

He blinked his eyes too slowly, a crocodile drawing her in before snapping. "But here I am. Public place. Looking after our son."

She whirled around. "Hannah. Where's Hannah? Quang?"

"What? What, Mum?" He jerked his head to his right. "She's there."

Thuy dabbed sweat from her neck with a handkerchief. "I'll look for Hang." She wrinkled her nose at Bac.

He shrugged. "I'm not going anywhere." He stepped toward her. "Oh, by the way, rumor is that you're looking at new jobs? Don't take him away from me." He stared at Quang.

"What?" She stiffened. "What're you saying? You're supposed to stay away from—"

"Getting clean. I'll show you. Just don't take him." His eyes narrowed, showing only black, like the young people in the propaganda poster in her office. But his were menacing. "If you do, I can make life difficult."

She recoiled. The dark tattoo on the back of his hand jarred loose a photo of him from the worst days: he had stood next to two men, all with cocky grins. They put their palms together slightly open, fingers pointing down to the ground, looking like a "V." The symbol, familiar among gangs, meant "Made in Vietnam."

An arm wrapped around her waist, and she jumped.

"You found them!" Hang squeezed. "They okay? Oh no. Him? What's he doing—"

Thuy grabbed Quang's arm and tugged him away. "Let's go." She glanced back at Bac and shuddered. *Might be the right time to make a move, far away. More independence for them, from him.*

Chapter 18

"Beautiful." Thuy spun around in the center of the museum's fourth-floor gallery. The room smelled of fresh whitewash, and late afternoon light spilled from windows just below the twelve-foot ceiling.

Thuy wandered the room with her layout chart. The collector's curator in Paris had requested forty running feet and suggested where to hang each piece. She had assured him the exhibit could meet those requirements and scanned the plan for the twenty-one pieces.

Footsteps behind her signaled Ngoc's arrival. He slipped off his black rubber sandals at the gallery's entrance, buttoned his blue custodian jacket, and placed his pith helmet on the floor.

"Chien, you know Ngoc, our custodian who's been here for a long time. He helps with uncrating and hanging. And knows a lot about some of our artists."

Twenty minutes later, Ngoc lowered Crate #1's outer wooden panel to the floor. He removed brown wrapping paper and bubble wrap.

Two envelopes fell out of the crate: one labeled "Notes on the painting" and a second with her name. She yanked off her latex gloves, opened the one addressed to her, and whiffed hints of Minh's favorite tea.

Ms. Thuy,

I hope you enjoy these paintings, chosen especially for you. For your museum. I'm sorry you did not receive all you wished for, but these are some of the best to show quality and depth of the artists. At least, I think so. I look forward to joining you for the opening. Maybe we can spend some time together.

Best, Minh

Her stomach fluttered. *Still thinking like a schoolgirl.*

"Exquisite." Chien stood in front of a portrait. His voice blasted her thoughts and brought her to the present.

Thuy joined him. Five women, maybe sisters, in a house, preparing a meal. The feeling was calm, almost gauzy and serene. "It's Trung Le Mai, one of the early ones to go to France. Minh does have pieces worth showing."

Over the next three hours, Ngoc unwrapped and hung the remaining twenty pieces.

Thuy walked the room's perimeter, straightened a piece that was crooked, and checked that all twenty-one were secured to the wall. "Wonderful work, Ngoc. Ready to head home?"

Ngoc swayed in front of one of the paintings. "Ms. Thuy. What do you know about the collector?" He stepped back and crossed his arms. Ngoc wasn't an art expert but had spent many of his off hours in the galleries and a few years back had begun drawing himself.

"Why do you ask?" She cocked her head.

"I wonder—"

"Let's look at all of them. Before anyone jumps to faulty conclusions." Chien frowned at Ngoc and set off along the wall in a clockwise direction.

"Ngoc, please join us," she said. "I want your thoughts." *But am scared of them too.*

Ngoc peeked at Chien. "I'm only the art hanger. Not the expert."

"I know," she said. "But you've been around art a long time. Please."

Thuy followed Chien, stopping in front of each painting, making notes: "Striking in shading; rhythm is lovely. Texture and tone—delicate and discerning."

Over the next hour the light from the upper windows darkened. With each review, she relaxed. She joined Ngoc in front of one painting. "Notice the balance in this landscape. Water buffalo in the corner, trees behind, and a small hut opposite."

"I like the way the shadows are stronger now that darkness is coming," Ngoc said. "You have a good eye, Ms. Thuy."

"You as well, Ngoc." She circled the room once more, checking the artists against the notes she'd made about each of them—from Minh's information and her own searches. "How are you two holding up? My back and my eyes are starting to fade." She glanced at Ngoc and raised her eyebrows. "All good?"

Ngoc gritted his teeth and looked at the floor in front of one of the portraits by Thu, the sole female artist in the group.

Thuy's stomach churned. "What is it? Have you found something?"

"I hate to say anything… sure I'm wrong. But…"

Chien strode over to him. "A portrait. Beautiful. I see nothing amiss. What do you see?" He scowled at Ngoc.

Ngoc scratched his neck.

"If you see something, say so," Thuy said. "We want integrity of this exhibit." She bit her lip. Maybe he was tired, like she was.

Ngoc stretched his arm toward the piece. "I know something about her. Especially her portraits, Mai was the best friend of my grandmother's mother. My great-grandmother—and she often drew her."

"That's far removed," Chien said. "How could you know that?"

"Because this is my great-grandmother. It is dated 1953, but that's impossible. At that time, artists—like this woman artist—worked for the war effort. At least that is what my grandmother always said."

"That's right," Thuy said. "Artists were war journalists. We have newspaper sketches."

"But women artists—and there were not many—were not war journalists. They were like other women soldiers. Carried supplies. A few were sappers who defused bombs." Ngoc tapped the wall. "I doubt she would paint peaceful portrait scenes in the countryside while everyone else was gone."

Thuy stared at the painting. *Peaceful. Happy.* Either this artist wasn't involved with war, or she was one of the best "art liars" around, able to paint the opposite of what most everyone was going through.

"How can you be sure?" Chien turned his phone flashlight on and got close to the painting. "Maybe the date's wrong. Or she painted between stints in the field? They weren't all out there, all the time. Did she take a break from war and make a portrait? Why are you questioning this one?"

She gaped at Chien. *Not sure where that defensive tone is coming from.*

Ngoc shrugged and rubbed his eyes. "Perhaps you're right."

Chien scoffed.

She plopped down on a bench and dropped her head.

"Ms. Thuy? Are you feeling all right?" Ngoc's voice punched through the fuzz in her head.

She sat up slowly. "We want this exhibit to succeed. But there can be no questions about the paintings. Mr. Ngoc, your thoughts, please."

"It is your exhibit, of course," Chien said. "Don't let Mr. Ngoc—or me—influence you. I'm sure every exhibit has pieces in question."

Damn. "But I don't want questions in my exhibit."

Ngoc inched over to her. "Please do not make yourself ill. I'm sure these are fine. Who am I? Just self-taught, with interest in a single artist. Don't mind me."

She looked at the window, now dark. This exhibit had to come off without glitches. She was partway there, as long as Ngoc's worries weren't real. She had to be absolutely sure, but her confidence had taken a hit. They couldn't see her waffling. "It's so late. My Shakespeare loving friend would say 'my necessaries are embark'd: farewell.' We are all exhausted. Let's look at this in the morning, fresh. Ngoc, I'll call in a few minutes to close up, but I'd like to sit for a bit, alone."

At 9:10 p.m., Thuy slumped in a corner of the gallery, exhausted and nervous. She couldn't shake Ngoc's comments. Even though he was the custodian, he'd also spent years looking at the museum's paintings. Once, five or six years ago, he had identified one that turned out to be a copy. *Maybe he's right this time.* She had to think about next steps. Postpone or go forward without the questionable painting. Weariness draped over her, and buzzing mosquitoes slapped the outside windows. She phoned Ngoc's office to take away the crates and packaging.

Chien answered.

"Chien! I thought you'd left. I need Ngoc to take the crates back to the vault."

"Can it wait until morning? He's stepped away."

"I'm sorry, but it needs to be done tonight. We need to clear the room so it can settle to its correct temperature and humidity. The pre-opening show is Wednesday. We need to get things set up."

"I'll find him and take care of it," Chien said. "Have you thought more about the painting he questioned?"

She skipped a beat. "I've got to decide if we open or remove it or what."

"You know, Ms. Thuy, I worked in a gallery long ago—also security—and sometimes they found problems, or what they thought might be, but in the end, it was always a mistake. Too many areas to question—signatures, style, materials. But false paintings are so rare."

"But I—"

"You need rest like the artwork does," he said. "Ngoc and I will be there in thirty minutes to pull the crates and lock up."

Swerving in and out of traffic, Thuy replayed the evening. She had to decide what to do. Keep all of the art pieces in the exhibit and hope Ngoc had made a mistake? Remove the one Ngoc had questioned? She worried about putting too much faith in a non-expert. Then again, Ngoc had identified a false piece years ago so she couldn't discount his concern. The beeping motorbike horns never quit, but tonight the crammed streets, sidewalks, and markets weighed her down. She veered to avoid a slow-moving driver hunched over his phone.

And then there were the misaddressed crates. Blog comments about Uncle Vu. The sketches in the vault. Hang's words hammered her brain—*"Don't decide until you have more information."*

She stepped off her motorbike in front of the house and plunked into a runoff puddle. Water splashed up to her ankle. *Drat.* Her brand-new Jimmy Choo look-alike alligator pumps were ruined.

A text from Anna jumped onto the screen.

Anna: Paris. Quite an adventure.

A pang of envy jabbed Thuy's chest, and she moved her thumbs across the screen.

Thuy: Will call later.

Maybe Anna could help her find more information about Minh. She'd be in Paris another couple of days. Thuy set her alarm to phone Anna at 3:00 a.m., which would be 9:00 p.m., Paris time.

Chapter 19

Thuy dialed Anna in the dark.

"Hey," Anna said after two rings. "What a city! When will you visit Paris? I've found good information about the immigrant groups… Oh, sorry. I'm rambling. What's up with you? Is the other museum job still in play?"

"Video call went well. They want me for an interview the day after our opening. But first, tell me what you're finding."

"The biggest is something that might help you. I found a ton—well, about fifty—vintage letters, Vietnamese and Chinese, all bundled together. I'll bring them when I come to Hanoi, but a colleague here translated a couple. Makes it sound like some of these early guys—writers, musicians, artists—were anti-colonialists. Vietnam's own Uncle Ho was the most famous. But others were on France's side. Vietnamese who spied for the French. In Paris and back in Vietnam. Controversial, so it's hard to find out much."

Thuy's mind raced. *Traitors.* If any of the special exhibit artists fell into that camp, it would be a huge loss of face. She had to know more about this collector and his paintings. And fast. "Is there any way you could find some information for me in the next few days? Before the opening?"

"Sorry. Been here a week and I'm leaving tonight. I wanted to be at your preview and stay for the opening."

The air-con was off, and Thuy's shirt clung to her back. "If there is a show—"

"If? What's that mean?" Chapel bells pealed outside Anna's window. "Hear that? Been a royal pain every fifteen minutes. But never mind. What's going on?"

Thuy's shoulders drooped. "I need information about the collector, about his paintings. About those artists you're learning about. I worry we might lose more paintings if there's anything wrong with them. We started with twenty-one and now have questions on at least one. "

"What? I thought you'd asked for forty something. What happened?"

"Tuan and Hai took out nearly all I wanted. Then the collector changed more. We got well-known painters instead of some of the lesser-known ones."

"God no," Anna said.

"Started out odd when we got the crates—they had the wrong address, but they made it to me. When we hung them, our custodian thought one looked off. He's not an expert but did discover a copy years ago." Thuy held her breath for two counts. "He might have uncovered… hate to think it or say it… a fake."

"No. That's awful."

"That's why I hoped you could look into—"

"Are you thinking about canceling? That'd be a huge shame. How about waiting to see what the preview shows? And then talk about postponing the opening?"

"Maybe. But I'd feel better if I had more information about Minh and his paintings."

"Shoot. I'm supposed to leave for the airport later."

Thuy's stomach growled. "I understand. Is there anyone else you trust who could do some digging?"

Anna let out a big breath. "Confound it. I'll rebook. What do you need?"

Thuy felt weightless and punched the air above her head. "You're a lifesaver. Again."

"You'll owe me one, my friend. So, what do you need?"

"More on the collector. Is he legitimate? Does he have a gallery, an office, storage unit? Of course, I did a Google search when we met. And LinkedIn. Generic information. Anything more on the artists would be great—I can send you the list. I'm curious about what those letters say."

"Whoa, whoa, slow down. I'm scribbling like mad. Not sure how much of this I can find. Can you send me your list in order of priority? I'll do my best."

"I do owe you. As always."

"But I have a favor to ask."

"Anything."

"An authenticator I've worked with—one of the best in Southeast Asia—wants to come to the opening. He's a fan of that era of art—from the thirties through the subsidy period. Could he join?"

"That'd be amazing. Then he could tell us whether we have any fakes—"

"That may be getting ahead of ourselves. He's touchy. And pricey."

"I'll have to get Tuan's permission—-"

"Hold it. Why are you asking your boss for permission? I thought this was your exhibit?"

"Only if something goes wrong. Otherwise, he'll take the credit." A lone motorbike went past the house.

"But what if we got him to do an informal review of the pieces in your permanent collection? At least we could ask."

"That'd be incredible."

"Now, just take charge. Stop feeling you have to prove yourself. You're good enough. Text me what you need, and I'll get on it. Until then, go after the Ho Chi Minh job too. I'd hate for you to be empty handed if this thing fails."

Take charge. At work. At home. In life.

Chapter 20

Thuy stood in the fourth-floor lobby at 6:43 p.m., waiting for her nineteen preview guests to arrive. An hour earlier, Anna had texted. She had news and would call later.

Her teal sheath and shimmery heels boosted her confidence. *Something other than black.* Dressing the part helped boost her chance of success, at least she hoped so. Her leg muscles twitched, and she stomped her heels to settle down.

Three guests wore dangly ceramic bead earrings and super high heels. Another sported a white and yellow linen tunic and looked like a sunflower. Two wore black tights and black mini-skirts—real or fake leather, hard to tell. A couple of the men sported white t-shirts and black jeans with sockless loafers. One of the newest hot artists carried off his man-bun well, standing in a circle of women in sleeveless cocktail dresses. Almost like a backup band. Light from outside faded to pink and grey, her favorite time of day.

The preview group's friendly faces also helped calm her. Hang wore a crisp white shirt and clean khaki slacks. In her ever-present red high top basketball shoes, she looked like one of the artists. Chien and Ngoc stood on the sidelines. "You don't need the custodian to be part of the crowd," Ngoc had said.

Tuan appeared in his crumpled day suit. "I came to say good-bye. I leave for New York in the morning. The Metropolitan Museum of New York conference." His breath smelled like shrimp sauce. "Good luck. I return in one week. Do not fail." He smiled at a guest and slipped out.

Back to his grumpy self. One last zinger before he leaves.

She shrugged him off and swept her eyes over the group. She was pleased that two journalists had joined—one from *Vietnam Reports* and the other from an art magazine. Good press before the opening couldn't hurt, even though it would be the artists' word of mouth she counted on. One man, angled face and soldier posture, stood to the side and saluted her when he caught her eye. *Familiar but can't place him.*

Someone tapped her shoulder. "Thanks for inviting me, Thuy. I love a good pre-opening." Quan Son Hoan was a well-known, quirky artist, thanks to his own efforts.

Hoan had been a rival when Thuy tried to become an artist, but once it was clear she couldn't cut it, their friction softened. He was an eccentric and opinionated influencer and she enjoyed him best in small doses. She'd invited him because he had a relative in this group of returning artists and, if he liked the preview, it boded well.

"So glad you could join. And you dressed for the party!" She winked.

Hoan wore black basketball shorts and a long-sleeved beige linen tunic, year-round. Long ago, he had told her that he lived in North Korea for a year. "No blankets, little food, and certainly no down jackets. Cold doesn't bother me anymore." He used his "year in North Korea" like a shield, never saying more but leaving a whiff that he was a spy or a soldier gone rogue.

She entered the center of the gallery and clapped. "Thank you, thank you for coming. This preview is to show the twenty-one paintings in our special exhibit, which we call 'Returning Home: Vietnamese Artists and Their Work.' Imagine that. Vietnamese artists' work that's never been in Vietnam or was taken out of the country for a long time and is returning. I asked you here tonight because you're connected to the art world, and some of you have relatives who were in this remarkable group of painters." She gestured to Hoan. "People like Hoan's great-grandfather." She raised her glass. Clinks sounded around the room.

Hoan tilted his head but didn't smile, so cool he seemed frozen. But he never smiled, so that was nothing new. The "soldier-posture-man's" eyes shifted around the room, not looking at her. *Almost like he's a security guard.* She glanced at Chien, who lifted his champagne glass at her.

"It's a huge opportunity for our museum," Thuy continued, "for the art world in Vietnam, and for all of us. The exhibit focuses on artists who worked in times of struggle from the early 1930s to the early 1990s—during wartime, the subsidy period, and into *Doi Moi*. For different reasons, some of their work left the country—or never was here at all—so we've not had a chance to enjoy it. But now we can showcase these 'lost paintings.' In Vietnam."

Applause erupted.

"Congratulations, Thuy!" Hang yelled from the side of the room. Several people cheered.

She bowed. "Now to practical matters. All of you, please give feedback on a couple of questions. We've hung the work in chronological order, broad time periods, rather than by artist. We've got the period just after World War II and during the French war—up to the Dien Bien Phu battle—from 1945 to 1954. The American involvement, until 1975. And last, the subsidy period and *Doi Moi* from 1986, up to the early 1990s. That's over fifty years of work from these artists. Tell me what you think about the arrangement, and what it brings up for you."

The crowd nodded, almost in unison. People turned toward the walls.

"And one more thing. Very important." She sucked in air. "Please tell me any stories about the art pieces or the artists. Because most of this art has never been here, we don't know much. If these men—and only one woman in the group, sorry to say—were relatives or if your elders knew them, I'd appreciate feedback. Now, please enjoy the exhibit."

The cacophony of the room rose, but through it, she heard her name.

"Thuy!" On the opposite side of the room, Hoan waved—palm out, fingers down. He stood in front of two abstract paintings and turned to squint at them.

She hurried to him.

"Where'd you get these?" Hoan leaned back, arms crossed, like a critic.

"I told you. A collector in France. Nguyen Son Minh." Her palms itched, and she rubbed her forearms. "His great-grandfather was part of the academy group in Hanoi. Why? Do you think he knew your grandfather?"

"Could be," he said.

She gestured at the other pieces. "What do you think of the layout?"

"It's the first time to see the progression of those artists so clearly," Hoan said. "We knew about the French influence, but this shows the artists almost 'talking' to each other in their similar approaches, techniques. As peers. And how they affected artists after them." Hoan's voice petered out and he turned away.

"Appreciate that, Hoan." She moved toward Hang. "Whew. He seems happy." If this preview came off well, she'd have even more clout going after another job.

Hoan flapped his arm. "Thuy! Come back!"

Dash that thought. "What?" Thuy darted across the cement floor, her heels clicking, with Hang behind her. "What's going on?"

Hoan pointed at a different abstract painting in front of him. "There. Look at that. It's my great-grandfather's." The abstract painting seemed cubist, stark grey and white shapes spread across the canvas.

Hang, arms akimbo, stepped in front of Hoan. "Yes. Congrat—"

"Look at it! The signature." Hoan put his finger almost on the canvas. "There." Hoan pulled his hair into a ponytail behind his head. "It's not my grandfather's. Blast it." He set his fist on the white wall and leaned his head onto it.

Thuy put her hands on her thighs and bent into the painting. The room darkened around her as a crowd huddled. She glanced at Hang and scrunched her eyes.

Hang turned to the group. "Give us some space. Please step back." Most people backed away, but a few hangers-on remained in place.

Hoan pointed. "I know this painting. It was in our house growing up. Great-grandfather made it in 1955 and sold it during *Bao Cap,* around 1985, for extra food one year at Tet. I don't know who bought it, but it certainly didn't have someone else's name on it."

Thuy's heart raced. *Slow down.* "What makes you think so? Same scene, different painting? Or different artists? You said a minute ago you saw how the artists influenced each—"

Hoan cracked his knuckles. "I can see it, can't you?" he hissed. "My great-grandfather was one of the leaders of that academy group, much bigger than your uncle. His work is better known. And I certainly know what's his or not."

Her insides tingled. *Not another one.* Perspiration dripped down her back, turning her sheath into a cold cloth. Definitely not her best clothing choice today.

"Don't be so dramatic, Hoan," Hang said. "Some foreigner probably bought it, you got more food, and the painting made its way to Europe, to France. And now it's home." She shook her head at Thuy.

"I am not dramatic. You don't know art, that's clear…and what you're not seeing is this." Hoan again put his finger close to the date and signature in the lower right corner of the painting. "P.B. Thuong. My great-grandfather's name was Vuong Bui Tho. And this painting is dated 1980, but he painted it in 1955. It's insulting to him. To my family."

"Who is Thuong?" Hang whispered. She ran her finger near the name, just over the paint.

Hoan flipped his hair back. "Thuong. That upstart in Ho Chi Minh. He signed his name on my grandfather's painting. Or made a copy." He leaned his face into Thuy's. "What's going on?"

She gasped. "Hold on, Hoan. Let's talk."

"I'm not going 'to talk.' I'm done." He paced in front of her.

A younger artist wearing royal blue boots tiptoed over. "Everything all right, Ms. Thuy? Can I help?"

Hoan scowled and raised his voice. "Not unless you know how to tell real from fake paintings."

The heads in the crowd turned in unison toward Hoan. Most people shrank back.

"My God. This is horrific. I can't believe you brought these 'paintings' here, when *this* one's a fake. What were you thinking?"

Thuy shook her head. "I'm sure it's a mistake. We'll sort it." Her mind spun back to Ngoc's comment during the hanging of the paintings, when he'd noticed something on the portrait by the female artist. She hadn't pursued it. Had that been the canary-in-the-coal-mine moment?

Hoan jammed his hands into his shorts pockets and stood defiant in front of her. "I know my great-grandfather's work. This is it but not his signature. If this happens to his, what about these others? If this one is a fraud, how do you know there aren't others?" He brushed against her shoulder as he left. "This is a hoax. You've got a fake exhibit." He stormed out of the gallery.

Two possible fakes. She needed Anna's information about Minh and his paintings. Fast.

Chapter 21

Drained, Thuy stood by the exit, thanking any visitors who dared to look at her. The room's noise had turned from guffaws to nervous laughter and whispers. Sidelong glances in her direction confirmed her fears. The preview was a disaster.

An artist congratulated Thuy on his way out, holding her hand in both of his. He said the right words, but his eyes were sad. Others turned away or looked down as they moved through the doorway, staying to the far side, saying nothing. *Cowards.*

She leaned her head against the doorframe. *Please let nothing else go wrong.*

The "soldier-posture-man" slipped to her side and held his hand out. "Sorry to meet under these circumstances. I am Viet. I saw you at the lake the other night when you looked alarmed at something. Gave you my card."

Thuy raised her hands into a praying gesture. "Of course. The policeman. I remember now. You were kind to notice. But why are you here?" She glanced around the nearly empty room.

"Secret art lover. Trying to learn more. My friend's a reporter and he told me about this, so I crashed your party."

"If you have any thoughts about how to fix it, I'll be glad you crashed." She put a hand on her warm neck.

"Nothing right now. But let me know if I can help in the future. I'll leave you to it." He bowed slightly and slipped away.

Hang squeezed her arm. "Interesting. Who was that?" She winked. "But back to the show. You know what Cleopatra said. Or rather what Shakespeare said she said: 'let ill tidings tell themselves when they be felt.' I worry there's more bad news to come."

"You're a bundle of joy."

"Afraid I might be. Come with me. I saw something before Hoan's outburst." Hang clutched Thuy's upper arm, guiding her to a Vu painting—the one of a neighborhood with whitewashed buildings, clothes lying on the windowsills, old men sitting on the ground in front of the building. "Your museum has more of these, right?"

Thuy caught her breath. *She sees something.*

"And this is Vu's work?" Hang faced Thuy, not the painting. Her eyes bored into Thuy.

Another nod. "Minh sent it from Paris. Why?"

"Check the date."

She waffled between wanting to look and not wanting to look but she had to.

Hang pointed. "What date to you see by the signature?"

Thuy braced herself on the wall and scrutinized the painting. Uncle Vu died in 1991. At least that's what Bo had always told her. And the thumb drive information didn't help since it said "no information after 1970." Her ears hummed like she was underwater.

She shoved herself away from the wall. "I want it to be 1991, since that makes sense. Uncle Vu would have been alive. So I don't want it to be 1999. But what do you see?"

Hang scooted toward the painting. "Maybe in transport it got scratched?"

"Oh no. That'd be even worse." Her breath came too quickly. *Can't believe this.*

"Breathe. In and out. Three times." Hang grabbed her. "At least that's what some meditation app told me to do. Let me get some chairs." She brought in two red vinyl and metal folding chairs from the guard's desk and placed them next to each other, facing Vu's painting.

"Now. Let's slow down. I'm no expert on art but I do know something about checking for counterfeits. At least in the software world. Developers leave their 'signatures' sometimes. Maybe it's like that?"

"What if there are others?" Thuy murmured. "We checked them all when we hung them. And…"

"What?" Hang grabbed Thuy's forearm. "What is it?"

"When we hung them, our custodian questioned one." She pointed. "That one. The portrait by Mai. He said his great-grandmother knew the artist and he grew up with some of her art in his house. He knew the painting technique and style and said he wondered if that one," she closed her eyes, "was real."

Hang sucked her cheeks in. "And tonight, Hoan raises doubt, and now… this." She raised her hand toward Vu's piece.

Thuy stared at her hands, limp in her lap like the dead fish in the fishermen's nets in one of Vu's paintings. "And that's the rub. What other errors might be here? What else could we have missed?"

"But your curator checked everything in Paris, right?" Hang asked.

She shook her head. "Mr. Hai has no real training. And he didn't see them all. Then he had to return early… sick wife."

"Let's be logical. Maybe it's not so bad," Hang said. "I mean, don't other museums have counterfeits?"

Thuy stared at the ceiling. "I wish I'd never gotten involved with this."

"Don't say that," Hang said. "You're doing good for the museum, for Vietnamese art. We'll figure this out. But I remember reading about some auction house that was duped."

Thuy's stomach ached but she leaned in. "Say more."

"A few years ago," Hang said, "in 2008 or so, I think it was Sotheby's that was accused of selling some paintings that were forged—"

Thuy squeezed her eyes. "No. Later. It was Christie's. I remember that." Her phone buzzed. *Bo. Not now.* She declined the call. "Around 2016. My friend Anna in Hong Kong told me Christie's wanted to sell paintings by two Vietnamese: Ngoc Van and Le Van De. Two pieces, each for over fifty thousand dollars. The dealer claimed one came from a private collection in Germany. Turns out, our museum also had one of the paintings. The director at the time said we'd acquired it in 1965. Not purchased. Artist donation. Of course, that was during wartime, so no one remembers. But still, the question was 'Who had the original?' No one could tell in the end."

Hang's red-clad foot tapped to a silent beat.

"Maybe it's a lifeline," Thuy said. "If our own museum had been conned, maybe I shouldn't be on the block for this mess. They must have known something like this had happened before." She felt goosebumps. "Tuan's final words were 'Don't fail.'"

Thud. Thud. Thud. Thuy's head felt like one of those vintage wooden rice-pounding mortars she'd seen as a girl. Her father had shown her how the real ones worked: a long log hinged near the working end of a large hammerhead that repeatedly crushed rice in a wooden bucket. *Thud.*

Hang waved her arm around the room. "Stop. Let's think. What've we got—how many possible fakes?"

Thuy put her head in her hands.

Hang lifted Thuy's chin to face her. "Your collector friend may be a 'carbuncle in your corrupted blood.'"

Thuy grimaced.

"Okay. No humor," Hang said. "So, what've we got?"

Thuy pressed her temples. "Let me think. The night in the vault, Mr. Chien—"

Hang tilted her head. "Who?"

"The security manager. He slipped in and out tonight. You saw him, but he's nondescript, so you probably didn't see him. Well dressed. Grey suit, metal rim glasses, thinning black hair."

"That describes almost every man over thirty in Hanoi." Hang chuckled.

"I suppose. But at the vault a few strange things came up. One crate was marked as having two pieces inside, but we found only one painting. The other was in a second crate but not marked. So that seemed odd."

"Unprofessional, maybe, but not sinister." Hang handed Thuy a glass of water.

"The main crate had the wrong address, wrong museum name. That was the night, after everything was on the walls, the custodian, Mr. Ngoc, questioned the Mai portrait."

"And tonight, Hoan says we have a real painting but a fake signature," Hang finished.

"Plus a possible third," Thuy added. "This one by Vu? So that's three by my count."

"But you know Hoan." Hang scoffed. "Every chance he gets, he tries to boost the legacy, even when his great-grandfather's paintings are trash. So do we believe him?"

"God, Hang. Maybe he did us a favor by pointing it out now, rather than at the opening."

"You're the optimist," Hang said. "And more… forgiving. As for the woman painter, maybe there's an explanation. Even though it was wartime, she may have painted portraits when she had a break from the front lines? Could we confirm her whereabouts during 1953? And, for what it's worth, I think the date on Vu's painting is 1990, or at least I can talk myself into that. If that's true, Hoan's may be the only one in question."

Thuy pointed to Vu's painting. "I'm not ready to accept that the date is just a smudge. What if it's not real? Bo will be devastated and the museum's reputation…" She walked to the wall and looked out at the room.

"My God, this is so big. The integrity of this exhibit, the museum. Even Vietnamese art as a whole. If there are fakes, I've got to get ahead of this." She shook her head and looked to the ceiling.

"Finally. That's the spirit." Hang pushed her fist into the air.

An artery in Thuy's throat pulsed. She pulled her fingers down her cheeks. An image from an American movie popped up: in *The Wizard of Oz*, a witch melts into the floor and disappears. She saw herself, her family, the museum, all melting in front of her friends and the rest of the world. She could lose everything. But she couldn't let that happen. *Take charge.*

Outside, she slumped on her motorbike and kicked it into gear. Other bikes buzzed and beeped around her like gnats, mosquitos, and even bats. But at least for those few minutes, her commute offered a bubble from the world to think about what was at stake. If this exhibit failed, so much mattered: not just her job, reputation, and future opportunities but Bo's respect, Quang's expectations that she could solve problems. Chi's love? So much more at a bigger level—the museum, the artists, the country. She had to salvage this.

She rolled past storefronts, Master Tan Herbalist, Klever Fruit, and Tired City. *How I feel now.* But she had to think through the options and decide what was next.

First, she could open the exhibit and hope. That meant showing all twenty-one, including the paintings under a cloud, and say nothing. Tuan would like this option because it would keep Minh happy. But with social media, the news of the disastrous preview probably was already out. *Strike that one.*

She halted at the intersection of Trang Tien and Ba Trieu. Lights twinkled in front of restaurants and gave the street a fairy-tale feel, less harsh than during the day. Far left, at the end of Trang Tien, sat the grand Hanoi Opera House, one of her favorite buildings in Hanoi. The French had built it—they left some good architecture if not good memories—and the dome looked like a Faberge egg, with lazuli blue tiles reflecting the last bits of light. A bike brushed up against her taillight, urging her forward.

Next option—open without the questionable paintings. Smaller exhibit but saved integrity. Hai, Tuan, and some of the artists would know they were down three paintings, but other visitors wouldn't.

In the wide turn onto Pho Hue, she gasped. It wasn't just the preview visitors who'd notice fewer paintings. She'd told Bo that there were two Vu paintings in the exhibit. He would notice if there was only one. She had to tell him if she pulled it. And, of course, she would know too. That nulled option two.

She slowed to five miles per hour and reviewed a devastating option: never open exhibit. Her shoulders drooped. But this exhibit was her chance to promote Vietnamese art, to let people see art that had never been in the country. One-of-a-kind opportunity. *That's what's important.* She screamed inside at the thought of the pieces never being seen.

But how had fakes—if they were—made it into such a collection at all? Did Minh even know? He deserved to know about her concerns.

But first, she needed a short course in forgeries. One of the journalists who had come to the preview had written about looting of art in Vietnam. Maybe he'd know about fakes as well. She had to reach out before she lost everything.

On the second floor of her house, kitchen lights blazed. Before she decided, she wanted Chi and Bo's input. Bo knew the art, especially Vu's, and Chi was a good balance, understood the importance of the exhibit. She'd take them to the gallery in the morning.

Her phone pinged. Probably a text from Anna. She pulled it from her purse, but it was Bac.

Bac: Open the exhibit. Quit messing around with questions.

She couldn't work out what he had to do with any of this. After their divorce, she'd been relieved not to have to interact with him. Now he was inserting himself into her life again— seeing Quang at the lake, and now this text. She shrugged. *If you take charge of the exhibit, do the same with him. Move on once and for all.* She stubbed her toe on the steps going up to the house, tripped but caught herself as a thunderclap roared, filling the sidewalk with the whirring sounds of hard rain.

Chapter 22

The next morning, Thuy led Bo and Chi up the staircase to the special exhibit gallery. *It's good of them to help.* She'd told them that the exhibit might have problems, that it meant a lot for the museum and for Vietnam and she needed some outside counsel. She wanted their thoughts on the exhibit, the fakes, and what to do. Their opinions mattered, up to a point. She had to make the final decision.

"My opinion? You may not like it," Bo had said the night before.

Today, she halted half-way up the staircase. Bo had stopped to cough so she descended four steps, tucked her arm through his elbow, and walked half-speed with him. Chi followed.

"Age is no fun," he said. "You'll find out." His eyes swooped around the gallery. "Very nice."

"Beautiful light." Chi smiled. "Good place for the exhibit. Tuan must value you to let you do this. Congratulations."

Thuy shrugged. *If it succeeds.*

"Which paintings give you concern?" Chi stood in the room's center, twisting to see all of the walls.

"Three in total. One has problems with style, technique, and content. The other two deal with signatures. Come. I'll show you." She walked to two paintings on the far wall marked with orange sticky notes. "Ten days before the exhibit opens, and we need to be sure of what we will show. I told you last night that at the pre-opening, an artist friend—Hoan—"

Bo started. "Hoan? The one who's great-grandfather never made a decent piece of—"

Chi tsked at him. "Now, now."

"Let's leave your view of him aside for now," Thuy said. "He said his great-grandfather made this painting, but the signature is not his. It's another artist—present day and very much alive—in Ho Chi Minh City."

"Who's that, dear?" Chi stared at the painting. "What's his name?"

"His name is P.B. Thuong. Hoan knew of him. Well, we all do. He's signed other paintings that weren't his, so this shouldn't be a surprise."

"Then it shouldn't be your fault," Chi said. "You couldn't have known. Or could you?"

"These paintings all came from France, so I assumed—"

"Pshaw. I wouldn't worry about that one." Bo waved his hand, dismissing the painting. "Not good anyway, so why would you want it here? What else do I need to see?"

Her throat went taut. *He does this too often. Tries to intimidate. Not this time.* She slowed down and breathed. "Two more could be in question, including one by Vu."

Bo glanced at Chi. "That must be wrong."

Thuy stood by the Vu painting. "I have to be objective." The vacuum cleaner roared in the hallway, echoing beyond the door. "Visitors must trust what's here. What they see. Not what I want it to be."

Gzzzzz. The sound grew louder. Hien pushed the vacuum into the gallery and stopped. "So sorry. I didn't know you were here. Let me do another part of the hallway—Ah! Chi! Good to see you!"

Chi strolled over to Hien, and they grabbed each other's hands and squeezed. "Good to see you, my old friend. Are you staying well?"

"Of course, at least when I can keep your daughter out of mischief." Hien winked at Thuy. "I've missed seeing—"

"That sounds like a full-time job," Chi said. "But we must not keep you from your work." She turned Hien around and gave her a nudge. "Tam Biet!"

Hien craned her neck back. "Yes. I'll see you next time." She guided the equipment out of the doorway.

"Have you seen her recently?" Thuy tilted her head toward the door.

"She just lives in the past. That's all." Chi said.

"Back to your problem, which is not a problem. Even if a few of these pieces are not real, does it matter?" Bo walked toward Vu's painting and lifted his arm. "That means the paintings are so good that others want to copy."

Thuy reached in her pocket for her lipstick and swiped her lips. *He doesn't get it.* "You need to understand, this is an exhibit of originals. Its success depends on its integrity and our reputation. And it's my responsibility to be sure that is done."

He turned his back to her, a wall of resistance. "Museums have trust already. That's why you can put what you want into them. And your suspicions… like a silent bomb." He swiped his finger on the Vu painting's date. "It looks like 1999, but you misread. A little extra paint next to the '1.' It says 1991, not '99." He stood at attention, unrelenting.

She glanced at Chi, who had walked away. "I… you have to—"

"Enough," he said. "I am glad Uncle does not hear this. I sold his work for many years so you could have a better life."

She was losing ground. "So, you think we should open?"

"Of course."

Chi stood ten feet away and nodded. "What does Mr. Tuan think?"

"He's gone to a conference. He's heard what happened but wants to move forward. It takes so much effort to get a permission to open an exhibit."

"Yes, yes. I see that." Chi bent toward a painting, her back curved more than it used to.

Could I really leave Hanoi? They'll need me. Maybe sooner. "Everyone wants to open. But it's a question of what's right—for the museum, the artists, for us." They didn't see, or maybe she wasn't making this clear enough.

"I'm sure you'll do what you think is best. You always do." Bo touched her shoulder.

She reeled. *It's a roller coaster with him these days. Positive, negative, compliments, and then none.* "I try. But if we do go forward, I have to know more about the artists."

Bo pulled his stained khaki canvas jacket tight. *Eight,* he had told her. *I wear a jacket with eight pockets to have plenty of room to carry Quang's art equipment."* He tugged a cigarette from one of the chest pockets. "Where can I—"

"You need to wait till we're outside. She glanced at her watch: forty-five minutes before the museum opened. She dropped to one of the benches facing the two paintings and straightened the wrinkles in her black trousers. *Always a struggle.*

Bo's head swiveled from art piece to art piece. Finally, he faced her, hands shoved into the jacket's front pockets. "How can I help? What do you want to know?"

Chi crept closer.

The whirr of the vacuum drifted further away, but a scent of fresh pine hovered in its wake.

"What about Uncle Vu and the art academy? When did he finish?" She squeezed an earring stud to keep it from falling out. She needed to know who was right, Bo or Minh.

"I assume the late 1930s, probably early 1940s." He rolled the cigarette between his fingers.

Minh's info had said Vu finished in 1938. Was Bo misremembering? Was he not telling her the truth? What could she believe?

She stood at a crossroads: knowing the truth but also knowing who was telling the truth, or what he believed it to be.

"Could it have been earlier? Maybe he was born earlier?"

Bo darted his eyes at her. "I know when he was born. 1926."

"OK." She bit her lip. "And what did he do after the academy?"

He ran his hand over his face. "I… uh… I assume he taught or went to the newspapers. That's what they all did."

"Did you know that for certain? From him or from others? It's important to be correct," she said.

Bo frowned.

"I think she's only doing her job." Chi stepped forward and touched Bo's arm. "She's the curator for this special exhibit and needs to know all she can about the artists. Isn't that right? Now tell us about how your security works here? Could someone have altered the signature on Vu's painting once it arrived?"

Her chest hurt like she'd been hit. "I… uh… no. We keep the gallery locked."

Chi stroked the silver pendant she wore—a dragon, her birth year animal. "You have mentioned some people who helped you. The custodian?"

"Ngoc? He hung the pieces. His great-grandmother knew one of the artists."

"Ah, yes. Did anyone else help you?"

Thuy paced and listened to birds chirping. "One other. Chien. The security guy."

"That's the one. And who is this Chien? Would he have an opinion?" She turned to look at a painting.

"Security manager. Been here about a year. He checks in on a regular basis."

"Where did he come from?"

"He was at a gallery, at other museums, was in security." Thuy stood and walked to Chi. "Lots of questions about him. Do you know him?"

"How would I know him?" Chi turned her back and stepped toward another painting. "I'm simply curious about your work, dear. We know so little."

Thuy wrestled her train of thought back. "Did Vu travel abroad. Outside Vietnam?"

"I doubt it. He had no money." Bo shoved his hands into his jacket pockets. "No one left, except to go to Russia for work or study. Some went in the *Bao Cap* time, after the American War. But he never left the north."

There's the problem. Contradicts Minh's information. "As far as you know, then, he never left Vietnam?"

Bo stood straighter. "Why? Do you have a reason to doubt that?"

She needed to tread carefully. If Minh had false information about Vu, that could put all of the other artists' bios into question. But maybe Bo just didn't know much about Vu, after all. "Is there a chance he went to Paris?"

He crossed his arms and looked away. "You ask the same questions. I told you. No."

She retrieved a leftover program from the night before, one that Ngoc hadn't swept away.

"Any more questions, dear? We need to leave before your working day starts." Chi strolled toward her.

"OK. Just a little more? What about Vu's time in the countryside?"

"I do know about that." Bo knocked his fingers on the bench. "About 1973. We had bombings in Hanoi, air raid sirens. One time Bach Mai hospital got hit; another time a school. Parents split up with their children—some going with one parent, the rest with the other, hoping that at least some would survive." He looked at Vu's painting and smiled. "During those hard times, he took his art to the mountains. Out of danger. Far from Hanoi. Many artists did so. To caves, out of danger. I visited when I could, and sometimes, he gave me some art to sell."

Let him talk. Like that time long ago when we walked around the lake. Feels like that.

He had said that it took a day to reach Vu's village. Then Bo had carried three or four paintings back to Hanoi on a Phoenix bike. Vu had lived in the mountains for several months when he wasn't in a war unit.

"Wasn't he really old? How could he live in the mountains alone?" she had asked.

Bo had laughed. "He wasn't so old, as you say. Maybe Fifty. Old to you, I guess." While they stood at the lake, Bo had tossed a pebble into the lake. "And he ate what he found in the forest. From his time during the wars, traveling with soldiers, he learned to catch small animals with his hands, and in traps. And he knew plants."

She had remembered holding her breath: He rarely talked about Uncle Vu, so she stayed quiet, not wanting to break the spell.

Back in the gallery, Bo sucked in a fast breath and sniffled. His voice, husky and rough, lowered. "Vu lived in Moc Chau, for a long time—"

"No, Bo. Not Moc Chau," Chi said. "Bac Son. You are confused." She squinted at Thuy.

"You're right. Bac Son. Bac Son. He was there. After the war, after the subsidy time. Even then, he gave us vegetables. We still had little in the city, bad rice, no meat. He grew sweet potatoes."

Food. Always food. Thuy stood next to Bo, studying Vu's painting.

"He had asked me to sell some of his paintings so we could have more food. We sold to the few galleries that sold to foreigners since Vietnamese had no money."

Chi touched Thuy's arm. "We should go," she mouthed.

"Just a few more minutes," Thuy said. She'd heard some of this but wanted more. "And did you sell the paintings? How did that work?"

The gallery guard entered and pulled her chair from the desk to sit.

Bo strolled toward the door. "In those days, a broker took them, paid me money. Sometimes I went to a gallery that sold to foreigners. Mostly Russians. Sometimes, when Uncle Vu visited Hanoi, he traded a piece or a sketch for food or coffee. You've heard about those times."

She shuddered to think of the art traveling on the back of a motorbike or bicycle—cold, damp mountain climate, humidity, dirt, no protection—for hundreds of miles.

She nodded. "How many did you sell?" She slipped her arm through Chi's to slow her down.

"Ah… many. After the *Bao Cap* time, the economy got better. Vu's cadre became more known. The broker and gallery had more buyers."

"Do you remember the broker's name? The gallery?"

"Broker, no. The gallery was… Bending Bamboo, I think. Vu brought several at a time, wrapped in burlap."

"Sorry to interrupt again, but the gallery was Yellow Bamboo, not Bending. Thuy wants accuracy." Chi patted Bo's hand.

Something's going on with them. Bo odd. Chi saying little. "I've studied the ones we have in the museum. I'm amazed so many survived, from what you describe."

He scowled. "Resilient. Like people.

He stretched his arm out to the walls.

She braced herself. "Well, the paintings, the sketches, they seem… it's like the style changed over time."

"And why do you say that?" His eyes narrowed.

"I know most artists have some core, some foundation, like a voice. But Vu's changed a lot. Did you ever talk to him about that?"

He rubbed the back of his neck and squeezed the cigarette he still held. "He was flexible."

Chien stepped into the gallery and froze.

She lifted her hand to wave him over, but he turned and left. *Odd.* Thuy lifted her hands. "I don't mean to aggravate. But his paintings of the 1970s, those alleys, seem so different from the later ones in the countryside. They seem lonely. Was he alone in that time? Do you think someone else made—"

"Who was that?" Chi said.

"The security guy. Head of operations. Thought he might come say 'hello.' Guess not."

Bo moved to the exit. "He'd lived in the city for a long time, then moved. That's all I have to say. We must go."

That hit a nerve. "I don't mean to upset you." *Slow down.* "I'm asking in my job as curator—for the exhibit, for the museum, for Vu's integrity. Vu is a famous artist, and people will want to know more about him." She sounded shrill, even in her head. "I'm sorry to ask so much but… just one more?"

He waved at Chi and then faced Thuy. "Go ahead."

"When did he die?"

He pinched his lips. "You know that. 1998. He was around seventy or seventy-five?"

She lurched. He'd said 1991 before. She licked her lips. "Are you sure?"

He whipped his head around. "Do you think I don't know my uncle's life? Born in 1926 and died when I said."

Thuy stopped where she stood. *His memory is slipping. Something had to be wrong.* She'd ask Chi next time she could.

Chi stroked his arm. "Let's go now."

Thuy winced and held her palms face out. "I'm sorry. I ask so that we can prove to others that the paintings are authentic. I heard about museums that have been embarrassed—"

He glared. "Are you saying he did not paint some of the ones in this museum? What disrespect. I've said that all you need is in the paintings. Quit saying, quit thinking bad things about him. About your own uncle. What do you know about him? You never met him."

A cannon ball dropped in her stomach. "And why was that?" She feared she'd be the cause of a heart attack. She should stop but couldn't. "I was born in 1979, and he died in the '90s. Why did you not take me to him?"

He caught his breath, and his shoulders lifted. "Too far. Too dangerous." He reached inside his jacket and brought out cigarettes and a lighter. "Oh, still can't do this." He crushed the carton and stuffed it back in his pocket. "It's time to go." He grabbed her shoulders. "Daughter, if you want me to find another painting for your exhibit, just ask. I have more in storage. But stop this nonsense discussion."

Her head fell back like whiplash. "Bo. We can't 'find' another painting and put it in the exhibit. The reputation of the art would be in jeopardy. These pieces have never been in Vietnam—"

"Like the ones from the countryside—"

This is going nowhere fast. "No, not like that. These are 'coming home.' Anything already in Vietnam cannot be used."

He slithered his hand through the air toward her, like a snake moving through grass. "You follow rules too much. Maybe your generation. Mine got things done. Of course, I kept some in the house. More in the cave. I offer a replacement."

The stomach cannon ball shifted side to side, making it hard to stand upright.

"No one has seen these. Who will know?"

Her words jumped. "I-I will know. My museum colleagues will know. The collector will know, for heaven's sake."

Bo zipped his jacket. "Your loss."

He left her no choice. She had to stand up for the integrity of the exhibit, the museum, and even if Bo didn't understand it, for her family. And that meant finding out why there were fakes in the exhibit, who was behind them, and removing them. Even if it meant going against Bo.

After Chi and Bo left, Thuy walked toward her office. She listened to the voice mail from the Ho Chi Minh museum assistant to the director confirming her visit the day after the opening. *Feeling excited more than scared. Good sign.*

"Ms. Thuy! Ms. Thuy!" Chien waved at her from the end of the hallway. "Stop, please. I have an idea."

She silenced her phone and tucked it away. No need to tell Chien about her interview. *Then again, he probably knew about the interview before I did.* "You should have come in to meet my parents."

"Oh, I could tell you were busy. Next time." His eye twitched. *Nerves?*

"I am sorry about the preview misfortune. I suspect you will have an authenticator review the paintings now? Maybe we should have done that when they arrived, but what about now?"

"If only. No one in the museum—"

"I have a contact. At a museum in Ho Chi Minh." He winked. "She's quite good, their authenticator, in addition to other jobs. I could get her here in a flash if you wish."

He seemed too eager to help. And she was too eager to say yes. But she couldn't. "I can't approve that. We need to wait for Mr. Tuan. At least a few days."

"Your decision, of course." He tipped an invisible hat and spun around.

Chapter 23

Later that morning, Thuy stood in front of Hai and twisted her silver bracelet. "You're the curator, you must go back to him, to the collector, to ask about the paintings."

"You must be joking." Hai's rumpled trousers and shirt suggested his wife was again ill. He dropped a stack of mismatched paper on his desk and watched sheets drift to the floor. "I cannot question Mr. Minh. Or his paintings. He made a generous donation and offered his best paintings. That would insult him. And the museum will lose face as well."

"But what if something is wrong? What do we really know about him? You met him in Paris. And you saw the paintings."

Hai lowered himself to his chair, like he was afraid he'd explode if he moved too fast. The shades on his window were crooked. "Why did you not ask questions before? When he was in Hanoi?" His radio played patriotic music.

Her head buzzed. *This man didn't remember.* "I-I *did* ask. Why our museum? Why these paintings? What does he gain? But you and Mr. Tuan refused to push him. Something seems odd behind it all."

"It's far too late. You received what he thought best." Hai studied his fingernails. Most were chewed short, except for the last finger on his right hand. Its curved nail was almost double the length of the others, to show he wasn't a farmer, that he worked in an office and so could have a long nail.

"The twenty-one that came weren't what I asked for. You or Mr. Tuan or Mr. Minh chose them. Not me. And now three, maybe more, are in question. It's not my doing. You saw them in Paris, you examined them. I assume you did?"

"Of course I examined them." His forehead and nose reddened, like it did after too many beers. He bent down to pick up some papers on the floor and clenched his jaw, barely containing what she assumed was wrath.

"All of them?"

"Only the ones from Paris, of course."

"What do you mean, only the ones from Paris?"

"He removed the ones from London."

Unbelievable. She rubbed her temple. "Why? Why did he do that?"

"No one to escort me, and I had to return early, as you know." Spittle built up on the corners of his mouth.

"But where did you see them? In his office? His house? At a storage room? Where?"

He wiped his upper lip, held his breath, and let it out slowly. "At a storage house. Some pieces were crated already, but I saw the others. That was most of them. Are we finished?"

He won't admit that he'd been had or was lying. Either way, this is bad.

"Even so, you must ask Minh what he knows. If there are fakes, we have to pull them."

Hai straightened, putting him nose to nose with her, and his face turned pale. "As I said, returning to the collector now would be dangerous, a huge loss of face. I will not. And if you continue to push, I'll inform Mr. Tuan. We have the paintings and must show them."

Adrenaline pushed her to a cliff edge. *Is my job worth this fight?* She didn't have the Ho Chi Minh job as a backup, yet. She needed to save this exhibit and do it right. "What if I approached Mr. Minh? I could be diplomatic. You would be safe, not involved."

"NO! You must not. We'll lose the exhibit and the donation. Is that what you want?" Hai raised his palms toward her and slowed his breathing down. "Let me think. Do nothing, for three days. Now, please go." He flicked his hand.

Chapter 24

Hai had requested Thuy wait three days before contacting the collector; she waited five. In the meantime, she'd arranged lunch with the journalist from *Vietnam Reports* who had attended the preview and drafted an email to the collector. At 10:15 a.m. Wednesday, she held her finger above the send button and reread her email. *Time to act.*

Dear Mr. Minh,

I trust you are well.

I am sorry to report, but we may have a problem. At a pre-opening for the "Returning Home" exhibit last week, questions came up about the authenticity of some of the art pieces. Do you have knowledge of this?

If there are any questions, we need to resolve them and consider options on how to go forward.

Best regards,

Pham Thao Thuy, Business Manager,

Hanoi Museum of Modern Art

She punched "send" and made a fist in the air. *Into the breach.* By the time she'd pulled up the blog to revise the latest one, her phone rang. She grimaced, expecting a tirade. "Mr. Minh, perhaps you received my email?"

"Ah, Ms. Thuy. So inspiring to hear your voice. Much nicer than words on a screen. Now what is the problem?"

Her ribs tightened. *He had to know this was coming.* "We have questions about some of the paintings. We've not decided what this means for the exhibit, but I need your input."

"We? Is that your whole staff? Mr. Tuan and Mr. Hai? Or just you?" His voice dropped.

Busted. She imagined him as an elephant, lowering his head, getting very still, ready to charge. She'd read that elephants pin their ears back to their heads and curl their trunks inward before they charge. "I wanted to alert you first."

He cleared his throat. "And which pieces are you talking about? I have the list in front of me, the pieces you chose."

Her pulse thrummed, and she willed herself not to take the bait.

"Three pieces. A portrait by Le Mai, the abstract by P.B. Thuong, and a signature on one of Pham Ly Vu's pieces."

"I see them now. I'll send you more documentation, of course. I purchased those—and really, many in my collection— from Mr. Morris Teller in Bangkok. An expert on Southeast Asian art. Worked for Christie's and in several galleries in Hong Kong and Bangkok and now consults. You must know him, if you're in the art world…"

She scribbled the dealer's name.

"…will set you right. I will contact him and introduce you."

"If he's in Asia, how are you sure the pieces were never in Vietnam?"

"He worked in France when I bought from him. I'm sure he'll tell you all about it."

Not good enough. She imagined a micro version of Hang, with her red basketball shoes, sitting on her shoulder. *Go in for the charge.* "We planned to open the exhibit in ten days but if we withhold the artwork that is in question, we'd be down to eighteen pieces. Very small for a major show." She waited, but the line was blank. If she had called on a land line, this would be the moment when the line would go scratchy, when the other person would say he couldn't hear her, but with a mobile phone, fewer excuses existed. He could, of course, claim to be entering a tunnel, but she heard nothing.

"…coming through a tunnel."

Of course.

"…didn't hear all you said. But please, think about this. If you do not open, if you withdraw some pieces, that will be a mistake. You will damage reputations—yours, your museum's, mine, but most importantly, the artists'. Visitors deserve to see these returning art pieces. Do you really want to jeopardize that?"

Energy seeped from her limbs. "Of course not, but I… Reputations would be hurt if we open the show with forgeries."

"Forgeries! How can you even suggest that? If there are copies, perhaps they came from the artists themselves, copies they made to protect the originals?" His voice oozed smugness. "Have you considered that?"

"Then why not tell us? Why let us believe they are originals?"

"We are going in circles. Mr. Teller will answer your questions. I must go to my next meeting." *Click.*

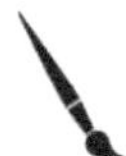

Thuy punched in Morris Teller's name and waited for Google to enlighten her. Her finger scraped down the mouse as she scrolled. He had a skimpy LinkedIn page and a short bio on his own website. No mention of education, degrees, certificates, or training programs. Just jobs. He had worked for a gallery in Paris from 1997 through 2013, for a major auction house in Hong Kong until 2016, and consulted with Christie's until 2018. He'd opened a gallery in Bangkok after that.

Ten minutes later, emails popped up: one from Minh and three from MTellerArt@gmail.com. She scraped her desk chair against the cement floor to get closer and scanned the email from Minh first.

Dear Ms. Thuy,

Regarding your confusion about some of the paintings. Let me promise you that they came from my great-grandfather or from reputable sellers, confirmed and verified by a renowned expert, Mr. Teller, of Teller and Associates, Bangkok. He has been my guide for over fifteen years, including when he worked for Christie's, so I can vouch for him.

To that end, I forward to you photos of receipts from several of my artworks that you have in your care. Also, from Mr. Teller, please find photos of four of the paintings. Notice one hangs behind a group of the famous artists represented. From a coffee shop in Hanoi in the 1980s.

Finally, I took the liberty of sending your information to Mr. Teller. He will contact you directly.

Yours sincerely,
Minh

She gulped her green tea and thought about Minh's Bhutan tea. *Wasn't especially tasty, but he was proud of it.* She opened the receipts file first—photos of hand-written receipts for pieces Minh had purchased between 1991 and 1997. The handwriting looked European—probably Morris Teller's—and the descriptions were vague. *Not helpful.*

The other three attachments were photos. She studied the one of the four Vietnamese men clustered around a coffee table. Behind them, hanging on a wall, was an abstract painting. One man blocked the signature in its lower right corner. The painting resembled one Minh had sent for the special exhibit, the one that Hoan had claimed was his great-grandfather's with a different signature. The longer she looked at the photo, the more the painting looked out of place. It seemed to stand away from the wall and was more vibrant in the coffee house lighting than she would have expected for the time period. *Photoshopped?*

She opened an email from Mr. Morris. In it, he boasted about his impressive career. *Odd thing to do.* If he was really culturally sensitive, he'd know not to brag in Asia. His second email included more blurry photos of documentation of what looked like some sort of certificates of the paintings in the exhibit. Surely, he didn't think she'd buy this as legitimate provenance. The notations, partly in Vietnamese and partly in French, were fuzzy. She opened his last email.

Dear Ms. Thuy,

These four artists are major Vietnamese painters from the French art academy. They painted during the subsidy period in the 1980s and through early 1990s. They sit in front of one of the paintings Mr. Minh sent you. This was in the Victory Café house in 1981.

I will phone to answer your questions.

Your faithful servant,

Morris Teller, Art Dealer

Twenty minutes later her phone whirred with a call from the 66-country code: Thailand.

"Mr. Morris Teller?"

"Ah, Mrs. Thuy, thank you for answering my call. You know who I am? It is easier to talk by phone, no? Mr. Nguyen, or Thomas as we foreigners call him, said you had questions. About some paintings he has loaned your museum."

"Yes. He said you sold him—"

"Sometimes people question the art, and they should do so. But I must tell you about myself first."

She put her phone on speaker and set it on the desk. Her ears rang, drowning out his bragging. "That's not nec—"

"I went to university in France, Perpignan, small town in the south. I worked in France, Lyon, where I learned art. And at Christie's in Hong Kong."

Her head pounded from the droning. "Mr. Mor—"

"And I came to love art from Indochina."

Her mobile phone moved on the desk, jiggling from another call. *From the Ho Chi Minh City museum again.* She pushed the do not disturb button and hoped for a voicemail.

"…searched for and sold art from Vietnam for buyers in Europe. Thomas contacted me many years ago." He stopped and seemed to draw upon a cigarette.

She breathed in. "How do you find art pieces, then, Mr. Teller?"

"Oh, call me Morris. I know in Vietnam you use first names and honorifics, but no need…"

A text pinged.

Museum : Interview in HCMC? Please call.

Heat rushed up her torso. *Maybe it's the right time to leave this drama and move on. I'd love a new challenge.* She shook her head. She had to stay present, in the now.

"…find people who are relatives of the artists. Who know about where the artists lived. You know, during war, many of them hid their paintings in the country, for safekeeping. If the family has found the art, and wants to sell it, I help. And since Vietnamese art is so popular, I have had much success. You are fortunate to be the beneficiary of Thomas's kind offer and his collection. The exhibit is soon, I understand."

A fire engine droned in the distance.

"We are not certain. He sent my museum only twenty-one pieces, and three of them may not be originals. So that leaves a very small exhibit."

"Twenty-one? Only? He has nearly 200, I think. May I help… loan you some from my current stock? Pieces that are for sale or auction but not claimed?"

She sank her head back onto her chair. "Mr. Teller, I don't know what you are offering, but we cannot mix pieces from other collections."

"Oh, my dear, happens all the time. I will help if it keeps Thomas happy and he buys more paintings. You know how it is."

Her mouth dropped open. *No, I don't know "how it is." First Bo and now this man offered pieces. Am I missing something? Another piece of this mysterious puzzle. Unsolved.*

She checked the clock. Time for her lesson on forgeries with the journalist.

Chapter 25

The fragrance of grilled fish with lemongrass, coriander, and noodles filled Thuy's nose as she sat in Cha Ca Restaurant on Duong Thanh, waiting for Mr. Son.

Trung Bui Son handed her his card: Senior Journalist, Cultural Affairs, *Vietnam Reports*. A few years before, he'd cracked a story about a looted statue from the central part of Vietnam. Stolen in the early 1970s, the Cham statue of the Hindu god Shiva, from the 13th or 14th century, was at last on its way back home from England, where it had been for fifty years.

"Mr. Son. I'm pleased you attended the preview, although I am sorry you saw the chaos. But that leads me to my request for a favor. I need a fast lesson about the Vietnamese art market, especially how the outside world sees it," Thuy said. "And anything to help me understand forgeries. As far as I know, Vietnam has no trained assessors yet—the Ministry says it wants to develop the talent, but for now, journalists like you seem to know the most."

"First, call me Sam. Trying to make my image more global, and foreigners can't pronounce most of our names."

The fish sizzled.

Sam leaned in, dropped coriander in his bowl, and added pieces of fish. He chuckled. "History of the Vietnamese art market in ten minutes." He glanced at the clock on the smoked-covered wall. "Here we go. To start, some people see the Vietnamese market as stages in history. I could give you the long-ago history—back when the Mongols and Chinese took pieces from us, but I think you're more interested in the last hundred or so years?"

She nodded and chewed.

"Got it. Okay. Start with colonial—when artists studied at the Indochina Art Academy—the one the French founded. That's your group of returning artists, or many of them. Later, government-directed art came during wartime—propaganda paintings, war sketches. The painters often didn't even sign their names since it was all for the motherland. Much later, the forgeries started, when pieces started to sell for more than ten thousand U.S. dollars. Nowadays, artists have a lot more freedom. They sign their pieces and decide for themselves where to show or sell, who to work with."

"Is that why a collector might loan pieces for a special exhibit—to sell more?"

"One reason. He could sell in Vietnam or back in Europe or Asia. An exhibit spreads the word. Gives the pieces credibility." Sam swigged his beer.

Thuy glanced at the table next to them: a group of men celebrating with frequent toasts and lots of jokes.

"But, with more buyers from abroad, Vietnamese art will leave the country. That means it could be forgotten, never seen here again. Some argue that's like the colonial days again—making art for outsiders."

Thuy spun her glass between her thumb and index finger. *Always money.* "That's why some artists boycott international exhibits. They want to show in Vietnam, so their work has a chance of staying here?"

"Exactly. And they can protect it more easily. I read about an artist who sent an original piece to a gallery, and the gallery swapped it out with a fake one. That made the artist so angry, he slashed the fake one and raised quite a fuss about it."

"Awful." Thuy shook her head. "Please. Keep going."

"Well, incidents like that are why well-known artists like Le Quoc Thanh and Dinh Quan deal directly with one or two galleries. They know their pieces and who buys them. A buyer can call the artist directly if there's any question. But, of course, forgeries in general are huge worldwide. But especially for Vietnam, after the scandal at the Cernuschi museum in Paris—"

Thuy's neck tingled. "Tell me."

"Well, in 2013, I think September? A French museum showed a Vietnamese painting that was going to be auctioned. By Vu Cao Dam—"

The server poured more beer for Son.

"Well-known," Thuy said.

"Or so they thought. Gouache and ink on silk. The piece was called, in English, 'Girls Drink Tea.' No date. From a private collection. The opening bid was around twenty thousand dollars."

Thuy scooped a spoonful of soup.

Sam lifted his glass in a toast. "But an art researcher in France called it a fake. If I recall, he said 'this piece is ugly and has a vulgar layout.'" He chuckled. "He thought the ladies were gossiping, not drinking tea on a nice afternoon. He said the lines were too clear, not what happens when you paint on silk. And he said the signature and stamp were 'vulgar.'"

"Not subtle."

"Exactly. He liked that word, 'vulgar.' Finally, he said that even if the painting was a 'draft,' that Dam—the artist—would never have made such a bad 'draft.' Some people say that to make a good fake, you have to 'see the work through the creator's eyes and, in a way, become that person.'"

"How else do they tell what's fake?"

"The provenance chain, of course. When and how a piece goes from the studio to a museum, from auction house to collector—receipts, invoices, letters, exhibition catalogues. The so-called 'lineage.'"

"But what about artists from here? We don't really have much documentation because of the wars."

"That's a huge problem, agreed. But fakes happen even in places where you'd think it wouldn't. Like France. It's strange, but museums in France have been especially vulnerable. And another case, in 2018, I think it was. A small museum in a town called Elne had more than one hundred paintings from a single donor. The donor loved the painter Etienne Terrus. Contemporary of Henri Matisse. After the donor died, the museum discovered that around 80 of the 140 were forgeries, which in total were worth about one hundred and seventy thousand dollars."

Thuy's head rocked back. "You're joking. That much?"

"That's what I mean—the question of fakes is not small."

The party of seven at the next table got up to leave.

"Now maybe I can hear you. Tell me more about forgeries in Vietnam, if you can."

"I'd say organized forgery rings started here around the time that a Ly Pho painting was sold for over a million. The artists of his era are dead and didn't leave much paperwork, so it's easier to excuse the lack of provenance documentation. For some time, collectors bought the pieces without knowing much about the artists or art. For instance, one gallery owner told me about a friend who bragged he had bought a Ming dynasty vase. He'd never seen one, though, so when she showed him a real one, he realized he'd been had. And some of those buyers are too embarrassed to admit they've been scammed so they never report it."

"So has anything been done to stop it?"

"A little. Collectors and good galleries have begun to notice crude techniques, colors that don't match what painters normally use, and people have shied away from buying them. Sadly, as they've discovered false signatures and techniques, it damages the artists' reputations, even if there are originals out there."

Thuy scraped bits of noodle from her bowl.

"That's why your exhibit has to be transparent—and real," Sam concluded.

Thuy put her chopsticks down and looked at the wall clock. "I appreciate your time. My director has returned from New York, and now I've got to tell him I think we shouldn't open till we get some sort of assessment. Dreading it. But your information helps more than you know. I've got to leave, but stay, please. Finish your beer."

She placed 400,000 Dong on the table and left. *A bargain at any price.*

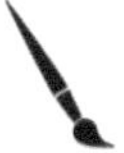

Thuy returned to the bustle of Hang Gai Street to retrieve her parked motorbike. She slithered between walkers and bikers, passed two older tourists wearing matching bright pastel pink and lime green shorts. Swedish, from the language. The man and woman stood at the base of the stairs in front of the Golden Silk hotel, transfixed, staring at the traffic. The man reached his foot out to take a step, but his wife yanked him back. "Wait 'til it stops," she yelled over the chaos.

Thuy chuckled. *First day here.* Anyone traveling to Hanoi got the same advice: learn how to cross the street. Most guffawed, until they arrived. Then they acted like these Swedes, frozen in place.

"May I help?" The tourists turned to her; their eyes scrunched in panic.

"Oh, please," the woman said. "Our first day here. How does this work?"

Thuy linked her arm through the woman's and turned to her companion. "Please walk next to her, not like a duckling following me, or you'll be wiped off the map."

The man's eyes widened, and he pursed his mouth. He grabbed his partner's other arm.

"Traffic never stops, so you must step into it, continue to move slowly across the road, and it will swerve and swarm around you. Never stop. Don't rush. Be predictable with a slow steady pace." She stepped onto the opposite curb with them, right in front of the Tan My store. "Here you are. And this is a nice place to shop while you get your courage again."

"You saved us." They hustled into the store, out of the heat and noise.

She glanced across the street and gasped. *Bo?* He stood on the stoop of the Pink Lotus Gallery. Tuan, from the museum, stood next to him and said something; they nodded in unison and shook hands. Tuan shifted his eyes along the street, but a pair of women holding parasols hid her from view. Bo touched his fingers to his head, saluting, and turned east on Hang Gai.

Tuan and Chi had worked at the ministry, so it made sense that Bo would know or know of Tuan. But that was twenty years ago. She'd never heard her parents talk about Tuan at home, except when his work at the museum came up. But here, Bo's interaction seemed casual, almost friendly.

She crossed the street once again, to the gallery.

"May I help?" A Vietnamese man in his twenties, wearing black rimmed glasses, a gamboge t-shirt, and tight black jeans glided toward Thuy. He could blend into Tokyo or New York as a fashion model, from the photos she'd seen of each place.

"Perhaps. Two men just left the gallery. I wonder what they were looking at?" *Blunt, but I need to get to the point.*

"Ehhhh… yes. And why do you ask?"

"I know them, or of them. They know art, and I'm curious what they were interested in. It might be a clue for my future purchases, perhaps from this gallery?"

Mr. Tokyo's eyes opened wide as if he saw fresh bait. "Are you a collector?"

"Something like that. Can you tell me anything?"

"One man worked here years ago and still does some consulting for us, especially bringing in older artists' work. The other man has several in his collection and is looking to sell them."

Her ears buzzed. *Selling art. Must be Vu's.*

"He's brought us pieces over the years and says he's found more in his family house that he could offer. They are from the subsidy period."

The front door clanged. A customer who could be the Swedish tourist's sister entered and hung by a piece near the front of the shop.

Bo had mentioned Vu's paintings during the subsidy period. Ones that he could 'loan' her for the exhibit. Maybe these were the ones he meant. "I know that period. Any artists in particular?"

"Several by Nguyen Do Cung and Duong Huong Minh. And then there is Mr. Pham Ly Vu. Any of those sound familiar to you?"

She pressed her tongue against the top of her mouth, to avoid blurting something unreasonable, and counted to five. "Yes, I have heard of them. I thought they were all dead? Are there undiscovered paintings still?"

"Oh, yes. Happens all the time. During wartime, people hid their work in all sorts of places: caves, friends' farmhouses, bunkers."

Thuy tilted her head and focused on Mr. Tokyo like he was the only person in the world.

"I've heard a little about that. Fascinating. Can you tell me more?"

He leaned toward her, glanced around, and lowered his voice. "Some people buried art. Unfortunately, some artists died without telling relatives where the work was and now it's simply luck to stumble across something. But these men seemed to know where to look. Would you like to look see what they offered?"

She placed her hand over her heart to slow it. "You are too kind." *Don't choke on your own smarm.*

He lifted his chin and reached into a cabinet for a set of photos. "These are from the gentleman."

She gasped. *He means Bo.*

The eleven photographs showed four different paintings—from the front, close, and far out—and the backs, which had scribbles. And one was identical to a piece in the Returning Home exhibit. *What was Bo up to?*

On the bumpy ride back to the office, she thought about whether to confront Tuan or Bo or keep searching until she had more information.

The loudspeaker screamed news of an unexpected impending storm.

She'd wait until she had more information before any confrontations.

Chapter 26

Back in the office, she called Anna. She was due in Hanoi the next day and must have information by now.

Anna picked up after one ring. "Always ESP with you. About to call. I'm at one of those romantic cafes, so if you hear clinking, it's espresso cups. How're you?"

"Wish I was there. I've had some adventures but want to hear what you're finding first." Thuy paced.

"Not great news."

Thuy's stomach churned. She let out her breath and counted to four. "Let me have it. All of it. Then I've got to decide how to move on this." She swung her head around. The propaganda posters offered up no inspiration today.

Anna cleared her throat. "The bottom line—your collector may not be who you think he is. I found no office at the address you gave me. It's a tiny grocery store. I did find the gallery, though."

"But he's a collector. He must have a warehouse, something."

"I did try to look for storage facilities but could not find any registered under his name, or his gallery's name. But at the gallery, his colleagues seem to like him, and I talked to the woman in charge. She said Minh was away on business. But she also said he was her husband."

Her chest tightened. *Married?* She clutched her chest. "I-I don't know what…"

Anna waited.

She pressed on her temples. "That's not what I expected."

"I was surprised too," Anna said. "The image and feeling I got was certainly different from the way you described him. I'm sorry, but there's a little more."

Thuy's chin wobbled. "More?"

"Not about him. About the letters I got. The vintage ones. I had some of the Vietnamese ones translated. Two of them refer to PLV—your great-uncle perhaps? And a Jean Agent, who sounds like an agent for the French. It's cryptic, and I'm not altogether sure what it means, but it could suggest Vu was working for the French."

Thuy's back jolted from pain, and she gasped.

"Thuy? Are you all right?" Anna's voice moved up a notch.

"I'm reeling. I can't imagine that. Are you sure?"

"As I said, not really clear, so you'll need to read it. The letters are partly French and partly Vietnamese. I'll bring them when I come. But I did want to ask—are there any other sources you have that might help clarify some of this? Any photos? Any letters at your end?"

The album. She should check it again, just in case. "I'll think about it. I've got to figure out what all this means for the exhibit. If it opens." She signed off.

She tapped her pencil on the desk, slowly and then faster. *Who to trust?* Vu might be a traitor. Bo and her boss seemed to be in cahoots about something. Minh wasn't who she thought. Teller in Bangkok seemed shifty. But she had to start with her own family. And Anna was right. The photos might tell her more than she'd gotten at first.

Chapter 27

That night, Thuy pulled the photo album from her desk drawer where she'd stashed it after her talk with Chi and Bo. *This needs to go back to the kitchen, but not until I've checked one more time. Maybe Anna had a point. Something else might be here.*

She'd forgotten that, in addition to photos, there were a couple of newspaper clippings taped to the last page. The tape had gone yellow and crackled, so she slipped her scissors under them to nudge them away from the paper. She opened the album fully, flat on the desk. The back cover seemed bulkier than the front. A tiny piece of paper stuck out of an inside back pocket she'd missed. She lifted the pocket with her fingernail and saw several pieces of yellowed paper. She pulled on one piece—thin as tissue paper.

Tweezers. Three minutes later, five sheets of paper lay on her desk, each the size of a postcard, folded in half. Letters. One envelope with a torn upper left corner revealed a partial address. Somewhere in Paris.

Quang and Bo cheered from below. Their team must have scored. *Chi might be with them or maybe not.* She closed her bedroom door and locked it.

Her eyes raced across the pages. The signature was PLV— Uncle Vu. The handwriting was the same, all in pencil, with smudges. The dates were 1938 and 1939. The letters were crumpled and smudged almost to the point she couldn't read them but they seemed to be a mix of French and Vietnamese.

The letters were addressed to "Anh," which could be any male, including Bo. The letters appeared to reference him: "*Would Lan support the effort…*" but it was hard to tell if they were to him or about him.

Her watch showed 9:12 p.m. The game would last another twenty minutes, at least. She needed time with these letters but not tonight. She skimmed the flimsy paper, but they didn't make sense. Just snippets that were readable.

"… support mon frere… asked to send information… need help from others… Lan?"

Lan was Bo. She had to decipher what Vu was referring to.

"… Paris cadre… join forces… sending money but need… return Hanoi… careful…"

The words read like a telegram—short, cursory, unclear. She could make out very few words, since most were missing or smudged. *What could it all mean? Who was Vu writing to? Why would Bo have these letters if they hadn't been sent to him? Unless Uncle Vu put them in the albums.*

The lamp flickered, and she froze. *No, no. Please no power outage now.* When it rained, often the power and sometimes the water went out. It had happened once last week, and she dreaded it. She'd have to handle these pages in the dark.

Pop.

The light came back on, strong as before. *Lucked out.* She plugged in her phone to charge it in case she'd have to rely on its flashlight.

One news clipping drifted to the floor. She scooped it up, careful not to tear it more than it was already. Two sketches, with Vu's name below. Dien Bien Phu. *He was there too.* March 3, 1954. Both sketches showed soldiers sitting or lying on the ground. One grimaced—*in pain?*—and others tended to him. One held his head; another touched his chest.

The back of her throat hurt. She paced, seven steps to one side of her room, seven to the other, and sat on the bed again. *Like the sketches that were stashed in the vault at work. No guns.* Her eyes swooped back and forth from one clipping to the other.

Neither drawing showed any sign of guns. She racked her brain to remember the sketches in the museum. She'd look at them next time she was in the vault, where most of the sketches were stored. She brought one clipping close to her face. *No weapons in this one either. He could have been making a statement, or simply focusing on faces, people.* She'd never noticed this before but now, given the questions the letters raised, and what Anna had found, she had to consider the possibility that her uncle—her famous uncle—was making a statement by leaving weapons out of his drawings.

Maybe he had sent messages, coded, through his art. Artists have done that for eons. Da Vinci wrote his notes backwards and tucked symbols into paintings. In some, like a painting by Domenico Ghirlandaio, a shining blob floats over the Virgin Mary's shoulder. Some people argued it was a UFO. And she'd read about how Pieter Bruegel the Elder's drawings and pictures indicated Dutch proverbs, like "swimming against the tide" or "the big fish eats the little fish."

But her arm hairs stood up when she looked at Vu's sketches. She set them aside and lifted the album pocket lip again to see if anything else was inside. Something was there, but not paper. A piece of cloth about the size of her little finger's nail. She tweezed it out. Red with a tiny swath of yellow. Silk. She'd seen medals in museums with red and yellow.

Bo said Uncle Vu had never been in France, but if these letters were from Vu, he definitely had been there. *Why lie about that? And what did the reference to Bo in the middle of one page mean? And whose medal, or part of it, had that been? Damn. Too many questions.*

Vu could have been a war hero and that could have been his medal ribbon. But the letters, those bits she could read, sounded like he was supporting France. When he said something about supporting *mon frere*, she knew that to mean "my brother." *Was that literally a brother? Or it could mean France?* He was a patriot—or a traitor. She couldn't decide if the letter sounded like he was recruiting his nephew, Bo, to join him.

Thuy had to think this through logically on paper. If her brilliant IT-Shakespeare quoting friend were with her, she would say "think it through." She grabbed her red FU notebook. *Not this one. Already got me into too much trouble.* The black "ideas book" would do the trick.

1. If letters were from Vu and he supported France = a traitor?
2. If true, family legacy = destroyed.

In the past, Bo and Chi would have been sent to prison camps for that.

Groans from the living room. The game must have turned the wrong way.

3. If true, her job = in jeopardy.
4. If true, Quang = banned from the academy?
5. What about the museum, if showing a traitor's work?
6. Vu could not be the only person in this situation. Other artists? In the museum?

Bo must have known about Vu in France, but refused to acknowledge it if he feared Vu had done something that could damage the family. She tucked the letters into the album and considered her options. She could ignore what she'd found, chalk it up to family lore that no one remembered. But she couldn't unsee and unthink what had happened. She could tell someone about the letters, but that wasn't an easy decision. Bo must know about them already, so that would force a discussion, shine light on a dark time in the family history. Or she could go to Minh—if she could trust him after this—and see if he had any knowledge about the artists in Paris who might have become informers for the French. *Informers. What a word. Shocking.*

She could talk to Hang or Anna, but she was queasy about bringing them in without more evidence.

A final, dangerous option would be to make the letters public—or partly so—on her blog. Open this potentially perilous question of what Vietnamese did in Paris so long ago and see where it took her readers, and her.

A knock on her door jolted her.

"Mum? You awake?"

She closed the notebook and album "Uh. Sure. How'd the game go?"

"Our side lost. And I don't want to go to school tomorrow."

"Why?"

"I wrote the four-page paper that Mrs. Quynh Chi wanted, but you won't like it." He thrust several typed pages to her.

She scanned it. "The words, they're not yours. They're too fancy. That's not the way you write. What's—"

"I used AI. Artificial intelligence. I don't want to spend my time writing. Since it's wrong."

Like I felt at your age.

He plopped on her bed and jiggled his legs.

"But this is not real. It's a machine's work."

"Who cares? It's a paper. That's what she wanted. All the kids do it, write like this."

And artists copy other artists. And museums have fake paintings. "When you do this, you give up your own voice, your integrity. You give up yourself. Would you ask a machine or some software to make a piece of art and then call it yours?"

He hung his head and tucked his hands under his thighs. "That's different."

"How?"

"What I draw is important. It's my idea, my pencils, my sketches. This is a dumb paper. It doesn't matter who writes it— me or AI."

"Where's the line?"

A rumbling of motorbikes roared on the street below. Teenage boys had taken to racing in the streets of Hanoi late at night, when the traffic was lighter. Police tried to stop it, but so many were sons of wealthy, powerful parents, that nothing stuck. The boys got off.

"If I tell you something, will you believe me?"

"Of course. You're my mum."

"Then I'll tell you I was wrong with Mrs. Quynh Chi. I should have fought back for you on this assignment. I believed you did not shove that girl. That your version—that she tripped—was right. But I gave in because she has power. But that was wrong. I'm sorry I didn't stand up for you."

His mouth hung open, and his legs stopped moving.

"We need to stand up for what's truthful, what's right, what's worth fighting for." She chuckled. "Sorry, I sound like I'm giving a politician's speech."

She pointed to the album on her bed. "I'm learning some things about Uncle Vu that make me rethink what's true. I want to know, even if it's not good for the family. It's hard but necessary. Seeing what's real, following a path that builds integrity and honesty… that's important. Do you understand what I'm saying?"

"That I can't turn in this paper?"

"Well, you have to turn in a paper, since we agreed you would. But it should be your own words, even if they are not what Mrs. Quynh Chi demanded. Explain the situation, why you should not be in trouble. Even if that doesn't work, you've followed your own path. And been truthful."

He smiled. "I'll do it." He sat up. "But I might get tossed out on my bum."

Chapter 28

The next morning, Thuy yanked a sticky note that Tuan had left on her office door. "Come to my office A.S.A.P." *Never a good sign when the boss leaves this kind of note.*

"Shut the door," he barked. He didn't invite her to sit.

This can't be good. She shoved the door to close it.

"You went around me."

If she had been closer, his spittle would have hit her nose. "Wha—"

"I heard from Mr. Minh. In Paris. He told me about your antics."

"I waited several days. We had to know about the paintings—"

"You had no authority. And you thought it a good move to provoke the donor? You may have cost us the exhibit."

Her mind went blank. "Mr. Tuan, I—"

Tuan lifted a hand. "You had concerns about some paintings, and Hai asked you to fix it while I was on my trip. But that did not mean you should accuse the collector of forgery." He lit a cigarette and flipped the carton around between his thumb and middle finger.

She screamed in her head and felt the pain of the carton's warning on the box: a photo of a man hunched over a smoldering cigarette stick. He looked like a skeleton—ribs, splotchy skin. She couldn't understand how Tuan could smoke those things with that photo staring out from the pack. But he didn't even notice. *We only see what we want to see.* And he saw her as an enemy.

"Have you looked at the paintings? One of Vu's has the date wrong, since it was after he died." She had to slow down, or she'd lose him. "And another one. A local artist says the painting was by his great-grandfather, but the signature isn't his. And a friend of mine tried to find Mr. Minh's office in Paris, but he doesn't seem legit—"

He slammed his palm on the desk. "You're making no sense. Are you still upset about the job? Is that why you're raising all of this?"

Of course not. I'm looking out for the museum, for the artists. The cigarette's blue-grey smoke irritated her nose. She fought the urge to grimace.

Tuan put his thumb and index finger on his eyeglass lens, smudging it more as he pulled them from his face and jutted his chin. "This exhibit is a once in a lifetime opportunity to show Vietnamese art to the world and build a relationship with a collector who could help us. Extraordinary chance for us. We have the government permissions. That means we must go forward."

No. You can't. "I see that but—"

He raised his palm. "Mr. Hai was in France. He saw the art, he inspected it, and he spent time with Mr. Minh. And I think Hai's a good judge of character."

Her knees shook. She imagined a racehorse in her head, straining. "But he *didn't* see all the pieces. Minh chose what to send, not what we asked for."

Tuan pulled back. "That's not true. Hai said only a few were replaced because some of the ones we requested were unavailable."

"No." *He liked the title but not the work, that was clearer all the time. He had no clue what was really going on.* "Minh removed several of the ones I asked for. And some that you asked for. He made the final selection."

He rubbed his forehead. "Really? This is new information to me. Maybe you are right to question, but we must not push too hard. I had hoped he would let us keep some of these paintings, donate them outright to the museum. Or even add some others from his collection. He could be important for us in the future. We need this exhibit, however we form it."

The glass doors on a grey metal bookshelf next to his desk stood halfway open, showing a space where a black marbled two-ring binder had been. Those notebooks were old school— they came from Russia and East Germany thirty years before, and one lay open on his desk. The plastic sleeves held photos of two paintings—a portrait of a young boy and a village next to a rice field.

He glanced at them, and her, and closed the binder. He squished his cigarette and blew a huge breath out.

She stepped toward him. "What are those? Are they in our collection?"

"Please do not concern yourself with these. Your father… no. No. To return to our discussion, you contacted the collector, the dealer, without permission."

"But only after Mr. Hai didn't get back to me. After five days. I heard nothing—"

"Against his wishes. And mine." Tuan blinked at her four, five, six times, very fast.

"All I did was ask if he knew if the paintings—"

"Enough!" He slapped his palm on a stack of papers.

She jumped.

"Mrs. Thuy, I gave you an opportunity. A chance. Few people have such good luck. But you are naïve. Sometimes what you say does happen. I heard at the conference that as many as forty percent of paintings in the famous Metropolitan Museum of New York City in America are not the real ones. The Metropolitan Museum! But these, in this exhibit, these are real. Pieces that have never been in Vietnam."

She sucked the insides of her cheeks inward and bit down, hard. She had to convince him. Her phone buzzed. *Not now.*

"Even the Ho Chi Minh National Museum has this challenge, but it shows the questionable pieces."

Her head jerked back. The museum with the job. The museum that might want her, even if Tuan did not.

"Speaking of that museum, I received an email." He stood behind his desk. "This morning. Someone who said you told her to come here to look at the special exhibit paintings."

Her mouth fell open. *What? How? Chien.* The only person she'd talked to about this was Chien. *He must have reached out to this mystery woman.* He'd made her bait for Tuan.

"I did not ask anyone to come in. You have to believe me." She sounded shrill inside her head, so she assumed it sounded worse outside.

"It wasn't your place. With that, with contacting the collector on your own, and approaching the dealer. You leave me no choice. I must remove you from the exhibit."

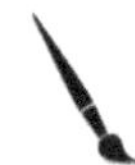

Thuy staggered out of Tuan's office like a zombie. Her vision blurred, and she shook her head to right it. *Oh my god. This makes it all worse…and harder.* Tuan accused her of going around him, of threatening the donor. All done for the museum, for the exhibit. And now he had accused her of inviting an authenticator from Ho Chi Minh City. That had to be Chien, but he hadn't told her he would do it. She had thought she could trust him, but obviously, that was a big mistake.

And now, she was off the exhibit. Whatever she'd done was for the good of the art, for the museum. But her hard work had bombed. And to think she was supposed to sell herself as a successful curator-in-training at the Ho Chi Minh job. She was as big a fake as any of the paintings she worried about.

Stop. Take charge. Her back straightened and she squared her shoulders. She had to fight, for the art, for the museum, for herself. No matter what.

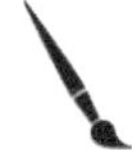

Thuy tramped up to the special exhibit. The door, supposed to be locked, was cracked open. She tiptoed in and inhaled.

Chien stood in front of one of the questionable paintings. He swiveled and bowed. "Security check, without people standing about."

"Tuan got an email from an authenticator in Ho Chi Minh and thought I'd asked her to come. Was that you?"

Hien poked her head in and waved a dust rag. "Need anything in here?" She saw Chien and backed out. "Oops. Sorry to bother."

"Oh… I've been a bad boy." Chien smiled, but it wasn't endearing on his round, pockmarked face. "Is he going to bring her up?"

"He's furious. He blasted me for going around him and may replace these with some my father donated that I've never seen or heard about."

"Now that's interesting. Your father? Paintings by your uncle?"

"I'm confused, but, in the end, he sacked me from the exhibit. I—"

Chien did a double take. "What?"

"Fifteen minutes ago."

"I'm so sorry if this is my doing. Should I talk to him? You're the right person for the job. You know that."

"Not anymore."

Back in her office, Thuy stared at the young soldier in the poster on the wall. He had gone to battle, like so many others, when his country called. Some of those fighters might have been excited to serve the motherland, fight for independence, and have the chance of meeting Uncle Ho on his travels through the country-side. Others may have felt fear but couldn't—or didn't—show it or say it. They stayed strong to make their families proud and to liberate the country. Still others may have felt some curiosity, after hearing their own fathers and uncles talk about fighting, at least the men who returned.

She ran her finger along and across the five-pointed yellow star. If young people like this, in their teens, could fight, then she could face challenges from Tuan and Bo.

She had no official power, but she knew what she must do: stop Tuan from opening the exhibit if he refused to pull the tainted paintings. *And only ten days to do it.*

Chapter 29

Thuy ordered a latte and stared out of the Cong Ca Phe front window across from St. Joseph's cathedral. An old Vietnamese woman pushing a bike stopped, grabbed a bouquet of plastic zinnias from her basket, and waved them in front of a tourist wearing a strappy top and dangly silver earrings. Ms. Earrings shook her head and turned away. The flower woman stepped in and pushed the flowers closer to the tourist's face. She probably said the price, "two dollah," or something in that range. The tourist put her hands up, but her companion laughed and pulled out a few thousand Dong and offered it to the flower woman. Maybe a dollar's worth. *Thinks he got a good deal. Little do they know.* The flower woman made a good show of insisting on more, they haggled, and at last, she pulled one flower out, handed it to Ms. Earrings, and left.

Thuy called Anna. "I'm watching some good haggling in the Old Quarter. Do you miss it?"

"Of course! I always thought I was a hugely successful negotiator 'til you told me I still paid one hundred percent more than what you'd pay. For some reason, those street vendors think I'm a foreigner and should pay more than you Vietnamese." She guffawed. "Good to hear from you. What's up? Can't wait to see you next week."

"Good news and bad news, as you Americans say."

Anna chuckled. "I'll bite. What's the good news?"

"I'm going to Ho Chi Minh City the day after the opening, to interview for the job."

"Congratulations! Wonderful news. Now what's the bad?" Anna slowed down.

Thuy sucked in air. "I was fired from the exhibit."

"What? Did you say fired?"

"Tuan didn't like that I contacted Minh without permission."

"I can imagine that didn't go over well. But that's not firing action, is it?"

Thuy scraped her fingers down her damp neck and pulled her shirt away from her. Her empty water glass reproached her: *Drink more water. Failed at that too.* "I also went to the dealer, another infraction. And he thought I had asked an authenticator to come up from Saigon."

"From Ho Chi Minh City? What were you thinking?"

"Wasn't me. I think Chien—the security guy—did it to help, but Tuan doesn't believe me now. But even scarier, he may try to swap out questionable paintings with some from the vault. Or even from Bo. Ones I don't recognize."

"Huh?"

"He had photos on his desk. Mumbled something about Bo but wouldn't tell me. I wonder if they were from Vu. And I also wonder if Bo is doing something he shouldn't, but I can't figure out what."

"You've got to find out more," Anna said. "And do not let Tuan replace paintings. That'd be awful for Vietnam, let alone the exhibit. Journalists from Hong Kong will be in town. You don't want fakes—or replacements—to be the headline."

"He insists the exhibit will open next week as planned. He's got government permissions, which you know are hard to get. If I could get him at least to remove the questionable ones…"

"You're in the right here. You're trying to protect the integrity of the exhibit and of the museum. Stand up for it. Remember that article you told me about how museums are the most trusted institutions? Make it true."

"I definitely want to do right by the museum, even if I'm not running the exhibit. I want to protect it. But we need help. Someone to check the paintings, to see if they're real. Even if I'm not on the exhibit, we have to protect the integrity of the museum. Tuan was furious at the thought someone would review the art. But we really do need someone to do it, even if he doesn't think so. For the good of the exhibit, and the museum. When does your authenticator come to town? The one from Singapore? We could use him."

"Could be dicey. We'd need a good cover story and something to entice him since I don't think he evaluates whether paintings are real unless he's got a commission. But in the meantime, you've got to get the government to help stop it or postpone..." Anna's voice faded.

"Anna? Are you there?"

"Thinking. Maybe I can help. I know someone."

"You do? You haven't been in Hanoi for years."

"You're not the only one who stays in touch with big names. I did that internship at the Ministry for a month when I was in Hanoi before. Stayed in touch with the unit director. Let me try." The phone went dead.

Chapter 30

"I'm doing this with you, not to you," Thuy said. She pulled a handkerchief from her leggings waistband and wiped her face and the back of her neck, under her ponytail. "You sit at a computer all day, argue with those IT developers ten years younger than you, and your blood pressure is probably off the charts. Here, we see scenery and remember history from grade four. And I wanted a safe space to talk. To pick your brain."

Hang panted alongside as they jogged around Ba Dinh Square. "Trying to test my photographic memory?"

"Go head and show off. What do you remember about this square, what we learned so long ago?"

Hang stopped, hands on her thighs, covered in leopard print leggings "Grade-four trivia—this square can hold 200,000 people. September 9, 1945, Independence Day, and Uncle Ho said, 'All men are created equal' and that bit."

Thuy chuckled. "Americans are surprised when they hear that's how Ho started that speech: 'endowed by their creator with certain unalienable—that's always hard to say—rights; among these are life, liberty—'"

"—and the pursuit of happiness." Hang pumped her arms to jog forward.

Thuy clapped. "And someone named Thomas Jeffer-sone wrote the words."

"Yup. And Uncle Ho tried to be a friend with America, and look where that got us." Hang stopped again, panting.

"OK, enough stalling." Thuy guided them along the north side of the plaza in front of the Uncle Ho Mausoleum. She nodded at two guards in white uniforms at the entrance. "They always ignore me."

Hang chortled. "I'll admit, my blood pressure was a bit high last year. But this running, it's too much. I may faint." Hang leaned over. "Slow down."

Thuy handed her a water bottle. "Drink, and then we'll walk."

She gulped for fifteen seconds. "Now, what's so important that we need a safe space?"

"I took Bo to see the exhibit after that disaster the other night. He just seemed confused and shrugged off any chance of those pieces being fake."

"That's a mistake. Don't get pulled into that one."

"I agree. And when I talked to Hai, he's terrified of losing face. Didn't want me to contact the collector. But I did. And his art dealer. I worry now there's something shady. So, Ms. Logic Brain, now that we're a few days away from the official opening, what do you think?"

"Nothing to think about. Expose him. Your collector may be a fraud himself."

That was Hang. Straight in for the kill. Thuy's hair on her arms raised. "Why do you think that?"

"Easy. From what you said, he pushed this exhibit on the museum. He chose the pieces. He's admitted to you he wants to sell them—so this gives him visibility. You're a well-respected museum. Should I go on?"

"But Minh may not even know if he's got fakes? He buys from a dealer in Bangkok, named Morris Teller. I talked to him and he strikes me as fishier than Minh."

Two soldiers' boots struck the sidewalk nearby. Changing of the guard.

Thuy looked at them. "No matter what I do or say, those guys never react. Like we're not even here."

"They're supposed to ignore us. Now, back to the collector. Whatever his motive is, something seems off," Hang said. "Your bosses must see this. And surely your father does?"

Thuy stretched her calves. "No one else seems worried like I am. Bo offered to replace the pieces with art from with what he calls 'unseen Uncle Vu pieces' that he's had for eons. From the time Vu hid pieces in the caves up north." *Ones that he took to the gallery the other day, maybe.*

Hang sprung on her toes. "You say you want to champion Vietnamese artists, but allowing fakes is not the way. And that's interesting about your dad offering unseen art from Uncle Vu. But why are you protecting this collector?"

"He offered us some incredible art. You saw them. Most are amazing."

"Quit being wishy-washy. The paintings are remarkable, but are they all real? With several that are in question, can you trust the others to be real?" Hang held her palms out, catching some rain drops. "Sprinkles. And a dark sky. I'm saved!"

"There's a Bia Hoi. Run!" Thuy sprinted to a ramshackle overhanging awning fifty yards away. She grabbed two spots at a low wooden table out of the rain and ordered beers. Rain pelted the overhead tarp and clumped to the ground a few feet away from the tables. The solid shush of the hard rain drowned conversation. "Let's just sit for a minute." She had to raise her concerns with Hang before the rain ended and they left. "What were you thinking when you talked about Bo and the paintings?"

"How is it that your father still has paintings from Uncle Vu? Ones never before seen in public? Do you believe him?" Hang stretched her arms above her head. "Geez. You look spooked. What's going on?"

A server poured beer in both glasses and plunked two big ice cubes in Thuy's glass.

"I... uh... I want to ask about some memories, about our childhoods. And Bo."

"Tell me. Can't be that bad. What is it?"

Here goes. Thuy swished her beer around in the heavy green glass. "Did your parents ever talk about my father in a not so good way? Did they ever see anything that seemed… odd to them?" She caught the server's eye.

"No idea what you mean."

The rain created a curtain of white noise to dull the conversations around them. Thuy leaned in. "Did they ever think Bo was up to something he shouldn't have been?" Water drained to a gutter beside her. Bits of leaves floated along the stream. She peeked at Hang.

Hang sat still, unmoving except for her mouth. "I'm shocked that you doubt your father. He's always been your hero. What's gotten into you?"

"You asked if I could believe him. I don't know right now. He's done a few things lately that make me wonder about the paintings he sold, about the money he got from them."

"Data. I'm an IT person," Hang said. "I need data. Give me an example."

Always the logical one. Thuy pointed a thumb in the air. "Okay. Almost weekly, he says Quang has the talent of my great uncle. So, when I didn't get the job, he brushed it off. Said it didn't matter since I don't have the art talent Quang does. Said it was fate."

"That seems skimpy."

"He has refused to tell me much about Uncle Vu, and what he does tell me might be wrong—like when he was born, whether he left the country. The collector had information that contradicted Bo's comments all these years."

"Maybe your dad doesn't know?"

"Or he's lying." Thuy caught the eye of the server and lifted her glass.

Hang touched her forehead. "Can't be that bad, can it? And after what you found out about the guy in Paris, why would you ever believe him over your dad?"

Rock music blared from inside the Bia Hoi. The pounding in her head matched the pounding from the drums. "I was on Hang Gai recently and saw him coming out of a gallery with someone from the museum. They seemed to know each other, which makes no sense. When I asked the gallery employee about it, he showed me photos of pieces Bo wanted to sell. My great-uncle's art. Some that I've never seen, and one piece looked exactly like one in our special exhibit. Of course, I can't be sure with a photo, but it looked the same."

Hang puffed her cheeks and let the air out slowly.

Thuy leaned toward her. "That's why I'm curious about what you might remember. Did my father ever do something that seemed off?"

Hang scraped her fingers through her hair. "My photographic memory works on trivia from school, but I can't guarantee memories of my own life. We were kids, for God's sake."

She's admitting it. "There is something. I knew it. What?"

The rain had slowed to a dull drizzle. Lighter, but still enough to stay under cover.

"I don't want to cause you trouble."

Thuy's arms felt weighted down. "I need to hear what you've got to say." Thuy wiped her hands on her thighs. "Or what your parents said."

Hang closed her eyes.

"Just say it." Thuy gripped the table's edge to keep from shivering. It didn't work.

"Please don't get mad," Hang said. "I remember a few times. They talked about your family having more food than we did. You had—"

"What? No one had food! What're you talking about?" Thuy gaped at Hang. "What did they mean?"

"Didn't you have a chicken a few times between Tet holidays? You told me that you had *Pho Ga*—not just vegetables. I was so jealous..."

What's this? Thuy put a hand over her mouth. "I don't... I don't remember that. I can't believe it." She drained her beer glass.

Hang patted her hand. "Maybe I'm misremembering. It was such a long time ago. Could be false memory. My parents are dead, so I can't ask them, and maybe they made wrong assumptions. I shouldn't have told you."

"Don't apologize. If there was even a hint of something wrong, I need to know." She wrapped her arms around her stomach. "If he bought a chicken on the black market, how was that even possible? We had no money. No one did. Chi made nasty comments about families who had better rice, not the rotten rice that we did. But a chicken? Shocking."

"I'm so sorry. What's this mean for you?"

Cataclysm. Pressure in her chest stopped her breathing. Suddenly, she restarted. "It means I don't know what's real anymore. But I've got to find out and make it right. "

Thuy's phone pinged. Voicemail from Quang. "Mum. I did what you said. The paper. And Mrs. Quynh Chi said it was okay. She said I showed strength. She talked to the girl again, and she admitted she'd lied. I did what was right. See you at home."

Maybe she could make it right too.

Chapter 31

The day that Anna arrived, Thuy stood in front of a series of doors at the Ministry of Culture, Tourism, and Sports. Above each door was a metal plaque with names and titles of a high-ranking administrator. She hoped Anna's contact could help them figure a fast way to assess the paintings or at a minimum, postpone the opening.

Down the hall, Anna waved to Thuy. "Here it is." She waited in front of a sign that read "Cultural Administration Support." She knocked and stepped into a large open room filled with cluttered desks. A dozen shiny black-haired heads and wide-eyed faces popped up from computers. "That always happens when I show up," said Anna. "A big non-Vietnamese woman." Anna waved at the group. "I'm here to see Bui Pham Nam," she announced to a young man at the front desk.

In the back of the room, Nam lifted his arm. "Auntie Anna! Over here!" His short-sleeved white shirt, navy trousers, and long brown leather shoes curled up at the toes matched most of the other twenty-somethings in the room.

Thuy shook Nam's limp hand. *You've not met many foreign men. They use firm handshakes as a negotiation starting point.*

"You asked about forgeries and what we are doing," he said. "I'm afraid the boss is away this afternoon, but I have arranged for you to meet with our crime expert."

At the edge of the open office was a walled, windowless conference room with an overpowering table, with five straight-backed wooden chairs on each side. *Probably made by the same tormentor designers who made mine.* Notebooks and sketches, books, and metal and stone sculptures that looked like they came from India and Cambodia covered the table. A small Cham head and bronze horse stirrups sat on a side table.

Anna and Nam caught up on family gossip before a Vietnamese woman in her fifties, with a triangle-shaped face and hair set in a bun covered with a crochet net at the nape of her neck, entered the room. Nam stood.

"Please meet Ms. Nguyen Thuc Anh. She is a South Asian expert—mostly India—but also studies looted and stolen art in Southeast Asia. She knows about fakes, at least some types."

Thuc Anh, square shaped in torso, wore a black silk *ao dai*. She leaned into the middle of the table and pulled a metal box toward her before sitting. She moved her arms over the tea paraphernalia with the grace of a ballerina, dropping tea leaves and steaming water into the pot in front of her. "Nam tells me you worked with his mum many years ago. I respect her very much. Now, how can I help you?"

"Thank you for meeting us, Ms. Thuc Anh. That's right. Many happy memories of those days. But now we have a favor to ask. Ms. Thuy." Anna gestured at her.

Thuy described the special exhibit and her concerns. "We received permission to hold the exhibit before we discovered possible fakes."

Thuc Anh picked up the stone head from the table. "Here's what I deal with," she said. "I bought this in a small antique store in Cambodia. It's supposed to be from the 15th century. What do you think?" She passed the five-pound object to Thuy, who gave it to Anna.

"Not my field, of course," Anna said. "But doesn't Cambodia restrict antiques from leaving the country? Like Vietnam?"

"Correct. Foreigners are not allowed to buy and transport antiques, so how could this store allow me to buy it? For twenty dollars?"

Thuy chuckled. "You got a deal."

"Turn it over. You'll see the small round indentation—it was part of a larger block of stone, created, and then sliced. The actual heads on real pieces were knocked off the bodies of the statues, so they tend to be jagged on the bottom. Not this one. Too clean. But you get the idea."

Hard to tell what's real and what's not.

"How many museums have such items, do you think? Fake ones?" Anna lifted the head and turned it around.

"Or stolen? Or looted? Probably most museums," said Thuc Anh. "Lots in countries that were on dangerous trade routes or went through colonization or war. Like we did."

"Are you saying it's common for museums to have such pieces? Not just tourists?" Thuy made notes.

"I am. You've probably heard that a director of the very famous Metropolitan Museum in America reported—I think in the 1990s—that up to forty percent of the pieces in his museum could be fake. When I heard that, I found it hard to believe he would admit it," Thuc Anh said.

Thuy nodded. "Shocking."

"But that's only his estimate. A professor who studies forgeries measures only the art hanging on walls and says that the number is closer to ten percent. But an institute in Geneva in Switzerland claims the frequency of fakes is much worse— between seventy and ninety percent are either fakes or what they call 'misattributed,' meaning they wrongly credit an artist with a painting. Of course, some critics say this is exaggeration."

"However you look at it," said Anna, "it's horrible."

A young man crept in and placed cups in front of Thuc Anh, Anna, and Thuy, and poured tea. Liquid splashed onto Thuy's saucer, and he grabbed tissues to wipe it.

Thuc Anh pulled her cup toward her. "I must say, if we are honest, we do not know how many false pieces are out there."

Thuy's energy plunged. "How awful it's so common. But how does this happen? How do fakes find their way to museums? Can't you prevent it?"

Thuc Anh raised her palms in front of her. "All valid questions. But before we go too far, may I give you a short history on fake art and forgeries? I promise not to lecture, but you need some facts."

"Please. We need to hear this," Anna said.

Thuy's shoulders curled forward. *What chaos. And, not just for us.*

"To be frank, art crime is a big business. Worldwide, recent thefts are in the billions of dollars in any given year. And forgery happens around the world, not just in Vietnam."

"I've read about wartime looting in Europe." Anna glanced at Thuy. "And stealing during colonial times in Africa. And excavations in Greece. Forgeries seem like one more piece of a very bad puzzle."

"Sadly, you are right," said Thuc Anh. "Much more is known about Europe and the Middle East… even Africa, because of colonization. Also, in South Asia. In India. But less about Southeast Asia. That's what I'll focus on in the future. I have an article by a famous Vietnamese professor—Professor Hoang-Quan Vuong—about Vietnam's art forgery. He's an expert in economics and business but writes about lots of top-ics. Let me pull it." She reached for her glasses. "Here we are. I won't make you read it but there are few key points."

"We don't want to take too much of your time—"

"This is important. First, please understand the crux of forgery is willful deception. But that's hard to prove. For instance, an art piece could be copied or made in the style of an artist, turned over to a gallery, or go to auction and be purchased by someone who believes it to be real. An expert could then expose it as a forgery but without the intent to deceive. That's a misattribution—"

Anna lifted her finger. "That's why that group out of Switzerland had such high numbers. Lots of pieces that were fake, but the collector or museum didn't know it."

"That's correct, Ms. Anna."

"But what drives this?" Thuy sipped.

"Good question. Here's what I think." Thuc Anh held up her thumb. "First, collectors in Vietnam desperately want ways to show off their wealth. We were such a poor country for so long, and now some people have more money than they could dream of."

"I've certainly seen that recently," Thuy said.

"Also, many of those buying art are quite ignorant about it, so they don't realize or even question that they might buy a fake. And then, they're embarrassed when they learn, so they may not tell about it." Thuc Anh's phone pinged. She peeked at it and turned it over. Her index finger went up. "A second reason for so many forgeries is that we lack the legal framework and infrastructure to find and flush it out. Our laws are weak. We lack a solid database of artists, but that requires curators, art critics, and art managers to maintain it. We don't enforce copyrights and professional ethics. As such a young art market, we have few resources for this. And many artists simply give up because they see no recourse, no support."

"And what about people who can authenticate? We heard about someone in Ho Chi Minh City."

"Ah, yes. Ms. Thu. She's self-taught, which is where we are in these days. We definitely need training and labs and technology. To be honest, we tried to set up a center to evaluate authenticity about a decade ago, but it has failed to attract many clients. And now… the resources are not enough." She pulled her shoulders back and stared at the table.

Ashamed that Vietnam is so far behind. Makes all of us look bad.

"And one final reason. Saddest of all," Thuc Anh added. "Sometimes those closest to the artists do the most damage. Too often we see cases of a relative, younger, copying a famous artist's work and passing it off as authentic. This happens when the artist has gained notoriety, and the paintings become more expensive."

Like what the journalist said. Once it's more than $10K, it's worth making a copy.

"And there's a part of our culture that forgives a younger person who may do such a thing. If he apologizes, we move forward."

Another shiver raced through Thuy's body. "I'm worried about our special exhibit at my museum. Artists' work that was in Europe and is 'returning to Vietnam.' The ministry granted permission for it to go forward, but now we worry that some of the pieces may not be originals. Is there no way to do a basic authentication review? What would that include?"

Thuc Anh's shoulders sagged, and she sighed. "Several steps: analyzing the appearance, establishing ownership and provenance, examining how it has aged, what materials were used to see if they fit the time frame. But as I said, we lack trained people and labs and technology. We have a few experts, and we go to specialists outside of Vietnam. But again, few resources." She spread her arms.

Anna put her hand on Thuy's arm and leaned forward. "But, since we came to you with the concern, is there any way you can help us find an assessor? Or what if we found one?"

She glanced at Thuy. "That's what you want, right? To keep the exhibit from opening until we know?"

Even if I'm not in charge, I have to maintain integrity for the museum. "Yes. Until we review the situation, all I can say is that you could postpone opening, voluntarily," Thuc Anh said.

"Ms. Thuy doesn't have a lot of time," Anna said. "If you could do a review, by bringing in someone, perhaps that could help slow it. How long does it take, and when might you do it?"

"An assessment usually takes two to three weeks since we must remove the paintings and take them to the lab." Thuc Anh flipped pages in her diary. "But, of course, we must gain permission from the ministry and the government to conduct an audit. Let me see, if we put the request in now, that usually will take three weeks, and so we could come to you in four weeks."

Thuy's stomach sank. "No, that's too long. The exhibit opens in a few days. Why does it take so long?"

"The lab. We send paintings to a lab in Bangkok."

Thuy's blood felt like it had stopped, and she gripped Anna's hand. "We're doomed."

Chapter 32

From the glass lobby doors, Thuy watched Anna and her authenticator colleague cross the museum's wide plaza. They stopped twice when Anna pointed to different parts of the building like she was giving a tour. From a distance, Mr. Geoffrey Tan Lee looked like an Asian Hercule Poirot, a mystery book character Anna had introduced to her when they worked together in their internships. A few years later, she found well-used copies of Agatha Christie books at The Bookworm. In those days, the bookshop hid behind the Western Canned Food shop on Ba Trieu and sold mild, non-controversial books like mysteries and cookbooks. These days, from its new location near Truc Bach Lake, The Bookworm sold everything from history and economics books to Nobel and Pulitzer prize winners.

Bow tied, rotund, with a bright yellow silk scarf dangling around his neck, Lee poked an ebony wood cane on the gravely plaza. His impeccable pale grey suit would doubtless become smudged with rain and mud over the coming days. Anna had sent Lee's *curriculum vitae*, so Thuy expected an English accent since he had studied in Cambridge years before. And some people from Singapore seemed to embellish a bit of an accent as well, if she remembered from her visit there seven years before.

Anna stood two full heads taller than Lee, and his determined stride was half the length of hers. Her brilliant white smile flashed. Mr. Lee had a hint of a grin as she talked.

Reserved? Arrogant?

At the lobby entrance, he burst into laughter and put his hand over his mouth as if he was embarrassed at his joy.

Thuy doubted he fully understood that she and Anna wanted him to authenticate paintings in the museum, so they needed to get his consent, without Tuan knowing. He was only interested in the glory not in the hard work behind something like the exhibit. Even if the government couldn't help, Mr. Lee would be the key to finding out what they had in the museum.

Thuy shook Lee/Poirot's hand. He bowed slightly and slipped his hand into his jacket pocket, thumb out.

"An honor to meet the grand niece of Mr. Pham Ly Vu. I have long been an admirer, an ardent one, for some time. My first encounter with Vietnamese art was during my student days at Cambridge." He peeked at her like he wanted to be sure she was impressed. "I spent two months in Paris and discovered Vietnamese art and artists. The artists in Mr. Vu's generation were such a bridge for the country of Vietnam. They connected the influence of the impressionists of France and Europe to Vietnam's style."

A pang of pride rose in her chest. "Thank you for that. Would you like to look around the museum? We, that is Anna and I, thought you might wish to see the museum and give us your impressions."

"Are you asking me to assess paintings? That is more than I expected."

Is he on to us? Thuy glanced at Anna. "We know this is an informal visit for you. As a patron of the arts, you will attend the exhibit. But if you have any informal observations on whatever you see, we are curious to learn from you. As a colleague and a new set of eyes. Always inspiring to hear what others think of our pieces."

Behind Lee, Anna made a small fist pump.

Lee pursed his lips and dipped his chin. "This is my first visit to Hanoi, and I do want to see the museum. Not only the special exhibit. You have a famous relative, and I certainly want to see his work. That is true. But first, may I have a cup of tea?"

Thuy led Lee and Anna to the gift shop, and they sat at one of the two tables set up for people who ordered drinks.

Chien filled three paper cups with hot water and brought a bowl of tea bags to the table.

"What's this?" Lee's head wrenched backward. "One should never drink tea from a… paper container." He glared at Thuy. "Never. In Singapore, we drink tea from a porcelain cup."

Chien swept the uncivilized cups from view. "So sorry, sir. Let me bring an appropriate cup."

"I'd forgotten this is still third world country," Lee sniped.

Thuy's throat clutched. *Maybe this wasn't such a good idea.*

"Mr. Lee, you have no idea how far Vietnam has progressed in twenty years; it's a marvel," Anna said. "Remember, your country had support from Britain for a long time before becoming independent. Vietnam has been on its own since the fall of Russia. It takes time."

Thuy's heart slowed. "Anna's right. Thirty years ago, we had no stop lights, or cars, or grocery stores. Now it is different."

He sniffed.

Chien arrived with ceramic cups, not ancient, not replicas. Instead, they were colorful cups with dragonflies painted in blue on a white background. He poured hot water from a matching tea pot and placed a bronze bowl of tea bags on the table. "Let me try again."

Lee studied the cup, looked at the bottom, and said, "From your ceramic village. I know it. Ba Trang. Very nice. Modern but nice." He stroked the teacup like it was a million-dollar piece of art. "This will fortify me for my review of the art upstairs."

Thuy clasped her hands. "Does that mean you will examine—"

"I need a contract for that."

Anna touched Thuy's arm. "Mr. Lee, we know how important and busy you are. My friend is grateful that you came all this way for the special exhibit. But she is concerned about some of the other paintings, in the permanent collection, and would like for you to take a look, if you would be so kind."

He frowned and picked at his bow tie.

Anna straightened her shoulders. "And I've been commissioned to write a piece, for the *Financial World*, on authenticators in Asia, especially since there are so very few like you."

You sneaky lady. Thuy glanced at Anna.

Lee sipped his tea and tried to suppress a smile. "Is there a chance you might include me?"

Anna swayed. "I would love to consider it. If I do, then I'd need to understand the difficult job you do. I could use your time here to learn what I could and tell our readers about your work."

Thuy held her cup midair. *Anna could pour on the charm.*

"I would certainly be willing but should start by talking with your director to get some context—" He turned to Thuy.

"Oh, I—"

Anna leaned forward. "I believe you said that he was out of the office today?" She nodded at Thuy.

"How could I forget? Of course. Does that cause you a problem? You'll meet him at the opening, but he's busy with arrangements right now. I'm sure you understand."

"I suppose. Where should we start?"

"Oh, by the way, Mr. Lee," Chien stepped forward, "would it be possible for me to follow you around too? I would like to learn how this works and if you could talk out loud as you go? I could listen?"

Lee's face turned red. "No one has dared ask. I do not talk as I work. Assessing is not a performance sport." He picked up his cane and tapped out of the coffee shop.

Chien lifted his eyebrows at Anna. "A bit pompous?"

Thuy's closed her eyes. *So pompous.* First, he makes a show about a teacup and now gets riled up by a simple request.

Anna put her hand on Thuy's shoulder. "Let it go. You need him. He's hard but he's good." She tilted her head at the door, where Lee stood.

Chien moved to Mr. Lee. "Of course, you work alone and on your own timeframe. That's what geniuses do, and I should have realized that." He swept his arms toward Thuy and Anna. "We all should. Please tell me where you'll be, and I will be sure you have fresh tea in an hour. And some sweets as well?"

"Very kind. I shall take an initial round to see what is on hand. Ms. Thuy, can you show me the way? We can reconvene this afternoon." Lee marched from the room, flinging his scarf over his shoulder.

Chapter 33

Thuy led Mr. Lee and Anna to the second floor of the museum's permanent collection. "By the way, Mr. Lee, do you know of a dealer in Bangkok, a man named Morris Teller?"

Lee stiffened. "We do not talk of contemporaries in my business."

Anna raised her eyebrows at Thuy.

"Sorry I brought him up. Please, on to your important work." *Bring me some news. Good or bad, I need to know.*

Lee left to roam the two floors that held Uncle Vu's art pieces, ranging from the 1930s to the 1990s. "Ms. Anna will return me to you in two hours. By then, I'll have some basic ideas about Mr. Vu's paintings."

At 3:30 p.m., Lee entered Thuy's office, smiling like he'd discovered a missing Leonardo. His bow tie was crooked, and he'd rolled his sleeves above his elbows. He played with the signet ring on his little finger and a paper fan hung from a bracelet on his wrist. He accepted more tea, which Chien had left earlier.

Anna followed, looking more nervous than pleased.

"I reviewed paintings on floors two and three. Many are from the war periods. I was especially interested in your uncle since the auction house in Hong Kong plans to sell some."

"Would you like to sit?" Thuy's head swished back and forth between her visitors. Given what she'd read in Vu's letters, she was desperate to know what Lee thought of the paintings.

"No, I think it's better to view the pieces together and I can give you my initial, cursory thoughts." He pulled a black leather notebook from his breast pocket and a stubby yellow pencil. "You have eight of Mr. Vu's art pieces at the museum, or at least on exhibit here. Mostly in Room 313, on the third floor. Two on the second floor. Shall we visit together?"

He unrolled his sleeves, buttoned his cuffs, and led Thuy and Anna up the stone staircase to two of Vu's war sketches. Lee flipped open his notebook and stood like a Nobel Prize winner about to give a speech, glancing around the room. He waited until two visitors left. "I believe there are five key phases for Mr. Vu." He stopped, as though waiting for an ovation.

"Please, go on." Thuy bent her head.

"From his short bio and what you told me, we know Mr. Vu attended the Indochina art academy in the mid 1930s, as a teenager. Most biographies claim he worked as a small-time artist and teacher until the academy closed, after the Japanese invaded Vietnam. I think that was 1940."

Thuy tensed her shoulders. *Small time doesn't sound good.* "And he spent time in France before being in the wars here."

"Yes. I understand. The Vietnamese had few journalists with cameras in those days. So, he drew." Lee pointed to the sketches on crinkled paper with his fan. "He signed these sketches with his initials in this lower right corner."

Anna snapped a photo of the signature.

"In those days, he used pencil. Or charcoal," Lee pointed. "And the paper that looks like newsprint, crinkled and rough."

Thuy leaned in. "I'm sure there are more of these. In newspapers."

"Not my area." He sniffed and made a clicking sound with his throat, drawing attention back to himself. "Back to the time-line. After the army, from about 1955 to 1960, he seems to be replicating some of his earlier training. With some French influence." He walked toward three more paintings; portraits of two different women and a child in one of them.

A small woman and child wandered in, at the far side of the gallery.

Lee spun and flicked his hand. "Not now, please."

The visitors scurried out.

"Now, we see influence from the French instructors that he studied with in Vietnam and later in France. By the middle 1950s, he was away from war and had oil paint and canvases. The pieces are not large. But at least he had access to better materials, sketch paper instead of newsprint. Pens instead of charcoal."

Anna leaned toward the portrait with the child. "The figures remind me of portraits out of Belgium or France."

Lee lifted his chin. "You know European art?"

"A little," she said. "I trained in Italy."

"Ahhhh." Lee bowed and led them to the next gallery, where more sketches clustered near a bronze statue of a woman soldier, holding a bayonet, ready to attack. Much of the room's art focused on fighting, both the American and the French wars. "Now you see that he went back to war sketches in the time of the 1960s and '70s. During the Vietnam War—"

"Called the American War in Vietnam, by the way," Thuy jumped in.

Lee touched his temple. "Of course, that would be true."

"We've had so many that we have to explain which war."

"Yes, yes. The American War sketches. Back to skimpy paper and pencil. Five of them here…"

Anna sidled up to the wall. "Men in fatigues. Exhausted."

"Maybe after a battle? This one looks like a man in pain." He pointed to a man whose head was thrown back, teeth clenched.

Thuy held her breath.

"Do you feel all right?" Anna bent toward her.

"Chills. I always get them from the sketches."

Lee cleared his throat. "Look at this one, please. A village, two soldiers by a small hut, or house." He held out his arm. "Walking toward us. Faces covered in mud. One laughing… Yes, he seems to be laughing or yelling."

Guns slung over their shoulders. Thuy looked at another one: a soldier lying on the ground, contorted, his gun lying next to him. His eyes were closed, and his mouth was open in agony.

She could hear the scream in her head. "Mr. Lee, these sketches have weapons in them. What about sketches that have none? No guns. No knives. Any thoughts?"

Lee squinted. "As we see, even when soldiers were in pain, they'd have their guns nearby."

"But could there be any artists who draw these types without weapons? Have you been in war, Mr. Lee?" Her throat tightened.

He pulled at his cuff. "I'm sorry to say—or rather, happy to say—I never fought in a war. Too young for World War II, and since then, Singapore has tried to stay out of fighting."

"But what about other wartime sketches you've seen? You must have some in Singapore? What're they like?"

"The ones I've seen typically have weapons or a plane or bombs in the background. Many show soldiers walking with guns, holding them in front, or slung over their shoulders."

But not Uncle Vu's. She tapped the wall next to the sketch. "I've seen some by my uncle, without weapons. Could that be normal as well?"

Lee tilted his head at her. "Forgive me, but do you know… was your uncle a pacifist?"

The pain in her throat returned. *If he could pick up on that…* "He couldn't…he shouldn't be… So many invaders. French and Japanese and Americans. And the Cambodians. Chinese." She backed away from the panels. "What are you saying?" *I don't want to hear. But I have to.*

Silence draped the room. If she followed Lee's argument, Vu had made a statement—no guns in his sketches, which could be seen as anti-patriotic. In the letters, Vu hinted at spying for France. If true, that could be why he didn't show guns. To make the Vietnamese soldiers look less threatening. The repercussions from those letters and Lee's insinuation would devastate Vu's reputation as well as her family. Let alone the museum for showing a traitor's work, if that's what he was.

"I suspect, if you have seen sketches without weapons, that was Mr. Vu's choice," Lee said. "Could be that his focus was on the faces of those he traveled with. Those soldiers."

She turned sideways, unable to look straight on at the men's expressions, especially those in pain. *Please never let Quang be in that situation.*

Children's feet rapped down the hallway. *Must be young.* A rule of life seemed to be that children under ten never walked, always ran.

Mr. Lee brushed his sleeves. "In the 1970's, Vu must have moved to an alley, because he made sketches of it. Did he live in Hanoi?" He fanned himself.

"Yes, in Hanoi. The neighborhood still looks like some of these. He lived there toward the end of the American War and after. You see the piles of rubble."

"In that period, he drew buildings, people from a distance, not close up. Again, another sort of shift in his style."

"What's the material he used? Can you tell?"

"I see a variety of materials. The normal ones for artists in this era—simple paper and pencil; silk and later oils."

Thuy moved away from the pieces and cocked her head. "These alley portraits, that's what made him famous. Some claim he used drawings like these as payment for coffee, for food."

Lee nodded. "Yes, that was during your difficult period? The subsidy time?"

"That's right. In the cities, we ate two or three bowls of rice a day. Some vegetables. A little fish sometimes, almost never meat or chicken. A little better in the countryside."

"But it's these portraits that are of interest. Two of them." Lee pointed his fan toward the paintings and then flipped the fan back open. "Seems too warm. Could you check the temperature?"

A few minutes later, she returned. "You're right. The temperature was two degrees higher than it should be. I've fixed it."

He nodded and moved toward two portraits. In the first one, a boy and a girl sat at a woman's feet. In the second, the same woman and boy sat together on the ground. The boy offered her a sunflower to add to the flower chain resting in her lap. He had a small scar on his left eyebrow.

Thuy gasped. *The boy in the painting looked like the boy from the Tet photos.* She'd missed it and had to check those again when she got home. She tugged her attention back to Lee.

"…1990s. Again, rural scenes but hazier, more impressionistic. Almost as though the artist was losing his eyesight and couldn't see as crisply." He turned to her. "Could that be the case?"

Thuy shook her head. "I've no idea. I know so little about him, and my father doesn't talk much about him."

Lee grimaced. "Not uncommon in Asian families."

"Maybe. But annoying when we want to know about an artist," Thuy said. "Mr. Lee, what do you think about these paintings? Is the same boy in each? And the woman?"

He removed his glasses, hung them from his lip, and stood four inches from the first, then the second piece. He stepped four feet back and then telescoped in and out from each piece.

"I see. Yes, you could be right. Perhaps some friends? Or relatives? Did he have a family?"

She shook her head. "Again, I have no verifiable information. But what do you think?"

Lee ambled from one painting to the next, lifting a foot and placing it down before he lifted the other foot. Five minutes of slow sauntering.

"Why did he do two of the same people?" she asked. "Monet painted the same scenes over and over. But why the same portrait? Why not different people?"

Lee studied his palm and turned his hand over. "So much to learn with painting… about the human body, the face, expressions, trying to tell a story about a person. Leonardo made hundreds of sketches of hands to learn how muscles worked and looked, under the skin. Mr. Vu was still learning at this time, I suspect."

The young mother and child who Lee had shooed out of the gallery a few minutes earlier returned. They stood at the entrance and scanned the room. When the woman saw Lee, she braced, then swept her eyes to Thuy.

Thuy shook her head. "Not yet," she mouthed. "Sorry."

Lee seemed oblivious to the potential visitors and stared at the painting. When he turned, his squint was so strong she couldn't see any whites of his eyes. "Where did these come from? Donations? Purchased? From where?"

"The accession information doesn't tell us much. I'm sorry. It was…" She peered at the label next to the painting. "Right, during the American War time and right after. Not much information during those years."

Hands behind his back, he looked more like a rocking egg. "I'm reminded of a situation when I consulted for Sotheby's. A few years ago. Two paintings by one artist in this same era. If I recall, it was 'The Letter' and the other was something like 'Reclining' or 'Resting Ladies.'"

Anna stepped forward. "I believe that's right, Mr. Lee. I remember this too."

He beamed. "The memory is still intact. Well, the two pieces were to go on sale for thousands of dollars. At the last minute, the auction pulled them because some experts had said that the characters in the paintings lacked the 'soul' that other paintings by the artist showed."

"The 'soul?' And no other way to authenticate?"

"It would have been a reputational slap if the house had tried to sell forgeries." Lee scowled. "I would hate for any such event to happen in your museum." He cleared his throat. "I do not wish to be harsh, but I must be honest. Do you know for certain that these are your uncle's artworks?"

When she blinked, spots appeared. *Afraid of this but should have seen it coming.* "That's what I've always been told." She gripped her forearms and swayed. "Do you have reason to doubt?"

Anna touched Thuy's arm. "Slow down, Thuy. We don't mean to question your expertise, Mr. Lee. It's just exasperating not to know which paintings may be real or not."

Thuy squeezed her jaw.

"Art makes people emotional." Lee retied his bow tie and flipped his head, as though he had a full head of hair to flip.

So dismissive. Thuy stood behind him and sucked in air. "Sir. Mr. Lee. Please. You must understand the importance. What you say will make a big difference for my family, my country."

Lee struck his knuckles against the wall and whipped around. "I knew this was important but not why it matters to your family. Let me look more closely, once again. Upstairs. The other set. I saw some that gave me pause there, and not because of their talent." He stared at her. "I think they may be forgeries."

Thuy wavered. *There it was. Fakes in the museum. What a disaster.* She slogged up the stairs, like a prisoner going to a guillotine.

Lee pointed out three paintings: a rural village with small, thatched roof houses and two or three people in front. For forty-five minutes, he scrawled notes, made sketches, and tapped his pencil against his lips. In between, he made grunts of comments.

Thuy stopped in front of paintings she looked at daily, but she'd never really seen. Paintings by contemporaries of her great uncle's and nearly mirrored ones she'd seen on the ground floor, the earliest ones from the academy artists. She noticed confident swipes of charcoal, shaky lines in pencil.

Lee squeezed his nose bridge and stretched.

Thuy's ribs tightened, keeping her breath shallow. She wanted—but didn't want—to hear his results.

Lee glanced sideways at the paintings. "The style, materials, as well as design elements—balance, contrast, pattern, and rhythm— lead me to believe that… I'm sorry to say… that two of these five pieces, on this floor and the one below… that two of these five pieces are by a different artist."

"What?" She felt heat behind her eyelids.

"Yes, the two alley paintings are by different people and the two rural paintings, portraits, are by another."

He scribbled in his black sketch book and showed her a matrix:

Artist	3 rural paintings	2 portraits
1	1 painting	2 portraits
2	2 paintings	No portraits

"I don't understand." A sour taste burned in her mouth. "All have Vu's signature. But you're saying these five are by two different artists? None of these are by Vu?" She'd known it was a possibility—the forgeries—but hoped the whole time that he'd say all was well.

Lee tugged at his cuff and repeated. "Two artists made these five paintings that you say are your uncle's."

Her mouth went dry. "Are you sure? You need to be absolutely sure. We have always said they are by Pham Ly Vu. And now you say a different artist, two artists, painted them?" She had a terrible urge to punch something—a painting, a wall, a person. Instead, she bit on her lips and stuck her tongue into her cheek.

She felt like she was running up a sand hill, slipping further down with each step. The paintings by Vu were not by Vu. The family legacy slipped like sand, sliding downward, nothing to hold it in place. Probably fakes in the special exhibit and now also in the permanent collection. She spun, walked into the hallway, and clutched her head. *Keep quiet? Go to Tuan? Expose all of this in a broader way through the blog?*

For her sanity and the integrity of the art, she had to come clean. Tuan first, then Bo.

Chapter 34

Thuy plodded to Tuan's office with her goal clear: convince him to halt the special exhibit and— worse—close the museum or at least remove any questionable paintings in the permanent collection. It could crush the museum itself, its history, and reputation. *He'd be furious.*

A bustle of school children, teenagers mostly, trundled through the hallway, blocking the door to Tuan's office. She twisted and moved sideways to get past them, but a few of the boys stopped in the middle of the hall to tell jokes and jab each other.

"Sorry, I need to get by. Sorry." She waited for the kids, but they didn't seem to hear her. They guffawed and leaned over, laughing. She pushed two apart to get to the door, knocked, and let herself in. The muffled voices continued with intermittent shrieks.

Tuan stood in front of a mirror combing his thin hair. He glanced at her, expectant, then irritated. "What? What do you need? There's so much to do before tonight."

She fiddled with her bracelet, trying to regain the confidence she'd mustered during the day. But it fizzled and she felt like a fifth grader being scolded. "I'm sorry to come now, right before the opening, but I have some bad news."

He twirled around.

Stay still, don't let him intimidate. "I'm sorry."

"You keep saying you're sorry! What could be worse than coming to me with a problem today of all days? This better be important." He tucked his comb into his pocket.

Thuy glanced at the office door, which was nearly closed. She pushed it shut and took a big breath. "Mr. Geoffrey Tan Lee from Singapore, expert in Southeast Asian art—came to

Hanoi this week. He wanted to attend the special exhibit since he knows about subsidy era artists. An auction house in Hong Kong that he consults for is offering some Vietnamese paintings in a month."

Tuan scowled. "His name is familiar. Is he some sort of evaluator? authenticator? The man I said shouldn't review the exhibit?"

"Well, yes. He didn't look at the exhibit pieces. But he came early—wanted to see the permanent collection, as a visitor. But you know how it is; he couldn't take off his professional hat and today. He…" She took a quick breath in.

"Hurry it up. He did what…?" Tuan stirred his tea with a vengeance, clanging the spoon against the edge of his cup.

"He found several, including some by Vu, that he thinks are forgeries in the permanent collec—"

Tuan's spoon spun too hard, and the cup fell over, spilling tea on his papers. "Now look what you made me do." He yanked open a drawer to pull out a towel and sopped up the tea.

She waited for more reaction. An insect scratched the upper window. Nothing moved—not the ceiling fan, not the window air-con unit that ran in the hottest months, and not Tuan's spoon. But sweat dripped down her legs.

He wiped his face with the damp towel. "You… he what? He found what?"

An artery pumped in her neck, and she assumed he could see it. He'd see how scared she was. Or angry. "Forgeries. Several. Not just a few. In our permanent collection. We must pull them, all of them, until we know—"

His mouth fell open, and his head jerked, like he was a marionette waking up.

She waited for him to say he knew… or didn't know. She also had to tell him about the sketches that had been removed— *maybe he did it*—and were in the vault. But she couldn't speak. All she could hear was that blasted insect on the window. *Tit-tit-tit.*

"I cannot deal with this. Not now. Why did you bring this now? You have no sense of professionalism. I could fire you right now, but this opening must go on. You have to be there if something goes wrong." He glowered. "But it better not. The collector will arrive this afternoon and he'll expect a flawless evening."

Her eyelids scraped over dry eyeballs, and she feared they wouldn't open again. But they did, and she saw his closed fist. "Did you know—"

"Get out," he whispered. "Do not speak of this. Not at the opening and not afterward. Get out, now."

She backed toward the door, grabbed and turned the knob, and pulled. It stuck. *No, no!* She yanked the knob again, and nothing happened. The humidity worked against her. She shoved her shoulder into the door edge, and once again turned the knob. The door sprung open, crashing against the wall. She peeked back at Tuan, whose face was red, highlighting the pock marks on his nose. She'd give herself a failing grade on that encounter. But she still had to fight. She had to find out who was behind the forgeries and get rid of them. Before Tuan fired her from the museum too, since he had already removed her from the exhibit.

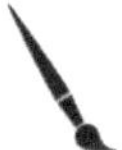

In the hallway, Thuy saw the Vietnamese Andy Warhol artist coming out of a gallery. No easel. No paints. Just a man in a daydream.

He waved and walked to her. "I heard your exhibit will open soon. I'm glad for you. We need more attention for the artists in those times."

She stood facing him, arms resting across her stomach in a respectful gesture. He was older; she wanted to learn from him about Uncle Vu and needed to woo him. "Very kind of you to say so. I hope you attend the exhibit."

"Don't worry. I'll be there. Not for your opening for the important people, but I will go later. I wish you very well." He turned to leave and then spun back. "By the way, I've thought about your questions about Pham Ly Vu. I will answer some of them, if I can. In the future. After the show. You are too busy now. And I must leave."

Her mouth fell open, and she felt her stomach flutter. She wanted to chase him down but forced herself to stay in place. She'd learn more. She had to make it soon.

Chapter 35

At 8:15 p.m., Thuy greeted visitors with a forced grin. Tuan had positioned her at the gallery entrance while he worked the room. His instructions: don't cause problems.

She had survived telling him about the possible museum forgeries and endured his wrath. But she couldn't shake the headache that came after. At this point, all she wanted was a drama-free opening. A night of people enjoying art that had never been in the country. She whispered to a waiter to approach a cluster of artists she knew. They raised their glasses at her.

Anna squeezed Thuy's hand. "Courage."

Several visitors congratulated her, which meant Tuan hadn't made public her removal from the exhibit. *So, he can still blame me if something goes upside down.* And if it did, she really wanted that job in Ho Chi Minh, simply to get away from him.

By 8:26 p.m., more than forty people—artists, government officials, gallery owners, embassy employees from Sweden, Germany, and America, among many others—had gathered.

She noticed a police officer off to the side. *Viet.* He had mentioned he'd attend as security support. She smiled, and he barely moved his head. *On duty.*

The guests sipped champagne, popped toothpicks of cheese into their mouths, and strolled through the gallery. A mix of jasmine, freesia, and coriander floated through the room. Minh's immaculate grey suit, with a bright red handkerchief, reeked of elegance.

Tonight, Thuy's black sheath and silver bead necklace rebuilt her confidence after Tuan's earlier thrashing. Every so often, she felt she "fit," and tonight should have been one of those times. Artists inspired her, and she wanted to help them; getting visibility through more exhibits would help build reputations. And that's what she wanted to do.

If it goes well. No guarantees.

A gallery owner pulled Minh aside. Thuy imagined he was asking Minh to show pieces at his gallery. On the far side of the room, two artists in their seventies, well known around Hanoi, shuffled toward Tuan, who stood in a gaggle of more gallery owners. The man hunched over almost at ninety degrees and faced the floor, forcing him to turn his head sideways to talk to his colleague. His companion's silver tinkled as she gestured. She beckoned Tuan toward a painting. The two whispered at Tuan, who rocked back and forth. He gripped his hands at his back, creating white knuckles.

Uh oh. Already a problem?

Thuy tried to lip read, but a patron asked her for directions to the toilet and another handed her his glass of champagne and asked for another. A friend congratulated her.

Next time she glanced, Tuan's mouth had become a straight line.

The two older artists leaned into Tuan; one grabbed his fore-arm. The man turned sideways, peered up at Tuan, and tapped his cane on the floor. Conversation noise and laughter kept her from hearing the cane or any of their conversation. Tuan shook his head, scanned the room, and wiggled his fingers at Thuy. "Come over," he mouthed.

She looked around for Minh and hurried to them.

Tuan grasped the back of her arm and edged her toward the artists. "These artists—who we all know well—think there might be some problem with this painting. I told them that you are our expert. Please answer their questions." He backed away.

Minh approached Tuan, with three patrons in tow.

Great. A bigger crowd to watch her go down in flames. She turned to the older artists.

"I'll try to answer. What can I do for you?"

"Surely you can see the problems. The colors, the strokes. Not what this artist did. The colors are too bright and wouldn't be available during the 1980s—"

"But please remember these paintings were made in France, where access to materials was much—"

"That may be." The woman flipped her long grey braid over her shoulder and reached for Thuy's wrist to pull her to her. "Come closer so we can hear."

Her companion tapped his cane. "And more than that. The texture in this piece. He never did that. Not in any of the pieces I've seen. But ask her. She has personal knowledge."

Thuy's headache took flight, pounding behind her eyes. She blinked quickly. "What personal knowledge?"

"I saw his work first as a young bride, after he returned to Vietnam from France. He was my father-in-law."

Thuy's energy drained. "I'm so sorry."

The woman glowered.

"Not that he was your father-in-law." She again wished she could melt into the floor, like that *Wizard of Oz* witch. She gritted her teeth, unsure how to react. She'd feared exactly this and had tried to warn Tuan, and now he'd sealed his fate, which meant her fate. She was done. "I'm sorry that there seems to be some misunderstanding. I'll discuss this with the collector and Mr. Tuan. I'm sure there's a re—"

"What the... I cannot believe you allowed this!" a man's voice screamed. "This wasn't in the exhibit last week. Where is it from?" Hoan, the artist who played on his North Korean experience, waved his arms in front of a painting. The crowd rushed to Hoan.

Thuy recoiled. *Surely Tuan didn't replace a painting.* She scanned the room for Tuan, for Minh. Tuan stood in the middle of the room, frozen, arteries throbbing on his neck. His arms were at his sides, hands in fists. *Am I to deal with this one too?*

"Mr. Minh!" Tuan beckoned the collector. "Let's see what the excitement is."

The hair on her arms lifted. No more than ten seconds had passed, but it seemed like a minute, five minutes. *What is Tuan doing? Calling attention to Hoan? Bringing Minh into the mix? Nothing can be salvaged now.*

"Mrs. Thuy, you too. Please join us with Mr. Hoan."

Sweat dripped down her torso. She'd be the sacrificial lamb. Minh glared at her as she lumbered into the crowd. The champagne glasses seemed to form a phalanx as visitors separated to let her pass.

Minh marched toward Hoan and the painting, his face pinched and filled with rage.

She followed in his wake, the crowd pushing forward with them.

An artist who'd been at the preview raised his eyebrows at her. "What'd you do?"

"I… I don't know what's going on," she said, forcing her legs to move forward.

Snippets of talk reached her. "At the preview, Hoan—he's the guy over there—found a fake of one of his great-grandfather's pieces. What's he found this time?"

Anna looked over the heads of the crowd and gave her a thumb's up, but her face was strained. "Courage," she mouthed.

No chance of that. Thuy's insides felt like ice, and her shoulders lost their perfect posture.

Minh reached Hoan's side. The room silenced, except for grating elevator music. He turned to her. "This isn't mine. You can't add one that isn't mine. Are you trying to sabotage the exhibit? You'll pay for this." He stormed out of the gallery.

Her heart raced as the crowd parted, revealing the painting. She reeled. It wasn't one from France. It was one of the pieces Tuan had photos of in his office. And Minh hadn't known, meaning he must not be part of the scam.

Tuan jammed his elbow into her ribs. "Go after Minh. You have to save this."

Her body went rigid, and she gaped at him. "I… what are—"

"Find him. Get him back here."

She wanted to scream. *You pulled me from the exhibit, but now it's my responsibility again.* She breathed hard and raced to the hallway, swishing her head around, looking for Minh. Half-way down the steps, he stood at the railing, wheezing over the balcony. His hands gripped the railing. She clicked down the stairs.

"You. What do you want? Trying to ruin me?"

She stood on a step above, which forced him to look up at her.

"All I wanted was to bring some paintings back to Vietnam. You've turned this into a farce, showing a painting that isn't mine, that probably never set foot in Europe but was here all along. Why? Why would you do that?"

She clenched the railing to keep from falling. "Of course, I never meant to hurt you or harm the exhibit. But fakes? Replacements? Not me—"

"I should pull the whole thing and sue you, the museum. You must close." He stomped down the stairs and yelled, "You'll hear from me."

When she'd started her evening, she wanted a successful, drama-free showing. *Totally blew that.* Now Minh was on the warpath; they'd found fakes in the special exhibit (serious enough); fakes in the permanent collection (more serious); and her father might be a part of some scandal (most serious). She had nothing left to lose.

She had to find out who was behind this mess and get rid of the forgeries, knowing full well she'd probably lose her job, her reputation, and her family's love in the process. She walked back to the gallery where Tuan stood at the door, sending people into the night.

"Leave." His hushed voice tried to hide his fury, but his face reddened and his body quivered. "You're finished. Go."

Her phone pinged a reminder. *Stupid of me to set the interview for the next day—Saturday.* She'd set it up thinking that

Tuan and company would be relishing the success of the exhibit and not notice if she were gone, but now, they'd probably cower in their offices and plot her downfall. *No need for them to plot.* She was already falling. She remembered another American movie— one about a plantation in the Confederate times. One where the main character said, "think about that tomorrow," whenever she faced a problem. That's what she had to do. *Tomorrow. On the plane. In case it went down. Which might be okay, the way things were going.*

Chapter 36

Thuy stood in front of the grand Ho Chi Minh Art Museum, a five-story former French villa renovated in the last three years. Snatches of curving stairways, filigree on wrought iron balconies and floral landscaping were as far from Soviet era functionalism as Thuy could imagine.

Ms. Nguyen Thi Linh, the director, had hair "set" in waves on her head that wouldn't move. The look was more 1960s than 2000s. Her rigid makeup stiffened her face.

"Thank you for bringing me here," Thuy said. "You have a beautiful museum building."

"So good of you to come. I understand you held your special exhibit last evening. Is that correct?"

"Yes. You're right." Thuy rubbed her thighs and said no more. *Maybe she'll drop it.*

"We appreciate that you came to us so soon after such a big event. But this job decision… we want to make it soon."

Tea arrived in an exquisite Chinese porcelain cup. "Tell me about the cup." It had to be a replica. If it wasn't, she'd put it down and never pick it up again.

"We have wonderful craftsmen in the south, able to reproduce to a high quality." Linh lifted the cup to eye level. "As with fine porcelain, you can almost see through it. We are fortunate to have something this beautiful, even as a replica."

Thuy ran her thumb over the enameled flower on the saucer's edge. "Thank you for the invitation. I am excited to hear about your plans for the museum."

"And we hope you may be part of that." Linh smiled. "You have a reputation as a very competent business manager. But

I understand from colleagues that you are ambitious to switch fields, to be a curator or at least on the path."

Thuy pushed her chair out from the table and perched on its edge, alert and ready. "I would love the opportunity." She brushed her skirt and looked at her feet. Her breath stopped. *Chet Tiet.* She wore ballet flats—easier to maneuver the airport and streets of Ho Chi Minh City—but each was a different color: right foot was black, and left foot navy. Her blood turned cold. A mistake like this could ruin the whole day. It made her look careless or foolish. Or like she was trying to be creative but couldn't pull it off. She grimaced internally.

Linh's red and black small bead necklace complemented her orange red silk blouse and both unnerved Thuy as much as her own mismatched shoes.

"I want us to become one of the world's top future-oriented museums. That means different types of sensory experiences, exhibits, technologies. We'd like to hear any thoughts you may have."

"Do you have any models in mind?"

A man entered the room. He reminded her of Minh: tall, well-tailored navy suit with a crisp white handkerchief. He winced and stretched his arm over the conference table: "Sorry for the lateness. I'm Thanh. Business manager. Like you." He placed his hands on the arm rests and used them to lower himself. "Broken rib," he said. "Hanging a new art piece, and I slipped. Museum hazardous duty."

Linh cleared her throat. "No models from us yet. Mostly, we're brainstorming. Any thoughts on your part?"

For fifteen minutes, Thuy talked about differences in museum experiences—mostly from what she'd read and heard from Anna: immersion experiences, interactive rooms, and virtual tours; events where visitors could create their own art and museums that collaborated with groups outside of art. She glanced around the room. Thanh fidgeted and checked his phone under the table. Linh stared at her, unmoving. *I'm losing them.*

Linh's frozen mouth barely moved. "All very traditional, really. We had hoped for some new thinking on your part."

No pussy-footing here. Then, go for it. "If you're serious… then I'd suggest going bigger. Maybe look to places like Dubai for ideas."

Thanh leaned forward. "Tell us."

Thuy stuck her feet under the chair and tried to forget her two-colored shoes. "I've done some research… on the Internet, since I don't have direct experience with these museums. But they are intriguing. Starting with Dubai's normal exhibits, experiences like virtual immersive tours of the International Space Station and the Amazon Rainforest. Something like that could open possibilities for 'immersive tours' in Vietnam."

Thanh leaned forward. "We could create virtual tours of the Son Doong Caves. How else could people see the world's largest cave? Or to the Annamite mountains and see a saola or muntjac deer?" Thanh's voice raised, and he winced. "Ouch. Better calm down."

"The deer that was just rediscovered?" Thuy pulled up a picture in her mind. "But also exciting about Dubai is that the museum plays a role in solving big, societal problems." The room smelled like frangipani. *Incense? Perfume?* She'd read that it made the mind sharper. *Need that today, for certain.*

"Oh? Solving big problems? How?" Linh poured more tea into Thuy's cup.

"It brings together designers and researchers, inventors and artists to solve problems in health, education, and energy. They're redefining what a museum is, and what it can be. Does your museum work with any academics or researchers now? Vietnam has loads of problems to solve—deforestation, river and ocean pollution. Or even poverty and aging. Finding ways to fit labor force needs with what students want to study— we have too many people going for university degrees but not enough in skilled trades. Yes, a museum can play a role in solving society's problems."

Linh's steely eyes drilled her. "Good brainstorming. Not the obvious environmental problems. Any other ideas?"

Thuy twisted her silver bracelet, pulling strength to move on. "I don't want to lecture—"

"I'll tell you when to stop. For now, keep going."

No nonsense again.

Another aide entered with a note. Linh scanned and tucked it under her phone. "Not now." She turned back to Thuy. "Go on, please." The aide opened the door and what sounded like casino pings came in. "A new exhibit on gambling," she said, waving her hand. "Back to your ideas."

"That's interesting," Thuy said. "Another museum to learn from may be the Grand Egyptian Cairo. The King Tut collection. Recently it opened a platform for the creative industry. It's called the art space—artists, designers, craftspeople work in the space and show their pieces there, on a rotating basis. There's a running theme for a time period—recently, costumes made from Egyptian cotton, using the Khayamiya technique. Egyptian-German artists spearheaded it. Over the long term, the museum will blend ancient and contemporary artwork. When I think of what Vietnam has—Cham and other ancient art, and what the new artists are doing these days, how different would that be?"

No one moved. Thuy stared at a series of wood block prints on the wall. *A famous artist but she couldn't remember the name.* She'd seen photos of his work and thought most of it was in Hue, but here they were in Ho Chi Minh City. The women's faces smiled with a sense of joy and kindness. *Surely not copies.* She'd have expected this fancy museum to have only originals, but she questioned everything now.

"This may be an unfair question," Thanh said. "But it's one business manager to another. You don't know our museum well, but what type of resource level do you think you'd need if we tried to incorporate some of the ideas from the Dubai museum? Especially the VR tours and collaboration?"

Thuy's mind stalled. "I have no idea. I could play around with numbers when I return—"

"Not necessary," Linh said, glowering at Thanh. "We will be able to offer whatever you need."

Thuy's head jerked back. *Whatever I would need? That sounds like paradise.*

"And confidentially, we expect to receive a major—the biggest in our history and maybe in the region—donation. One of the country's top businessmen. You'd know his company, if we told you."

Thuy's mind raced through possibilities—Trung Nguyen Coffee, Bitex, Vin Group, any of those had entrepreneur leaders who'd made a fortune during the last twenty years. The Hanoi museum's budget was like an ant in the midst of what sounded like an elephant here. "That's wonderful."

"We're close but not there yet." Thanh smiled.

"Back to our business, though. I like these ideas," Linh said, tapping her fingers on the table. "But more than that. I like your thinking. You've done your research but not stopped there. You're thinking about what we could do using the base of those ideas from elsewhere. That's what we need. Now, let's have a tour and talk more later."

Thuy rushed to the toilet. She grabbed a handful of tissue and stuffed it in her mouth before she let out a silent cheer. No one had asked about the special exhibit. Since the museums were rivals, the managers likely wouldn't be talking to each other, so she had hoped they wouldn't know Tuan had removed her from the exhibit. No one had mentioned possible fakes in the special exhibit, or the permanent collection. *Maybe I can pull this off. For now.*

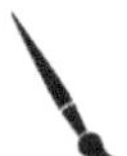

After a brief tour, Thuy, Linh, and Thanh settled back at the conference table.

"We're impressed," Linh said. "We feel positive about your ideas. You work hard. All very good. We have approval for the position. If you are interested in talking more, we should discuss timing. But first, have you questions for us?"

Thuy swallowed. *Sounds promising, but don't get ahead of yourself.* "One question—different from what we've talked about but important to me. How do you handle any possible forgeries or copies in the museum?" Her eyes swept to the wall.

Thanh swiveled to look at the wood block prints. "You worry that's not real?"

"I can't imagine an original in a conference—"

"Rest your worries. We have no counterfeits, no fakes, no forgeries in this museum." He sniffed. "We've an in-house authenticator. One of the few in Vietnam so far."

Chien's friend, the mysterious assessor.

"…Ministry wants to establish a unit to appraise art, but we don't have enough people who can do that yet. The one person who does it, with us, learned on her own. She reviews everything that comes to us. We do not want a scandal before our donation comes."

Thuy put her palms on the table. "That's encouraging."

A different aide—young woman with knitted brows— entered and stood by the door. Linh nodded, and the aide brought over her phone.

She raised her eyebrows and turned the phone face to Thanh. Linh took a big breath and looked at Thuy. "Anything else you would like to ask? Or tell us?"

"I think you've answered my questions very well. I appreciate it."

"Very good. Thank you very much for coming to see us today. We will be in touch." She hurried from the room.

Thuy's stomach sank. *Something just happened.* Thanh's expression wavered. He looked hurt, like his ribs had flared up. But he'd done nothing in the last few minutes to hurt his chest, except read a note.

Thanh waved his arm toward the woman standing by the door. "She will show you out. Have a good trip." He left the room almost as quickly as Linh had.

She'd lost.

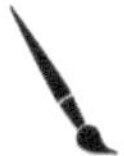

In bed that night, Thuy's phone pinged and then rang. Her fuzzy head didn't want to answer but she took a peek.

Bac: Please answer. Quick chat. Please.

He'd added a heart emoji, as if that helped, as her ex-husband. She clicked "call."

"What is it, Bac? We're not supposed to be in contact." Her voice sounded low, what she called her "whiskey sour voice," like Lauren Bacall whose movies she'd loved.

"Thanks for calling. I wanted to hear how your interview went—"

Her chest constricted. "How did you know about that?"

"I try to stay up on your life, even if you don't want me to. I only want to be sure you and Quang stay safe."

"I'm going back to sleep, leave me alone."

"Wait. Please. One minute. Please, for your sake, don't push this investigation about the art. There are bad people behind it, you could get hurt."

"Why should I believe you?"

"Because I'm probably not around for long myself and I want you and Quang to get the bit of money I do have."

"You're not making sense. I'm hanging up."

"Please, Thuy. Don't push it. You'll be sorry. Think of our son." He hung up before she could hang up.

Chapter 37

On Sunday, Thuy went into work, knowing she needed to debrief with Tuan about the exhibit. Even though he'd sacked her, she felt an obligation to the museum, to the integrity of the art and the artists. In the lobby, she saw a voicemail from Ms. Thuc Anh from the Ministry and stepped into a supply closet to listen. *Maybe they've found an authenticator sooner. At least that could help save the museum—if not the exhibit.*

"Ms. Thuy, I have bad news. We learned about your exhibit—more possible forgeries—and also that you have problems in your permanent collection—"

What? She knew that already. Someone's feeding info…

"… no power to postpone the special exhibit, but you need to shut down the museum until you resolve your questions on the paintings in house. I'm sorry."

The closet's shadows draped over her, and she felt an anvil had sunk in her chest. *What the…? They'd refused to help close the exhibit but now say they'll close down the whole museum?* Tuan would be out of his skin with rage. She trudged up the stairs to his office, anticipating a list of what she'd done wrong. *This might be the last straw.*

Tuan wore his "serious meeting Italian glasses," the ones without tape holding them together. His "How could you damage the exhibit so badly?" glasses.

She sat on her hands so he wouldn't see her quiver. The office smelled of fear, sweat, and disinfectant. She stared at the Golden Buddha sculpture on his desk. *Has to be fake, like the one on my desk. Nothing seems real anymore.*

"You left the opening and were away all day yesterday. I don't know what to think or how to understand your actions."

"I… it's… my fami—"

"I do not care about your personal life. I care about this museum. Our reputation was attacked. Mr. Minh may take legal steps against the museum for damages to his reputation. He pulled the collection and wants it shipped to France this week. He was most upset with you. I wonder if you engaged in some kind of inappropriate behavior. I remember your actions at that first meeting."

She felt like a hammer had hit her between the shoulders and she nearly lurched. "You can't think—"

"As I said, I don't know what to think." He squeezed his nose at the top of its bridge. "You've ruined us. Minh demands an apology, in the newspaper. As a government entity, our actions are reviewed carefully. The museum could be shut down. The end of my career." He gripped his Bic pen.

Her fingers scraped the chair under her legs, and her hands stayed icy. *What about the museum? Vietnamese art? But he had replaced a piece that wasn't in the collection. That was damaging.*

"And your Mr. Lee? The famous authenticator? He also phoned yesterday. He was under the belief that his visit was official, sanctioned by me, by the Ministry. And expected to be paid. You lied to him. And to me."

A sharp stab in her chest joined the heavy, dull pain between her shoulder blades. She imagined some medieval torture technique that squeezed her. "But… but I had to be sure of what we had. I wanted to save the museum, not hurt anything. Since the government couldn't help us—"

"Your actions have ruined so much. I can't have someone who sabotages an exhibit—"

She flinched. *I was trying to help.* Any confidence from the upcoming Ho Chi Minh museum offer vanished. She stared at the buddha, wanting calm thoughts but hearing only Tuan's muffled words.

"And then I learn about the interview! The reason you skipped town yesterday? What am I to think? You go on an interview with our rival? I'm dumbfounded."

Her shoulders collapsed and she felt smaller second by second. Her ears plugged up. *He heard. How did he? Next he'll tell me—*

"…fired. Collect your things and leave by noon."

A flash of heat raced up her neck. *It was for the museum! For the artists! Even for you.*

"You can't. You asked me to oversee it, and when I tried to uphold the integrity of the museum, of the exhibit, you ignored me. You put that replacement into…" *And now I'm the scapegoat.* She crumpled.

"How dare you accuse me? Our museum does nothing that others have not." His neck arteries throbbed. "And now your actions destroy me, the museum, and those precious artists you care about."

She willed her legs to stand and pushed up from the chair. It felt like she was lifting a fifty pound sack of rice. Limp, dull, uncontrollable.

Tuan mumbled something.

"Excuse me?"

"I said before you go accusing me, look to your own house." He glared at her. "Now leave."

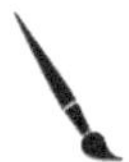

Thuy's office door stuck, like Tuan's had. *Darn humidity.* She shoved her body, the door flew open, and she stumbled her way in. Her perfume filled the space. *Should be called the scent of failure.* She sank to her chair. *Time to go home, where they have to take you in.*

She grabbed her briefcase, ran her hand over the front fold, and stiffened. *Who am I kidding? I'm part of the problem.* Fake Ferragamo shoes, fake Mark Cross briefcase, fake Ray Bans.

She'd gotten so used to them she didn't even notice the small mistakes that branded the pieces as counterfeits. The spaces of the stitching. The crooked label. The leather that wasn't really leather. Now, fired, she was no longer of the art world. *A fake and failure even there.*

And worse, her family was also fake. Her father traded in Uncle Vu paintings that he claimed were original, long ago stashed in caves.

She stuffed her notebooks, tablets, laptop, and pens into the briefcase. She had hoped the Ho Chi Minh job interview would come through, but now Tuan might torpedo it before she had a chance. That could mean she'd need a new career. She shook the idea from her mind. *Too big to think about that today.*

A single bird tapped on the windowpane. When she was a kid, people had killed and eaten birds anywhere they could find them. Over the last decade, the birds had returned. They'd come back from what seemed like extinction. If she were philosophical, she'd have to think that way—how to return from being completely dead, everything finished.

But that was too much for right now, this moment. She thought of Quang and how his willingness to stand firm and tell the truth paid off. She had to do the same, and that meant solving the mystery of what was going on with the fakes and rid the museum of art pieces that weren't real. She played back Tuan's comments, after he'd trashed her. The last thing he'd said was something about looking in her own house. *Bo. He must be part of this scandal of fakes. Heartbreaking, but what did Tuan mean? Other than offering paintings that had never been seen, there had to be something else.*

There was also the problem of getting those counterfeits out of the museum, and now that she was no longer an official employee, any chance of that dissolved. *Maybe time to give up.* Bo—and Tuan—would prefer that. *End this nosing around, asking questions, putting the museum at risk of exposure.* If she wanted to get her job back, that might be the only option. *It would be easier. That's for sure.*

She leaned over the desk, picked up the Cham head, and ran her fingers over the rough stone. She wanted to believe that it was real, that some person 400 years ago had created a statue to gain wisdom or be closer to spirits. *But it wasn't true.* This head, the one in Tuan's office, they were all made up, counterfeits. So many articles had talked about pieces like this having been looted during wartimes over a thousand years. But this one had been made a couple of decades ago. She ran her thumb over the nose, the eyes. The same stories would come out about Vietnam too—that the paintings, the sketches, and statues were fake because that's what brought in tourist money and that's what the place needed. But she loved this country, its art, and artists. She had to help tell the right story, the true story. *If I don't, who will?*

The bird tapped at the window again. *He saw something, maybe his reflection. Something that looks like food in my office?*

Shooosh.

It flew in and zipped around the ceiling. He seemed lost, confused, looking for the way out again. She watched, mesmerized. At last, he sat on the top of her bookshelf, chest panting. *Tired, friend? I feel the same way.* He looked up at the window again, flapped, and disappeared. *Made it.*

He hadn't given up but, at last, found a way out. I can't give up either. If I do, what will Quang think? What will Anna think? Or Hang? What will I think about myself?

She had to find out what was behind the counterfeits, remove them from the museum, and save reputations—of the museum, artists, her family. Herself. If she could crack the museum case, she'd have options. She might even be rewarded for it. *Don't get ahead of yourself.*

In the meantime, she had to confront Bo. Tuan's accusation to "look in her own house" made it clear: Bo had been complicit somehow, certainly in replacing those pieces in the special exhibit, and now she worried about the ones in the permanent collection. She swiped her bookshelf top with a tissue. *Birds. Leaving a memory of themselves.*

She tossed the tissue and grabbed her briefcase. And gasped. *What if Quang had played a role and was painting copies?* She grabbed her chest and scrunched her shirt.

A text popped up.

HCM Museum: Hello, Ms. Thuy. I am Thanh from the Ho Chi Minh Museum. We reviewed your interview. I'm sorry but we must halt any more discussion. Thank you for your time.

Chapter 38

Thuy raced home, shoving down thoughts about the job in Ho Chi Minh. *Not now.* Distracted, she ran two yellow/red lights on the way, realizing she'd likely have to point the police to Tuan and her own father. But first, she had to talk to Chi about how to talk to Bo.

She pulled up to the house. The ground floor space where they stored the motorbikes was empty. No motorbikes. "Lang! Are you there?"

"Hello, Ms. Thuy," he called from the back courtyard. "Fixing a broken wheel."

She breathed out. The bikes were here—or at least one since he was fixing it. She rushed to him. "Is my family at home, upstairs?"

"Out."

She took a step back. "Out?" Almost never was the house empty. "And Quang?"

"With your dad." He pulled his arm out of his sleeve and looked at his watch. "Left about an hour ago."

"Left? Do you know where?"

He shrugged.

She sprinted up the stairs and into the kitchen. "Chi? Are you here? Chi?" Nothing.

Two letters sat on the kitchen table. She grabbed the one from Bo.

I feel shame like never before. Your actions destroyed the family legacy. There's nothing more for me. Or for Quang. I and Quang go to the countryside. I must think. Do not come.

Bo

She tumbled into a chair and reread the letter. They left an hour ago with no clues as to where to look. She pulled Chi's letter toward her.

I will try to salvage things. You find Bo and Quang. Try Bac Son. Ask for Mr. Tan. Please tell someone you are going. To be safe. C.

Gone. All of them.

Chapter 39

Thuy grabbed a water bottle, jammed a day's worth of clothes in a plastic bag, and rushed to her bike, on the front sidewalk. She blanched.

Standing next to it was Bac, smoking and looking like a Vietnamese version of that old American movie star, James Dean: leather jacket and jeans.

In this heat, what's he trying to prove? "What do you want? I'm leaving."

"Nothing much. Just a reminder. Please be safe. Leave this crazy idea about fakes and counterfeits. Nothing to it. All smoke." He blew smoke at her.

"I don't know what you're talking about. But I am going to look into this. It matters to the museum and to me. And remember, you're supposed to stay away from me, from us."

He grabbed her forearm and squeezed. "Listen to me. I'm trying to protect you and Quang. Stay away from this." He shoved her arm and walked away.

She rubbed her arm. *Bruises. Don't miss that. Shake him off. Just go.*

As he swung his leg onto his bike, he looked back. "I'll try to keep people from hurting you, but I may not be able to for much longer."

Tell someone you're going to Bac Son. Chi's voice now seemed urgent in her mind. Thuy pulled Viet's business card from her phone case and called. He answered before the ring finished.

"Thanks for answering."

"What's going on? You sound agitated? Did something happen?"

Must be what police officers do—get to the point fast. She stood up straighter. "Yes, I'm worried about my family. My dad has left with my son and my mum is also gone. I think my father might have gotten into some sort of scam, maybe stolen some art. I don't know yet but I'm going to try and find him. In Bac Son."

"Really? Art scam? Why would you go there?"

"For some reason, my mother thinks he might have gone there. She suggested I let someone know that I'm going, just in case I need help."

"Good decision. Should I go with you? I get off work at 3 o'clock."

Lang stepped out of the back courtyard, wiping his hands on his work trousers. "You okay?"

She nodded and put her hand on her chest.

"Ms. Thuy?" Viet's voice sounded strained.

"Yes, I'm here. No need for you to come. I've got to go now anyway. I'll let you know if something comes up."

"Where's your mum? Is she going up there too?"

"To be honest, I don't know where she is. Wrote me a note—said she would try to make things right, but I don't know what she means. I need to go."

"I'll be by the phone."

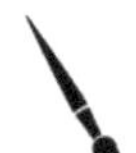

Within thirty minutes, Thuy had left the cramped city streets for a two-lane paved highway heading north. Even a decade ago, rice paddies lined the road and changed with the seasons, from a brilliant Kelly green to a musty grey green and finally to brown shafts after harvest. Now, orange-roofed brick houses dotted the landscape.

Chi's words haunted her. *I will try to salvage things. You find Bo and Quang. Try Bac Son. Ask for Mr. Tan. C.*

Bac Son. One hundred kilometers from Hanoi. That would take three to four hours since the roads in that direction weren't great. She'd heard that name before but couldn't remember the context. She crossed the Red River and it hit her. Bo had said that Uncle Vu lived in Bac Son for years. And now Chi said to ask for a Mr. Tan there.

Chi had said she should salvage things. *What a thing to say. Surely, she doesn't suspect anything.* Her mom had always believed in the good of people. She'd never understand that if Bo was living a lie, through art forgery, that would end the family legacy. Even if he didn't believe copying was a real crime, the rest of the world did.

Thuy tightened her helmet strap and lowered the eye shield. For years, mosquitos had pelted her teeth and clogged her throat when she swallowed one, but since the helmet law went into effect, she wore one, despite the discomfort. The putty-colored sky, with buzzy grey clouds, promised humid and warm weather, even in the mountains. Her body dripped perspiration inside her "sun protection uniform" of long pants, a long-sleeved shirt stretched over the backs of her hands, along with a hoodie pulled onto her head. Face mask. Sunglasses. She'd heard about an American movie called "The Invisible Man," and from the photos, that's what she looked like, covered and obscured.

After an hour and a half, the road disintegrated from recent landslides and woeful lack of maintenance. Some potholes were the width of her wheel's diameter. Boulders the size of small goats dotted the center of the road. She slowed to ten miles per hour and held the handlebars loosely as she bounced her way through.

If she found Bo—or rather when she found him and Quang—she had questions. What was his role? Why did he run? How did this man Tan know him... and Chi? Too many. She'd know what to ask when she saw him but needed to be sure Quang was safe first. When she had Quang, they could start a new life somewhere. *But not Ho Chi Minh. That door had closed.* And other art institutions would have the same reaction once the story got out. She doubted she'd be able to work in art after being fired. She'd probably lose her parents… and maybe her mission to bring Vietnamese art to the world. *Was all of this worth it?*

The immediate question was what to do about her father. Turn him in—or save him and the family. She dreaded the thought, but it bounced back each time she tossed it. She had to decide.

A surge of dark grey clouds billowed, and rain plunked on her helmet. She nudged the bike to the shoulder and rummaged through her bag for a plastic poncho and water bottle, which she half emptied. Another hour and a half or so to go. Longer if the rain turned to mud, which seemed likely. She pulled the poncho over her helmet and spread the back of it over the seat behind her. Raindrops now pounded her helmet and shoulders, and the bottoms of her drenched pants clung to her ankles. She ran her handkerchief along the handlebars in an effort to dry them. *Futile.*

Her phone vibrated: Hang calling. Hang, the logical technology wizard who always looked after her. "What's up? Been trying to reach you. What's going on?"

"On my way to Bac Son. Trying to find Bo and Quang," Thuy said. "I suspect Bo's involved with art fraud. I'll explain it all when I see you. But I have to find them."

"Please be careful. As The Good Bard, Mr. Will Shakespeare would say, 'the truth will out.' But as I would say, don't kill yourself in the process."

For forty-five minutes, she slogged up a winding sludge-filled road. One and a half lanes wide, the road would have been nerve wracking in good weather, but the mud raised visions of sliding down hundreds of feet. She hugged the inner rock wall even though that was the wrong side of the road, but with no guard rail or fence on the "right side of the road," she'd avoid slipping over the edge. The steep drop could have ended it all. She wracked her mind for the name of that American motorcyclist who liked to soar over big canyons. *Even Knees? Evil something?* On one of his leaps, he fell into the big hole, and this reminded her of that jump—one she did not want to experience. *Evel Knievel. That was it.*

Her handlebars—and arms—lurched when she bumped over a rock and then hit a slippery patch. The bike tilted, fell on its side, and began a slow-motion glide toward the far edge of the road. She gripped the handles hard, screamed, then gave in to the slide, half knowing nothing could stop her from catapulting. She tensed, squeezed her eyes, and gritted her teeth.

Suddenly, she jolted to a stop. The bike's spinning front wheel whirled. For ten seconds, she lay stiff, waiting for the inevitable slip into oblivion. A sharp pain spiked in her knee, and she sank into the muck. She blinked fast, trying to clear her eyes. Over her shoulder, she saw the bike's back wheel, lodged into the saddle of a tree trunk, which had split into two trunks, each leaning onto, into, and over the road. The tree formed an anchor and kept the bike from taking its Evel Knievel leap. The bike lay on top of her, pinning her left leg.

She dropped her head into the mud and licked her lips of the raindrops that struck her. *Drat. No traffic. Probably none for a long time. No help. And nothing fake about this trip.* If there was a time to give in, give up, this could be it. Her breath slowed. *I can lie here, feeling sorry for myself. I've ruined so much, hurt people, and will be run out of the city.* Finally, she forced herself up to her elbow. *Wallowing won't get me out of here… or help figure things out.* She did another audit of her body for pain or broken bones. The knee pain had lessened. *No excuse.*

She hoisted the bike upright and shoved it to the inner road. Every part of her—from legs to poncho to cheeks—was covered with slimy mud. But other than mud clumps and a broken kickstand, she found no other damage. She rearranged her poncho to cover her body and guzzled the remaining water in one of her two bottles. The rain had slowed to a lazy pace of plops into water holes.

The tree loomed, overhung the road like it was reaching for safety, avoiding the abyss below the cliff. *Look at that.* An Acer campbellii. She'd seen photos but never the real thing. Forty feet tall, brown bark, and five-fingered leaves. Tree of the mountains. *And rescuer of wayward women.*

Thirty yards of muddy road in front of and behind her, but patches of sunlight danced in and out of the clouds. She leaned against the rock, squinted, and raised her damp face. *First a miracle tree, and now sun? Maybe some gods, somewhere, trying to tell me something.* She pulled on her helmet and swept her hand along its top, shoving rain away from the front of it. Calm descended, and she quit thinking. Almost quit. She couldn't shake the residual fear that, for the sake of a tree, she'd have hurtled down a jungle-covered mountain and probably be dead by now. Instead, she closed her eyes again, sniffing the scent of rain, and chewed bits of mud.

A tree branch snapped. She checked both directions—still no traffic, of course—and strode to her miracle tree. Blossoms the size of her watch face rested at the tips of a branch—brilliant red-orange and yellow. The colors of Vietnam's flag. *Another sign?* She had to stay strong and get what she needed from Bo this time.

Time to find Bo and Quang.

Chapter 40

Thuy slid down the dicey mountain road and reached the valley as the sun dipped over golden hex rice fields. It was 3:45 p.m. when she coasted to a small wooden sign: Bac Son. She'd arrived.

Beside a grey-flanked water buffalo, a boy in pants rolled to his knees ambled in front of her. The boy's head reached the buffalo's shoulder. He and his charge plodded at the same pace.

Thuy placed her feet on the ground and rocked her bike side to side. *A boy out of school on a Wednesday afternoon.* She turned to the fields. *A farm child.* Children often missed school during the September – October harvest; maybe this boy had been in a rice paddy all day. She drifted up beside him and slipped off her helmet.

His eyes looked empty as he trudged past, beat and bedraggled, whether from work or the rain.

"Hello. Do you live here?"

The boy nodded but didn't stop. His feet squished in the mud with each step.

"I'm looking for a Mr. Tan. He has lived here many years."

The child stopped, and the buffalo followed suit. "Teacher Tan? "

Thuy shrugged. "I don't know if he's a teacher. Maybe."

"End of the village. Ask there." He spat and tugged at the nose ring.

Two minutes later, she entered the village center—a communal house, several mud-sided huts on stilts with straw rooftops. A scrawny dog sniffed a mound of buffalo dung. Two men in their sixties squatted in front of one house, smoking cigarettes.

"Xin Chao." She nodded.

The man with sunken cheeks twirled a cigarette between his index finger and thumb as the inch-long ash fell to the ground.

"I'm looking for Mr. Tan. Do you know him or where he lives?"

The second man rubbed his hand over his face and stroked his chin, which sported spikes of a grey beard. He lifted his arm away from his body. "End of the road. Don't think he's there, but some other people are."

"An old man? A boy?"

"We mind our own business, but the man has a funny accent and smokes fancy cigarettes. The kid with him doesn't talk."

For minding his business, the man had noticed a lot about Bo. But then, small villages were filled with a few nosy people, unlike Hanoi, which was filled with a lot of nosy people. She squinted down the dirt path. Nothing stirred. Back on her motorbike, she moved slower than ants could scatter. At the end of the short stretch, two one-room huts on stilts stood opposite each other. "Hello? Anyone here?"

Someone grunted, and an elderly woman poked her head out of a window with no shutters or curtains. "Yes?" Her upper blackened teeth peaked out from her lips. "Yes? What is it?"

"I'm looking for Mr. Tan? And a boy and his grandfather. Do they live here?"

"You're not from here?"

It's my sophisticated look, of course. "No, I'm from the city."

"I can tell. You're looking for Tan? Teacher Tan? Not here. In the fields today. The others? Don't know them." She retreated into the dark shanty.

"Wait, please. Perhaps you've seen them, though? An older man, in his sixties, wearing a beret hat? And a boy? Twelve? Black glasses?"

The woman tucked a wad of betel nuts in her mouth. She lifted her crinkled face to the sun. "Sixty? A young man, then?" She chuckled.

"Are they here?" Thuy rolled her stiff shoulders.

The woman straightened, bringing her height to what Thuy guessed was a full five feet.

"Ask Mr. Tan when he returns."

Thuy checked her watch. "It's already half past four. When does he come back?"

"Not my business. He teaches during the day and sometimes goes to the fields after. But he usually comes about now. You could walk toward the paddy and meet him on the way."

Thuy leaned her bike against the other hut and started down a footpath toward more fields. She stopped after ten yards and gazed at the sunset.

Small white flags stood in the field, looking like scarecrows. A tiny figure, thirty yards from the path, bent over in shin-deep water, surrounded by rice plants. The woman straightened, took off her *non la*—cone straw hat—and fanned herself. Her shoulders hunched forward as she trundled toward Thuy.

Thuy waited for her. "You work hard."

"It's in my blood. Five generations." The woman walked to her bicycle, laying in the grass on the levee. "What's someone like you doing out here?"

"Looking for Mr. Tan, from the village. Do you know him?"

The woman, hands on her bike, pointed with her elbow. "Over there." She stepped on her bike and wobbled away.

Thuy stared at the woman and shivered, even in the warm afternoon. *This might have been my life.* During the American War, Bo and Chi had moved to Hanoi, where she was born. But if they hadn't, she could have been that boy with the buffalo or this woman, doing soul-breaking physical work. In the field below the mountain in the distance, the subtle yellow of corn and rice awaiting harvest reminded her of an impressionist scene. One hundred yards away, a man in black stood on the levee between two paddies.

She walked along the levee. "Excuse me, sir. Are you Mr. Tan?" He didn't react, so she drew closer. "Hello?"

"Yes. I'm Tan." He thrust his face toward her like a turtle pushing its nose out of a shell.

She caught her breath. One of his eyes had something wrong. And his bushy, nearly white, hair reminded her of something. She'd seen him somewhere, but she'd never been here before.

"I am Thuy. I'm looking for a man and child, from the city. I wonder if you've seen them."

"Who are you after?"

"The man's name is Pham Cho Lan, my father. And my son. They are supposed to be here."

"Who sent you?"

"My mother. For some reason she thought you would know where they are. I don't know why."

Tan scowled. "I know why, but what you want to know is that yes, he is here."

The strength in her muscles released, and she felt like rubber. She let out a huge breath. "Thank you. I'm so glad. I need to—"

He scowled and sauntered past her, slowly but deliberately. "No, you cannot see him. I'm doing what your father asked."

She gasped. Something about him rattled her, beyond his rejection. "Wait!" Tan's eye had a silver rim, like one she'd seen before. *The Vietnamese Andy Warhol artist from the museum. The man who copied Uncle's paintings.*

He stiffened but did not turn toward her. He took another step.

She jogged after him, willing her legs to move forward, kicking up mud droplets. She wanted to pull on his sleeve but dared not touch him. Instead, she circled in front to face him and stop his forward progress.

"Y-you're the painter in the museum. You copy paintings."

"The same." His shoulders drooped. "And you're the arrogant niece. Never noticed me in the museum. Why should I talk to you? All my life, you ignored me… pretended I never existed.

And now you want my help?" His eyes narrowed and he spat on the ground.

Her blood pulsed. "What? What do you mean? I... don't understand."

A flock of geese flapped past her, dipping into the water.

His turtle-like neck stuck out again, and he curled his lips over his teeth. "Stop it. You want me to believe that your father, who visited my father and me every month for years, never *talked* about us? Never *told* you anything?" He turned his back to her.

Her leg and arm muscles trembled. Dizzy, she stepped back, nearly tripping, and the world around her fogged up. *His father? Was his father Uncle Vu? The painter in the museum? Uncle Vu's son?* She dropped to the ground and pressed her palms into the mud. "Wha-What are you saying?" Her words toppled out, but her arms and legs remained still, unable to move.

"You are shocked," Tan said, standing above her. A lip curl played at his mouth. "Yes. My father was your Uncle Vu. The painter. Your father knew."

Her mind spun. *Ah! The photos. The Tet photos.* Now they made sense—Tan was the teenager in the photos; awkward, skinny, dark skinned, perhaps from working in the sun? But he looked so old now. She stared at him, her mouth sagging. Snatches of his muffled words reached her, as if she was in a coffin or room that stifled sound. Even the insects' buzzing seemed lower, muted.

"...embarrassed by a bastard child. Before my father was famous. Only later, your father wanted to live off that fame."

"Your mother?"

"Died in childbirth, or at least that's what I was told. He said he loved her. But she was too young and it was wartime." The mountains in the distance disappeared as fog drifted down.

Her chest tensed, making it hard to breathe. She studied her mud-caked palms, placed them back into the dirt, and leaned forward to push up. Still weak, she slunk back down to the ground, sitting on her calves.

Tan stood even taller. "What do you want, really?"

She tilted her face up, squinting. "I don't know what to say. Honestly, I didn't know about you. My father has told me almost nothing about Uncle Vu." *Can't apologize for something I never knew about.*

He leaned forward and squatted, putting their heads on the same level. His feet were flat on the ground, and his left arm rested straight forward on his knee.

She suspected he could sit like this forever. She was out of practice, using chairs so much, and had about ten minutes worth of squat in her.

Tan leaned into his thighs, trapping his arms between his thighs and chest. "You're stunned. I can see."

"I didn't know. You have to believe me. I didn't…" Thuy popped her jaw to clear her hearing, but the fogginess remained. "We must talk, but now… today. I want to find my family."

He stared at the field. A fly landed on his sleeve, and he gazed at it rubbing its wings and twitching. "Pests. No matter the time of year." He blew air on the insect, and it flitted away.

Of course, once he mentioned it, she felt them on her face and swatted. She counted to sixteen, waiting for him to speak.

"Your father is here, but you have come for no reason. Lan does not wish to see you."

She choked. "What? No." Panting, she squeezed her fists. "He has to see me. I have to bring—"

"His decision." He stood up and looked down at her. "He said if you came, to send you away." He gestured toward the village. "Please leave."

Thirst wracked her. The rice field water tempted her. *I must be delusional.* "I…I can't. I must see them. I have to talk to my father."

"Who does not want to see you. Are you deaf? Just go." He glared at her for ten seconds.

Thuy struggled to get a decent breath and stood. "I've come so far. You must help me. Please." Her head hung, and she moaned. "I can't go back."

He cleared his throat but stared ahead. "He said that he did not want to see you. How did you make him so angry?" Tan turned his lame eye on her like she was one of the pesky flies.

"I questioned him about Uncle Vu. Asked if some of his paintings could be forgeries. And if Vu had ever gone to France. He refused to talk and then left. With my son."

Tan rocked forward and back. "Ahhhhh. Why do you worry about the paintings?"

How many times must I try and convince people? "If they aren't real—in the exhibit, the museum—people won't trust us. It could eventually harm Vietnam's reputation. It's our moment to shine on the world stage. People want to see the art, want to buy it."

"Let them. They can see all kinds of art—"

"But it has to be real. We're already known for knockoffs, counterfeits—shoes, fashion, DVDs, and even masks during the coronavirus, for God's sake. We can't slip into that with art. What would that make us? As a country? As a people? I do not want us, the country, any of us, to be known as fake. Not to be trusted."

"But what's that got to do with your father?" His jaw tightened. "Or me?"

"If there's anything he did that smacks of forgeries, that'll ruin our family, which I guess is you now too. Our reputation. Uncle Vu's. Your father's reputation could be destroyed." She lifted her palms to the sky. "But right this minute, I want my son to be safe and I worry about him being with Bo."

Tan tapped his hand on his chest, like he heard an internal music beat. He held out his hand.

"Come with me."

Chapter 41

Darkness dropped suddenly in the tropics. By six o'clock, Thuy stood on the edge of a patch of forest, facing Bo and Quang, their faces dancing in the light of a small fire pit. She heaved a sigh. *He's safe but something is so wrong.* She needed to stay calm.

Ten feet from her, Bo hugged the boy and then nudged him toward her. "Take him. But I refuse to leave. I will not be shamed in my own home, in my own town."

Quang turned and hugged Bo. "Do I have to?"

Bo nodded and gestured toward Thuy.

Quang walked toward her. "I'm fine. No need to worry, Mum."

She grabbed him and squeezed. He coughed. She clutched tighter, but he twisted his shoulders, and she had to loosen. One more jerk, and he was free. *I am losing him.*

"Mum. I'm fine. Please. We wanted to visit the forest. And I met a nice teacher. Mr. Tan." He pulled his Real Madrid t-shirt over his hips and broke a twig off a tree. "What's the plan? Do we stay here or go?" His head swiveled. "You two sort it. I'll wait in the hut with Tan." He meandered through the darkness.

Bo shrugged. "Do what you need to. I'm staying."

Quang reached a dark structure, and a door slammed.

She jumped. "Who's house?"

"Tan's. And before that, Uncle Vu's. Where he painted."

She squinted but couldn't make out more than a shadow outline. "I never knew."

Bo leaned against a tree stump and said something, drowned out by chirping crickets.

"Sorry?"

He leaned forward. "I will not return. If you make this public, I will be punished, go to jail. I reject that. I will die if I am in prison."

"I don't even know what you mean by 'this.' But I need to do what's right. What's right for the family. For the art. For Vietnam."

"The family? I'm your family. You seem to forget." He sat on a log, refused to look at her, and smoked.

She wobbled and felt faint. *Lack of food. Or his harsh comments. Always throws me.* She stumbled toward a tree for balance and sat on a stump. *Breathe. Stop and breathe.* The fire hissed. "Let's slow down. Could you tell me what happened and why?" He was a silhouette against the blackness of the trees. She'd decided to go to the police but now, she waffled. It was the right thing to do, but it devastated her to think of turning him in.

"Please. Let's talk about this," he said. "Maybe we can then understand each other."

The wind rustled the leaves. She squatted by the fire and poked it.

Bo reached for a can of beer on the ground next to him and wiggled it at her. "Want one?"

She reached out. "Thanks. Now tell me. How did we get to this point? I need to know. Especially if there's any way for me to help."

Bo looked at the sky, one of the few in recent days where the stars blinked. He lit a cigarette and blew a smoke circle. "In the American War, I worked in a munitions factory outside Hanoi. Two hours by bicycle each way."

She'd heard stories about the "family bicycle." Most families had them, a prized possession. When a family's bike was stolen, the whole family grieved.

"…very little food in the city. The rice we got sat in a warehouse for a year, so it was rancid. Vegetables stale, often rotten. We ate filth."

"And not much of it."

"And not much—are you going to tell this or should I? " He scowled.

"You. Sorry. But we don't have all night." She popped her beer and gulped. Warm. *Why does he retell these stories?* She'd heard some of them a hundred times. An irritating habit to talk in history and long circles.

"And, during the wartime, Chi worked in the Ministry of Culture and Information. They feared the bombings would demolish places like the Opera House and museums. Chi's job was to evacuate art works to the countryside… to caves and small villages. Many artists did the same. Some museums asked artists to make copies to exhibit while the originals stayed hidden."

She stared at the fire, not moving. *Be invisible so he'll get to the point sooner.*

"After the fighting, some artists brought pieces back to museums but not all. They had no money to travel to get the work. Or forgot the locations."

She wrapped her hands around her upper arms. "Yes, we've talked about that. and Uncle Vu did it too. But what does this have to do with us, with you?"

He glared at her. "Patience was never your strong suit."

She put her palms up. "Sorry. You're right."

"Then the subsidy time—rations for housing, for food, for cloth to make clothing. No one had time for art."

Two pairs of clothes for the year. Two shirts, two pants. One pair of rubber sandals. Always hungry.

He shook his head. "Always hungry."

She jerked. *Reading my mind.*

"Children starved. I didn't want that for you."

She took another slug of warm beer, swallowing without joy. Waiting for the punch line. "And this goes to the art."

He shot an eye-dart at her. "We have time here in the dark." Another cigarette. "During the war, Uncle Vu had moved some work to the countryside. He brought some here—to Bac

Son—and took other pieces to Nam Dinh, to hide them in the old Catholic churches. And some in caves. But he never told us where everything was. Only some. I feared he'd forget, but he said he knew all of the hiding spots and was happy his art was away from the bombs. But some bombs never exploded."

Sweat beads dripped down her temples and ear lobes. A friend's father had lost an arm in an accident, years after the war. And worse, two of her friends from university said their own children had found what looked like buried metal barrels but were still-live bombs. One child had lost a leg; the other had died from the explosion. Periodically, the government reported statistics on deaths or maimed children. She shuddered. "Sorry, what did you say?"

His head quaked. "Please listen. I will not say this again."

Her arms chilled as the air temperature dropped.

"In the early 1980s, Vu and I went to collect some paintings in the countryside, ones that he could find again. A gallery in the Old Quarter sold them to foreigners. Russians, Swedes. Some British. Twenty dollars for a painting; five or ten dollars for a drawing. To you, today, that is very little. But in 1980, twenty dollars was a whole month's salary for a factory worker."

She let her breath come in slow, low, sniff-sized pieces. *The most he's said in years.* "How did it work?"

"When the gallery sold a piece, they paid me. I used the money for food. Better rice. One time, a chicken. You had more to eat."

She braced. In those days, any food not given out through the ration shop was black market. Fines, even arrests if people tried to get something they weren't due. And he'd done it. The family had eaten; she'd had more food and didn't starve, but they had eaten food that was illegal.

"Everyone—everyone who was able—did it."

Her chest felt like he'd whacked her with a branch. The argument that "everyone did it" didn't hold, since no one was supposed to. *But he did it for us.*

A loud rustling in the bushes startled her. *Tan? Quang?* She twisted and strained to see through the muggy air. She gasped. A rat slinked through the grasses. She grabbed for Bo and opened her mouth to scream, but nothing came out.

Bo stood up and darted toward where the rat had passed. "Off! Scat! I think it's gone." He sat next to her and rubbed her arm. "I remember. You were always terrified. It's just a rat, but I'm here, just like when you were little."

She couldn't stop shivering. "I can't… breathe." She wheezed, hand on her chest, willing her heart to slow down. He'd saved her then and calmed her now.

He crossed his skinny legs, and his black rubber sandal slipped off his foot.

"Those things terrify me. Still."

He leaned back, grabbed her hand, and looked into the tree canopy. "Happy to help." He slurped beer. "Shall I continue? I want this to be over."

"Please. You said you sold paintings for Uncle. At a gallery. How much did you get?"

Bo's face sagged. "If I sold a painting for twenty dollars, I told Vu it sold for fifteen. He gave me five dollars and kept ten." He slapped his upper arm, creating a cemetery of mosquitos. "Every month or two, I sold a painting and used money for food, until the subsidy period ended. When the new economy came and life started to get better, I found a job at a foundry, making good money. I could have stopped selling the art."

"Could have?" She wrestled with how far to push.

His mouth opened and closed, and he swatted at more mosquitoes. "The gallery wanted more." He began to sway side to side.

"What happened?"

He shifted and glanced away. "In the early 1990s, the government said that market renovation was working. But it was too slow. We had a little more to eat. A few more clothes, but still struggled. I made twenty-five dollars a month, your mother twenty, to take care of the family."

The cicada's high-pitched clicking rhythm filled the air. "Then I was born."

"Then you came. Indeed. Our only hope was selling those paintings." His voice drifted off.

The night air draped her arms. She nudged. "Bo?" He couldn't leave this unfinished.

"That was it? No other way?"

He jolted, alert again. "You will never understand."

"I want to try. Please go on."

"It was a time of change. More foreigners came to Hanoi. They wanted paintings to buy. The galleries wanted more to sell." He sighed. "Vu had to find more and make new ones." He stood up and poked at the fire. "His art supported our family. Maybe I skimmed some, but there was nothing wrong. Vu didn't mind."

Her stomach flittered. *Bo took advantage of his own uncle and thought he didn't mind? How did that work? Be patient. Hear him.* "Tell me. What happened?"

"1991. Chi's job changed. Less money. I sold cigarettes on the street." He stared at the cigarette in his hand. "Like this one. One stick at a time." Burnt stubs rimmed the fire pit.

"Then, suddenly, no word from Uncle Vu. Like he had died. Nothing. Finally, a letter from Tan."

Invisible weights pulled down her shoulders. She wracked her mind. Nothing stuck with her about that time. *Where was I? How did they keep it from me?* "I don't rememb—"

"We told you nothing. You were in middle school, very busy."

Her chest ache joined the heaviness in her shoulders, and her mind jumped, flashing to fuzzy memories.

"I tried to find out what had happened, but Tan said everything was okay. He brought me paintings but didn't want me to visit."

Her tight chest kept her from getting a deep breath. *Doesn't make sense. He could have stopped this earlier.* "But how could he keep you away? Why didn't you go?"

"I did go. Finally. I went to the same place they lived for years, but they'd gone. Vanished."

She leaned back against a tree, squeezed shut her eyes, and rolled her head against the trunk. Grit ground into her hair.

"Tan brought older paintings to sell… less refined. Ones I hadn't seen, of course, so I didn't know the age. But they came from caves, from twenty, thirty years before. We sold maybe one every few months."

Something nagged. She thought she knew Vu's work, old and more recent. They had changed in style, true, but with all that was going on, she now wondered which might be the real ones, which forgeries. *And Bo became part of this swindle.*

The fire popped against a night of mossy frogs chirping to each other, like birds.

"I was glad to have them again. Our situation had changed, once more. Chi worked in a different part of the Ministry, where her work was not so important. Our income had fallen again, so we had less food, and you wore the same clothes for a long time, even ones that were too small. Chi unraveled sweaters from older kids and made a new smaller one for you."

She could barely see her father in the darkness. *He is a voice, softer every minute, without a body.* She slid closer.

"In the 1990s, Vu was better known. Foreigners, but also rich Vietnamese wanted his work. Old pieces became very valuable. We had to find more. I went to see Vu and Tan and, on one trip, and Tan told me, finally, that Vu had had a stroke, and we had to find his paintings in case he would die. Vu sent us to a cave to search."

She froze and heard ringing in her ears. *A stroke. And he didn't know.* "That must have been awful to find out about Uncle Vu."

"Shocking." Bo cleared his throat. "But we had to keep going. We had to find his early work in places where he hid them. It was for survival."

Nausea worked its way up her throat, and she slumped over.

Bo grabbed a bottle. "Here, water. Drink."

She had to hear this, hard as it was—to think of the poverty, to imagine trying to make enough for extra food. She'd never asked her parents to tell her what it was really like. *Was I so self-centered that I missed what my parents were going through?* She'd been a child but in all the years since then, she'd had no excuse.

Once again, she tried to remember his absences but couldn't. She pushed herself up from the log and paced in a circle by the fire, nearly stumbling over a tree branch in the dark. Unable to see him in the darkness, she pretended she was talking on the phone, disembodied from this man she loved and scorned at once. "Where'd you look?"

"Caves out of Moc Chau. On the first trip, Tan and I spent two days on the motorbike to find them. Of course, we broke down two times."

Of course. Nothing works when you need it to.

"Hills, mud, rain. Then when we got to the Son Moc Huong cave, we couldn't find anything. Spent three nights inside, where it's cool. Shared the space with bats. Actually, quite beautiful. It had those sticks from the ceiling—"

"Stalactites?"

"That's it," Bo said.

He continued, "And kerosene lamps, and it got smoky inside, so we ran in and out when it wasn't raining. Finally, about 20 meters inside, we found some pieces behind a large stone. Maybe ten. A few were damaged, but most looked good. Then we had to come back down, carrying those paintings and drawings, wrapped in burlap. That's what I have in the house. Or did, until I sold some."

She slapped at the bites on her ankles.

"We found six or seven pieces in four different caves," Bo said. "Hard work to get there and then harder to bring out the pieces. We took what we could. Sold them. But we needed more. So Tan made them, pieces that we said were Vu's."

Whack. She gasped and put her hand over her mouth. She'd suspected but now had confirmation. She stepped on a twig and pivoted to him. "Tan made them?" She stared into the canopy of the trees. "Of course. The stroke. Tan took over."

Bo's orange cigarette tip moved up and down with his nod. "Tan had lived with Vu for years and could draw. Not as well but to people who didn't know, it was Vu. At first, even I didn't know. He told me the paintings were from Vu's early days and I believed him. Tan stored his paintings in the caves to let them age for a year. Then he asked me to help search. He pretended he didn't know exactly where at first and said they were pieces hidden during times of fighting and war. By then he was painting for Vu, as Vu. We continued, as a way to make money."

And he'd done this for a long time. Fake paintings. Galleries and collectors who believed him. A mosquito nipped, and she slapped her thigh. "No one asked for proof?" She imagined him in the dark, hanging his head in shame, but doubted he could feel it.

"No. It was for money… to survive. To save us. And I didn't know what was going on at first. He lowered his voice. "Sometimes, a person does something once and stops. Stops lying or deceiving. Forever. But other times, that first act, especially for something positive—like food for the family—makes it easier to do the next time."

She felt exposed—her insides went cold. *That was his excuse always—he did it for survival.* In a time when he had no control, no chance to make changes or choices in his own life, he did something to take control. To rid the feeling of helplessness. *But he didn't stop. He could have. They had what they needed. But he didn't stop. How could he…?*

He puffed, oblivious to her outrage.

It was a crime. He continued doing something he knew was wrong, even after they were in better shape. "By then, we had enough. We had the house. I was in university. But you still sold fake paintings?"

"Where do you think the money for that house came from?"
His voice rose.

She imagined him staring at her.

He shoved himself up from the log. "And your university? And now your son's art supplies? From savings, from those sales." A slapping sound pierced the dark—his fist pounding his palm. "Grow up. It was from those sales you criticize me for." He threw his cigarette butt toward the fire, but it landed in the dirt, still smoldering.

"But gained through illegal means," she whispered.

He blew air out.

"How could Uncle Vu let you do that? His reputation… it will be shattered." A rustling in the brush made her shudder. Nothing more.

"Was what I did as bad as what the people who bombed us did? Or others who stole from their neighbors? I did it for you. And if you ever talk about it—if it becomes known—you will destroy us: Uncle Vu's reputation, the family's, *mine*. Surely you don't want that."

She grimaced and scratched the nape of her neck. She had always wanted his approval and love, but it wasn't easy, never had been. *Now it's impossible.* She held her breath, slowly counted to five, before a slow exhale. "What was Tan's role then? Only painting?"

"Ask him." Bo said. "He's there. In the trees."

Chapter 42

A light flashed on and off in the forest not ten feet from Thuy. She arched, leaned forward on the log, and squinted. "Tan?"

He stepped out of the darkness.

He's been here all along. "How did I miss hearing you?"

"You're from the city and know nothing of the forest night. You and your father should come to the studio, the shed, to continue talking. Quang is asleep, and there are fewer bugs."

Bo lit a cigarette.

She shook her head. "Not good for you to smoke so many."

Bo shrugged. "A moment of peace. And, you know, it's not real—it's chicory," he said, staring at the stick, "Not tobacco. A counterfeit cigarette."

Tan chuckled. He'd changed out of the clothes he wore on the rice field into a black smock, like the one she remembered from the museum. She couldn't imagine how he could wear such a heavy, dark color in this heat. He pulled a match book from his pocket and his own cigarette.

Oh God, a counterfeit cigarette? What's real? And who can I believe? She shuddered. *Stay on task.* She followed Tan and Bo down a narrow pathway, under massive banana trees. Gnats and bugs too small to see snatched at her ankles and calves. She waved her hands in front to keep from being surprised by webs or bats.

Tan held open the door, and she slipped into a softly lit space, littered with easels, paints, and art paraphernalia. In the glow of chunky candles, he offered chairs to her and Bo and squatted across the room. His white hair glistened, but he squinted, hiding the strange silvery eye. The room was littered with drawings and paintings leaning against the wall, on two easels in the room's center. At least twenty books squatted on a crooked shelf, and four metal cans sat on the floor, holding brushes of different sizes.

She brushed her hair from her eyes. "Tell me what you two did."

Tan glanced at Bo, who nodded. "It's simple really. We sold Vu's earlier pieces for a couple of years. After his stroke, we knew that those would dry up eventually and decided to create more."

Quang snored on a blanket next to a wall of the room. Innocent. The way she remembered him as a child. His teenage years beckoned, and she hated the thought.

Tan handed Bo a beer and offered one to her.

"Not this late. I need to get some sleep so Quang and I can leave by daybreak." She sneezed and sniffed. "But I should hear what happened." She tried to keep her emotions from showing on her face but didn't know how she looked to them.

"I tried to sell them as my own. No success. I became Vu, in style, in media, in tone. I had learned how to make portraits and some landscapes, so I made those. Not exactly the same, of course, but close enough."

She'd noticed a difference in style over time. *Because it wasn't Vu doing all of the work.*

"But the galleries wanted more," Tan said. "So, I painted Vu's work, or at least called it that. When foreigners came, and some auction houses from outside Vietnam, they wanted art, and sometimes it seemed that they didn't care if it was real. The 'market-oriented economy under socialist guidance' pushed ahead. And I tried to provide what they wanted."

She glanced around the workspace. He'd captured the essence of Vu, or what she thought had been Vu's style. Rather than edgy, there was a softness, a gentleness to the portraits, especially the one with the mother and son, who she now realized must have been Tan. The confidence in strokes, the different materials—from pencil in the sketches to oils on canvas of the portraits—he'd done well imitating the master. And yet, some of Tan's work had a playfulness, some risk taking in them. Gentle but playful. If some of those pieces she saw were his, he had competency and skill in his own right. *He is good. Really good. He could've left this charade behind and gone out on his own.* "Why didn't you tell them that the paintings were yours? If they liked them, you could have become a famous artist."

"I was unknown. If they knew I made them, then I would be a copier only. Not a true artist. And by then, we were in too far. I was angry, but we had no choice." Tan pointed to Bo. "And we were forced to continue."

They must have known what they were doing and chose to continue. Her jaw tensed.

"I dropped off paintings at a gallery one time, instead of your father." Tan glanced at Bo. "A new gallery worker questioned them; said they looked better than Vu's."

Better than Vu's. Someone else had recognized how good Tan was. *That must have been hard for Bo.*

Quang shuffled, stretched and threw the cover off his chest.

"I was surprised and asked what they would go for if it was a different artist. And the man brushed me off. He said, 'Vu is too big now. We're selling his name. Even if someone else is better, he's hot now, and we need more.' Then he asked if I could get more of Vu's."

Bo shook his head. "He knew. The gallery guy knew they weren't Vu's. But he forced us to keep making them."

"Oh God. You were selling fakes; some random gallery worker knew that and then he coerced you into making still more for him?"

Tan paced the edge of the room and stopped to cover Quang and straighten his pillow. "Yes. I did more for him. He paid well because the sales in the galleries were skyrocketing. Customers, especially rich Vietnamese, bought these paintings to show off, to let people know how much they had made. I split the money with your father." Bo smiled. "We were partners by then."

Her head spun. *I knew it.* "Let me guess. This was in the late 1990s."

"Indeed," said Bo. "How'd you know?"

"That's when you bought the house. It seemed that you had more money all of a sudden."

Moths flitted around the candles. She slid off the chair and sat against the wall, legs outstretched. All she wanted was sleep. This was too much, but she had to stay awake. Alert. She felt her anger draining but she had to keep a clear head. They'd done something illegal and would have to pay for it.

"And then that man from the gallery went to the museum." Bo tossed his beer bottle to a pile in a corner, where it clinked with the other glass. "And blackmailed us."

She felt like she was underwater again, voices muffled, movements slow.

He stared at her. "And you know him."

"Blackmail?" She stuffed her shaking hands between her legs. *This bad dream keeps getting worse.* Forced to paint, threatened with blackmail, they had come up with a scheme of replacing originals.

"And I know him? You must mean Tuan. I know he's involved. He's got to be the one."

Bo and Tan looked at each other.

And yesterday, he fired me. News for another day. Too much already. "But blackmail—"

"Tuan? You think it's Tuan? He's not smart enough to be behind this," Tan said. "He's a toady and does what he's told. No. Someone else is the mastermind. Surely you understand that."

She reached for her bag, yanked out tissues and rubbed her nose. *Stalling. Not sure what's happening.* "Well, who else—"

"That gallery person was Chien." Bo slapped his thigh.

Now her vision warped. Bo was blurry. Chien? *Chien?* Always on her side, had her back, had helped her find the new job. What were they saying? That he was a crook? "Chien? The security and operations guy? Chien from my museum?"

"The same. He sold Vu's paintings in the gallery. Before he joined the museum."

She placed a hand on her forehead. "I don't follow. Has he known about the paintings… and me… all this time?"

"He knew about it all because he organized it." Tan walked to the doorway and flicked his cigarette to the dirt. "He found out about Vu's stroke and figured out that I was doing the copies when I brought some in and he asked me specifics about the materials and style. After that, he came to me directly, cutting your father out of the loop."

Her mind blanked. *Cut out of the loop. The illegal loop. That could be a good thing, but that's not what Bo is saying.* "And you agreed? To do this on your own?"

"I had to. Chien insisted. Would blackmail us both if we talked."

Her mouth fell open, and she gaped at Tan. She spread her fingertips across her chest—to keep her heart from jumping out. "Let me get this straight," she said. "After Vu's stroke, you sold his old pieces. Then you painted fakes, and Bo sold them to a gallery—"

"To Chien, at the gallery," Bo said.

"To Chien." She sat back. "And he sold them to tourists. And collectors. But then he went to Tan." She looked toward him. "He asked you to bring them to him directly, so Bo was out of the loop."

"Right. So far." Bo nodded. "Once Chien went to the museum, he got Tan to copy the originals there, then he replaced the originals with those copies. And he sold the originals, some through the galleries, some through the black market, I suspect."

Her head whiplashed. *Unbelievable. And all under my nose.* A few weeks ago, she'd noticed something "off:" a painting had been crooked, and the frame had been smaller than the area it was hanging in. *A replacement. And when they'd first hung the artwork and Ngoc had questioned a painting, Chien had assured them it couldn't be fake.* She shuddered at the thought of how many might be compromised. *That would destroy the museum's reputation. And if Vu's were part of the scam, the family's legacy would melt. Like that wicked witch.*

"He was able to get much higher prices since the market had discovered Vietnamese art."

She leaned over her knees, afraid of fainting. "Then he must have put the originals in the vault. And changed the documentation. You said he'd come up with fake provenance, which I guess is also in the vault."

"You got it."

"I… no. How could he? I know that we have originals. We have the provenance for…" She shoved herself up from the floor. "I need some air."

"Stop, Thuy. Listen to him," Bo said. "We are trying to tell you."

"Wait a minute. Let me get outside."

The forest had a light tint through the trees. The moon or a tiny hint of sun. She glanced at her wrist: 2:23 a.m. Just as the darkness fell fast in the tropics, morning would come early and fast as well. She needed sleep before she drove back to Hanoi. But first, as much as she hated this, she knew what she had to do.

Tan and Bo stepped outdoors.

"Let us tell you the rest." Tan faced her. "Chien made me forge provenance papers. Documents. The ones that the museum had—the few that it had—he brought to me to copy. He put them in the museum's vault and gave the originals to the gallery, along with the real paintings."

"Then cut us out," Bo said.

"Sorry? Now I'm confused. What are you saying?"

"Chien learned how to make counterfeit documentation himself or got someone who did that. Receipts, the artist description, some photos of the paintings. Then he could sell the original paintings, but with forged provenance papers. So few had clear provenance—with the war and all—it was hard to know their backgrounds." Bo grabbed a twig and spun it, then stuck it between his teeth like a cigarette.

She wiped the back of her hand across her forehead. "Meaning the customers got the real art. And the museum had the fakes. And who knows where the real documentation is?" But Chien couldn't just walk a painting out of the museum or bring another one in. Even if he was head of security. *Someone else was involved. Tuan, of course.*

"Chien chose the paintings to copy, Tan made them, and then Chien put the fakes in the museum and sold the originals. For at least the last year."

"That's why I go to the museum to paint," Tan said. "I study the paintings—and copy some."

She stumbled and sank to the ground. Her mind whirled in zigzags. *Some Vu paintings are real and some not real. Documents supporting them are real…and not real.* "What you're saying jeopardizes the integrity of the whole museum."

"I'm not a museum expert." Tan lifted his palms. "I don't know what you mean."

"It would bring down the museum. Its reputation. All of us who work there." *Worked there, if I'm honest.* "But Chien? I trusted him. He supported me. Why would he do that?" She shook her head.

"Money. Ego. The chance to have people look to him as a big wig, at least in his criminal world," Bo said.

And the people with access to the vault, with the opportunity to change paintings without anyone thinking twice. Chien, Hai, and Tuan. And me.

"Tuan… he's part of it."

Bo nodded. "He was the go between. The footman. Took paintings from us. I assume he and Chien worked together to hang the fake ones." He moved toward the forest again.

She followed him to the dead fire pit and sat on a tree stump. Her heart broke, but she had to do what was right. "Bo, selling forgeries as real, passing them off that way, is a crime."

"You still don't see. How is that a crime? The paintings went to a gallery."

"But they were still fakes."

"The gallery sold them, not I. My job was to help Uncle by selling paintings and getting money for him. And for my family." His chin quivered. "And it was a way for Tan to learn more about paintings. All good things. No one got hurt. Until we were the victims. Blackmail."

Another stomach punch. *Doesn't matter. Don't waver. Exhausted.* "You think it's a crime without a victim, but that's not true. You lied. You took money for something that wasn't real. You hurt Uncle Vu's reputation, and now we don't know which pieces are real. The value of his work will be in question. When people learn what you did… it could all be worthless."

He hung his head, and his voice dropped. "You think the wrong way. Some money belongs to me. I helped Vu's legacy. I helped make money for him and for the family."

"But in a criminal way." *He has to see this.*

"But many people do what they must to save their families. I did that. So you could eat. To get money for Chi's medicine. To send Quang to art school. Surely…" His eyebrows pushed together. "Everyone does it."

Everyone does it. She'd never accept that from Quang.

Tan went inside, returned with a glass of water, and plunked it down by Bo.

She sighed. "But everyone should *not* do it. Especially someone like you. I've been proud to be your daughter while you've fought for the legacy." She made a fist. "But… you must turn yourself in."

His head whipped back, like she'd struck him.

"She's right," Quang stood in the doorway. "She says to tell the truth. Mum's right. I did and you must too."

Bo stood and moved toward Quang. "My grandson, you're a child. You don't understa—"

"I heard what you said. I heard you and Uncle Tan. And Mum. We must not live with fakes, or live fake lives. Please tell the truth. It is bad but we are a family."

Pain in the back of her throat stopped her swallowing. She faced Bo. "You must go to the police... Or I will."

Bo hung his head and reached for Tan's arm. He choked and nodded. "Tan will take me. I will take Tan. We promise." He stared at Quang through wet eyes.

"And I must confront Tuan and Chien." She looked at Quang. "And our truth sayer comes with me. After I sleep."

Chapter 43

At six o'clock, Thuy brushed the sleep from her eyes and woke Quang. Grey mist lay low to the ground and weighed down her damp clothes.

She had combed Quang's bushy wild hair but it sprang back into its own shape. She strapped him to her, almost as she did when he was toddler, to keep him from slipping off the motorbike if he drifted back to sleep. Turning Bo and Tan into the police was the right thing to do, but it pulled her insides apart. *If only they had stopped when they ran out of Vu's paintings. Then they'd have been worth even more because they'd be so rare.*

She stopped on the road an hour from Hanoi to call Viet at the central police station. Once again, he answered before the ring finished.

"Thuy. Glad you called. Are you all right?"

"Thanks again for answering. I'm about an hour from the city. I'll drop my son at home and go to the museum There are people there I need to see, to confront. Unfortunately, I was *right* about my father."

"Are you okay?"

"Shaken, betrayed, but physically okay. But I need your help—"

"Anything. Tell me—"

"Bo confessed to being part of an art fraud scheme, said he'd turn himself in to the police, today, along with his nephew. They've been trading out originals in the museum for copies. Then someone else sells the originals for loads of money. They claim the museum director—Mr. Tuan—was complicit. And that the security manager was behind it all—"

A Russian-made truck, probably from the 1980s, rumbled by, overpowering her voice and spewing dust on her already gritty poncho.

"Yuck. I'm a mess."

"Sounds loud. Are you on the highway?"

"Yes, lots of traffic today. What was I saying? They were blackmailed into making copies that were put into the museum in place of the originals. Then a dealer—I think I know who—sold the real ones. Some went on the black market. Many went overseas. I'm on the way to the museum, but the director might leave before I get there. I can explain it all when I see you."

"I can try to slow him down. I can get a few of us and visit—we'll do an impromptu inspection."

"Better than nothing."

"Who else is involved?"

"Head of security. Mr. Chien. I think he was behind it all."

"No others?"

"Not that I know. Why?"

"I… No. I'll take it from here and head to the museum."

She revved up her fueled bike and handed a snack to Quang.

"Where are we?"

"Nearly home. Please try to hold on. We can go faster if I'm not worried you'll fall off. I'll drop you at the house and you can sleep there. But then I need to talk to you later, so please don't leave."

He nodded and his chin fell onto his chest.

Her bike sputtered. It sounded puny in the open air; in the city, all bikes sounded like Harleys. *Hold tight.*

She bumped and jostled through villages and hamlets, a repeat of the day before, with sore arms from trying to stabilize the bike. Definitely not a fashion plate today—her head hurt from the jolts, her hair had stiffened from dust and grit, and her pant legs felt heavy from hardened mud.

She dropped Quang at the house and arrived at the museum at about 11 o'clock, groggy but ready to fight. Two police bikes;

Viet must have brought backup. *No sign of the guys.* She raced upstairs to Tuan's office, where the door stood ajar. *Maybe I missed him.* She knocked and pushed it open.

"Tuan. We need to talk."

He squatted behind his desk, back to her, with a small safe door open and papers strewn on the floor. "What the—"

"My father confessed. Said you're part of this—"

Tuan stood, still holding an armful of what looked like receipts, spreadsheets, green papers, and notebooks. He dumped them on the desk. "You have no idea what you're—"

"You switched the originals with fakes paintings. You've ruined the museum's reputation."

"I fired you," he hissed. "You can't come here and—"

"Of course I can if you're doing what you seem to be. My father says—"

"You believe your father? Him?" He sank to his chair. "The guy who's losing his mind? Forgetting everything? You have to be kidding. He knows nothing. He does what he's told. Why do you think he's involved in any serious way?"

"Because you bloody well told me! You said to look in my own house. Because he gave you paintings. Because he admitted being part—"

Tuan guffawed. "So naïve! You have no idea what you're talking about. You're as clueless as your father is. How can you be such a fool?"

She heard the vacuum cleaner roaring down the hallway and looked at the Ho Chi Minh photo. *He'd hate this.*

"You missed the entire thing. I said, 'look to your own house.'" He plopped to his chair. "You didn't suspect? It's her. That's the one in your house who's the criminal. The rest of us took orders. It's her. And Chien."

Thuy couldn't get enough oxygen and wheezed. "Wha—"

"It's your mother, you dullard. She's the brains behind it all. It's her. Your precious mother. She's on her way here to plan the next gig. If anyone deserves prison time—"

Chi! "What? You're wrong. Can't be."

"Talk to her. She's coming this morning." He sneered and brushed some crumbs from his shirt. "We're meeting in…" He glanced at the clock above his door. "Right away. She should be in the lobby about now."

Her knees buckled. She sank to the floor and felt a swish of trousers race past her.

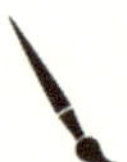

Thuy put her hands on both sides of her head, a "hear no evil" gesture, and whimpered. *No. Not Chi.* She stood and grabbed the doorframe. *Got to get there. Downstairs.* Her feet sounded like bullets moving down the stone steps. *Tat-tat-tat.* She peeked over the railing to the lobby and glimpsed a woman in the lobby. "Chi! Wait! Chi!" *Get down there. Find her.*

The woman looked up. *Not Chi.*

She reached the bottom of the stairs and, in a frenzy, swiveled her head around the lobby. *No sign of her. He lied.* She spotted Chien in the coffee shop and sprinted to him. "You! You and my mother, for God's sake? Where is she?"

His eyes shifted to and from her, over her shoulders. "Your mother? What's going on?"

"She's coming… to see Tuan… and you. So are the police." She grabbed hold of a table to steady herself.

"Uh… so sorry. I need to go check on something." He raced out of the shop, glancing toward the lobby doors and slipped toward the back of the building.

There. There she is.

Chi stood in the lobby, regal. Clothes she rarely wore. Black sweater, long red skirt, black boots.

"Chi! Stop! Chi!" Thuy rushed toward her.

Chi opened and closed her mouth and looked up the staircase and turned toward Thuy. "What are you doing here? Supposed to be—"

Thuy grabbed her by the shoulders. "What is going on? Are you involved in this scheme? Art crime? Not you. Please not you."

Tuan reached them and nodded. "Her. Told you. She's behind this all. Copying art, replacing it, selling on the black market. I didn't come up with it. Not me." He waved his palms in the air. The few visitors in the lobby had stopped and moved away from the action. But they didn't leave.

At that moment, two police officers burst through the doors. One remained there and the other rushed toward Chi and Thuy.

Thuy blinked her very wet eyes. "Are you looking for her? My mother?" She gestured. "And this man. Both involved in an art fraud scheme." She teared up and took big gulps. "Oh, how could you do this?"

Chi clutched her upper arm. "I don't want to slap you, but you must stop this emotion."

Thuy reeled. *She's crazy. Get away.*

Chi grabbed Thuy's chin like she was a child. "Look at me. Thuy. Look at me. It's not me. Tuan, yes. And Chien. He's the one we're after."

We? We're after? Thuy's cheeks burned. "Bo told me everything. It's Tuan. And they said Chien was involved—"

Chi pulled Thuy toward the side of the lobby. She nodded to the police officers. Viet walked to them and nodded at Chi.

"Ma'am?"

"Around back," Chi stuck out her thumb. "Maybe dangerous."

Viet sprinted toward the door.

He knows her. "You know these police people?"

"Of course I do. I've been working underground trying to catch Chien since he came to the museum. And you helped us crack this. We couldn't prove anything until you uncovered the replacement paintings scheme. That was Chien. Your father, Tan… they were pawns. Even they didn't know the whole story. Tuan's the middle point, but Chien is the big boss."

"I'm confused."

"Let's sit. It's all because of you that we found these guys, that we have the pieces of the puzzle to charge them. Once you started to question things. We've been trying to catch Chien, and your work made it happen. You discovered there was a scandal—replacing originals with fakes, that Bo had something to do with it, and also Tan. You pursued the dealer in Thailand, even though it was for the exhibit, but he's Chien's main outside contact."

Thuy's stomach fluttered and her mind went fuzzy. "I still don't follow. I simply wanted to save the museum, the artists—"

"And because you did, you brought in Mr. Lee. Got him to identify the fakes, or some of them. To at least raise attention to this. Brilliant."

"Then why are you… What did you—"

"All I could do was watch from a distance and hope that you would stay in this job for a while. Every time you told me about what you were finding—the fakes in the pre-opening, the questions you had about the shipments, the dealer's shadiness. That's what we needed, but I could never have found all of that out."

"But what about Uncle Vu?"

"Chien tried to calm you about the paintings, but you wouldn't be deterred. So then he wanted to make you think Vu was a traitor. That would harm the family. He made sure you saw those sketches from Uncle Vu that had no guns in them—he probably removed them and put them in the vault, to make you consider the possibility that Vu spied for the French? Again, he used you to keep the scheme going, to make it seem like it would be bad for any fakes of Uncle Vu and the others to be found. I've reviewed letters from Vu and so has the security police—he was a double agent—the French thought he was spying for them, but really, he was spying *on* them."

"I can't believe this."

"And Bac, your ex..."

"What about him? He's been trying to intimi—"

"He's one of Chien's henchmen. His job was to steer you away from investigating. Obviously, he failed." Chi stroked Thuy's hair. "Look at all the mud and twigs. You poor dear."

"So, it was Chien and Tuan. Not you."

"Of course, not me. But as I said, you did all of the work, dear. I just nudged you along." Chi handed her a comb. "Oh, Anna showed me the letters she found in Paris. From Vu? They were also fake. His name had been added. All made to compromise Vu. You're a genius, my daughter."

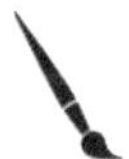

Bo and Tan turned themselves in that day but were released to house arrest. Chi expected they would likely receive light sentences because of their cooperation and information about Tuan and Chien.

The next day, Laotian police caught Chien on a remote roadway, trying to cross the border. He sang like a mossy frog, giving up Morris Teller, who was really Francois Allon, a long-time art criminal from a tiny town in France.

Three months later, Minh sold one of the questionable paintings in the "Returning Home" special exhibit for $30,000.

Bac disappeared. Three months later he was still on the run.

Chapter 44

Shortly after Tet holiday, Thuy and Quang stood at the entrance of his new school.

"I will not wave because artists do not." In the damp drizzle of late winter, Quang huddled in his poofy jacket and scurried up the steps to the door of the Vietnamese Academy of Art on Hang Bong Street. The newly opened art academy had overtaken an old government office building, with its high ceilings, tall windows, and tile floors.

Thuy zipped her fuchsia jacket and pulled her pashmina scarf tighter around her neck. She glanced at her black leather Sam Edelman boots. These were the real thing, although she'd bought them on sale, but they were sturdy and good looking. The best she'd had. She peeked up at Quang, who flashed a look. He faked a small wave by reaching to push his hair back from his forehead and wiggled his fingers in the process. She offered a tiny flick of her index finger. *So only he can see.*

His confident walk reminded her of Bo, who despite his flaws, never quit doing all he could for his family, even crossing a legal line. Chi had told her that Bo drew on connections to get Quang an interview with the senior academy leaders. The academy didn't usually take students younger than fourteen, but Quang, at thirteen, was on the borderline. Bo had offered to donate some of Uncle Vu's sketches—and showed letters to confirm they were really Vu's—if the men would look at Quang's work and then decide.

Later, Thuy saw the portfolio of Quang's drawings. Most were neighborhood sketches in the style of Uncle Vu but clearly with Quang's touch. Vibrant colors, sharper lines, and a touch of whimsy from the modern era, like three birds sitting atop a mess of wires on a utility pole. *Now we have birds and don't have to eat those.*

Mr. Nguyen Van Thanh had invited Quang to join the spring inductees, where he would spend two hours daily working with mature students who acted as mentors, and two hours with instructors. He'd learn about drawing, of course, but also about the history of art in Vietnam.

Kumquat trees on the backs of motorbikes passed through the narrow street, with blooms that had come out for Tet. Students—all who looked at least sixteen or seventeen—entered the building, dwarfing Quang. He looked like a newborn antelope learning how to get his feet under him. She sucked in a breath and sent a virtual hug. He must—and could—prove himself, on his own. *Today is the first day.*

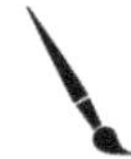

Later that afternoon, Thuy and Hai stood in the museum lobby, staring at a raucous rainstorm pounding the plaza tiles. No dainty raindrops, just the *shhhhhh* of a deluge of water.

Rain—a sign of good luck.

"I talked with Mr. Tuan, even while he is in jail," Hai said. "Now is time for you to move up in the museum. I will retire this summer to spend more time with my wife. You will be the new curator... and lead the museum into a new era. We need young people who speak English, who can compete with big museums, who will do what is best for artists from Vietnam."

Her eyes, half-closed, scanned the lobby.

"Even though the exhibit failed, we cannot stop showing our artists. You must do this job."

Adrenaline rushed through her chest. *Too late.* "I came to tell you good-bye."

Hai's mouth fell open. "But you wanted this job. What has changed?"

"I need a new start. On my own. Without your approval, or Tuan's, or my father's."

Hai cocked his head.

"The Ministry asked me to start a new unit for authentication of artwork in Vietnam. They want me to help train our own band of experts, set up a lab, all that we need to join the global art world. No more fakes in Vietnamese museums."

Hai grinned. "Very good for you. Very good for Vietnam. And you start when?"

"Next week. My first assignment is to assess our own paintings. Here."

He clapped. "Imagine that."

"Yes, imagine that. I can't wait to get started."

References

This work of fiction drew upon much that is real, or at least I think it is, but after writing about fakes for so long, I question everything. I relied on numerous articles and loads of books. Some of the references that were most helpful follow:

On Forgery, Fakes, and Lost Art

Casement, William. *The Many Faces of Art Forgery.* Lanham, MD: Rowman & Littlefield, 2022.

Charney, Noah. *The Art of Forgery: The Minds, Motives, and Methods of Master Forgers.* London: Phaidon Press, 2015.

———. *The Museum of Lost Art.* London: Phaidon Press, 2018.

Hebborn, Eric. *The Art Forger's Handbook.* London: Cassell, 1997.

Innes, Brian, and Chris McNab. *Fakes, Scams & Forgeries.* London: Reader's Digest, 2002.

Koldehoff, Stefan, and Tobias Timm. *Art & Crime: The Fight against Looters, Forgers, and Fraudsters in the High-Stakes Art World.* New York: Seven Stories Press, 2020.

On Vietnamese Art and Painters

Ciclitira, Serenella, ed. *Vietnam Eye.* London: Thames & Hudson, 2016.

Goebel, Michael. *Anti-Imperial Metropolis: Interwar Paris and the Seeds of Third World Nationalism.* Cambridge: Cambridge University Press, 2015.

Noppe, Catherine, and Jean-François Hubert. *Art of Vietnam.* Paris: Assouline, 2021.

Quang Phong and Quang Viet. *The Fine Arts College of Indochina.* Hanoi: Fine Arts Publishing House, 2022.

Taylor, Nora A. *Painters in Hanoi: An Ethnography of Vietnamese Art.* Honolulu: University of Hawaii Press, 2004.

Vuong, Quan-Hoang, Ho, Manh-Tung, Nguyen, Hong-Kong T., Vuong, Thu-Trang, and Manh, Toan Ho. Paintings can be Forged, But not Feeling: Vietnamese Art—Market, Fraud, and Value, *Arts,* (2018) 7 (4): 62-99

On Museums

Bringley, Patrick. *All the Beauty in the World: The Metropolitan Museum of Art and Me.* New York: Simon & Schuster, 2023.

Bosker, Bianca. *Get the Picture.* New York: Viking, 2024.

Acknowledgements

So much goes into a book—from the ideas to the research, from the writing to the rewriting. I am happy to report that after fifty-three or so drafts, I'm starting to learn a little about writing fiction. Much more to come.

I'd like to acknowledge the country and people who made this book possible.

First, I give much thanks to Vietnam. I've been fortunate to spend some thirty years working on and off in Vietnam. I went in March 1994 to teach in a three-week training session, going to a country that had much I hate: bugs, humidity, hazy skies, and power outages. I came away in love—with the people and their hunger to learn, their kindness, and their wisdom. I've since spent time teaching, researching, and for the last fifteen years, taking Boise State Executive Masters of Business participants to Hanoi, where they do business projects. Many of them fall in love with the country and people, just as I did.

I came to this book with a wish to help people who don't know Vietnam well or at all to learn a little more about it. It has become my second home, with all of the wrinkles and flaws that any country or person might have, but I love it and the people I know there with all my heart.

I was fortunate to speak to several outstanding artists in Hanoi, Vietnam: Dang Xuan Hoa, Dinh Thi Tham Poong, Trinh Lu, and Dinh Quan. Many others in Hanoi were also gracious and informative: Pham Phuong Cuc, Dau Thuy Ha, Luong Ngoc Khanh, Suzanne Lecht, Tran The Viet, and Deputy Director Mdm. Nguyen Thi Thu Hoan and her staff at the Vietnam History Museum. For context, I also visited The

Vietnam Fine Arts Museum, The Vietnam Women's Museum, The Vietnam Museum of Ethnology, and The Hanoi Police Museum (who would have thought?).

Nguyen Hoang Anh and Vo Nguyen Dang Nhan were kind enough to read an early draft and look for cultural mistakes.

Thanks to the art expertise and generosity of Melanie Fales, Lisa Hunt, Emma Kirks, Susan Moreman, and Kathy Saloman, who offered early help to kick start this project.

Heledd Priest, formerly of Heywood Hill Books, sent me incredibly helpful books I would never have found on my own.

Once again, Kristen Wise and Maira Pedierra brought the book to life and jumped in to help whenever I tumbled or whined. Thank you, ladies.

The editing and proofing magic of Zora Knauf and Kerri Doyle helped make this book the best it can be. Thanks also to Kerri Doyle for the title idea.

Lisa Poisso, editor extraordinaire, consistently offers inspiration and very practical advice. Some of us in her Story Incubator coaching group think Lisa should be a co-author on our books!

The Called to Write sprint group was there, every day, whenever I needed them. Thanks, all.

Thank you to the many friends who offered sympathetic ears, reading eyes, and brilliant thoughts to keep me going. Thank you all: Hildy Ayer, Stephanie Camarillo, Linda Clark-Santos, Elisabeth McKetta, Cheryl Larabee, and Eileen Roulier.

Angeli Weller, in particular, offered early ideas for plot twists and turns and constant scaffolding when I needed it most.

And, of course, Tony Olbrich and our dog Matisse walked me through another project with grace and humor. I couldn't ask for more.

Meet the Author

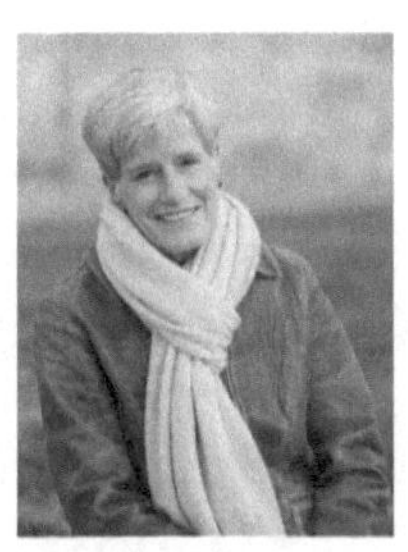

Distinguished Professor Emerita at Boise State University (USA) and former Adjunct Professor at Aalborg University (Denmark) and the National Economics University in Hanoi (Vietnam), N.K. Napier has taught strategy and creativity, coached executives, and helped create Vietnam's first international standard business school.

Napier co-created and hosted Idaho Business Matters on NPR's local affiliate (Boise State Public Radio), was a regular guest on KTVB Channel 7's Noon News, and wrote for Forbes Vietnam. She continues to blog for PsychologyToday.com. Her long-time work as a teacher, researcher, and writer has led to several awards, including a Medal of Honor and a Medal of Friendship in Vietnam, the highest awards given to foreigners.

After 35+ years in the academic and research world, N.K. Napier has embarked on something completely new: fiction writing, which offers her the joys and challenges of being a beginner again, with opportunities to do in-depth historical research and create fun new worlds and characters.

To check all her published fiction and nonfiction books, visit NancyKNapier.com.

Dear Reader,

Thank you for reading my second novel, *The Art of Lies*. I hope the story drew you into the world of art, deception, and the wonder of Vietnam and its people. If you were enticed by the drama and its twists and turns, I encourage you to share your thoughts with other readers via a review at the retail outlet where you purchased the book.

If you haven't yet read my first novel, *A Case of Too Many Deaths*, you can download a free chapter from my website or buy it directly at your favorite book retailer. To learn more about my other published books, upcoming projects, and to stay connected through my blogs, visit NancyKNapier.com.

COMING SOON: As a thank you for reading *The Art of Lies*, I am excited to include a sneak preview of my next mystery novel, which is also set in Vietnam:

> *What happens when a lawyer from Hanoi learns that her devout U.S.-born Catholic father, who died by suicide, had a life she never knew about before he married her Vietnamese mother? As Lien uncovers layers of mystery and betrayal, she faces a dilemma: come clean to her family about her father's past, which included serious crimes, or keep his good name and family reputation intact? Her search for truth takes her from Catholic churches in Nam Dinh to the mystical, mountainous region of Ha Giang in the far north of the country. Along the way, she encounters a shifty church historian with a dark past, uncovers a former soldier friend, and learns more about U.S. soldiers who did not leave Vietnam after the war ended. Meanwhile, her brother's wife is pregnant, which raises the stakes because they too have begun a search about Dad's past and health.*

More soon,
N < N